EYE FOR AN EYE
MOLLY SUTTON MYSTERIES
BOOK X

NELL GODDIN

For the wonderful and patient readers of this series.
I raise a kir to you!

An eye for an eye makes the whole world blind.
    —Mahatma Gandhi

I

M *arch 2008*

IT WAS EARLY SPRING, but in Provence the air already smelled rich and full of the promise of fresh growth and flowers. Redheaded Molly Sutton, standing at the railing of a luxurious rooftop terrace in the historical center of Aix-en-Provence, turned her face up to the evening sky and inhaled deeply, unable to stop smiling. Dearly as she loved her own village, who could turn down an invitation to someplace new ... especially in Provence.

It had been a glorious few months since marrying Ben Dufort on a snowy afternoon in Castillac. The couple had enjoyed every second of their honeymoon in Nice, even finding, as perhaps only happy newlyweds can, that a case of stomach upset was hilarious instead of annoying, that a winter sunburn is an opportunity for the delectable mutual slathering of unguents rather than an annoyance, and best of all, that tying the knot had not dulled their feelings for each other one bit.

They had returned home renewed and contented and begun their married life without any difficulties on the horizon, save not quite having enough work for Dufort/Sutton Investigations, which was not an unusual state of affairs. After the wedding, the gossips of the village (which, to be honest, included nearly everyone) were quiet on the subject of Molly and Ben; after all, happiness and contentment do not offer much in the way of juicy news. They tried to stir up some interest in the fact that Molly, only a scant few months after the wedding, had traipsed off by herself to visit out-of-town friends: *really, so soon? Was there trouble in paradise?* But Ben had responded to any such hints with a hearty laugh, and the talk had eventually dwindled away.

The sun had long since dropped below the rooftops, but Molly could see perfectly well thanks to the streetlights. Just below, *rue* Niccolo was narrow, and peering down without leaning out too far, she could see into the building on the other side of the street: an older man stood at a stove, stirring something in a saucepan. Farther inside the room, a beautifully-set table lit by candles.

The terrace was the top of a stunning house belonging to her friends Adèle and Michel Faure, brother and sister, whom she had met on a case early in her career as an investigator. The stylishness of the apartment was testament to their very good (and expensive) taste, but to Molly's mind, the real achievement was the roof garden, which when they had bought the place had consisted of nothing but a desultory café table and a couple of uncomfortable chairs parked on a flat tarpaper roof. But now it was a green paradise right in the middle of town, with trees in enormous *jardinières* just beginning to leaf out, as well as an extensive herb garden already bursting with a wide variety of herbs ready to snip for an omelette, a stew, or a cocktail.

Well, luxurious roof gardens aside, if I'm going to be honest, I *do* miss Ben rather badly, thought Molly, letting her eyes drift over the herbs distractedly, and allowing herself to get a little misty-eyed. He told me I would and he was right. She smiled again, remembering how he had teased her when she told him about her plan to visit Provence.

"It's not that I'm restless by nature," she had said. "Well, maybe just a little. But I don't have all that much in the way of *gîte* bookings at the moment. I mean, yes, someone is coming every week, but it's not like we're full up the way it will be in summer. So ... it seems like the right moment to skip town, just for two or three weeks. Adèle and Michel were the first real friends I made in France, and I haven't seen them in so long. I don't want the connection to lapse so long it fades away, you know? Adèle is all hot for me to come to the music festival and listen to some opera. But please, be honest—do you mind staying home and running the *gîtes* while I'm away? Would you rather come to Aix with me? Because we can find someone to run things while we're gone, I'm sure."

Ben had reassured her that the honeymoon was enough travel to last him for a while, and he was more than happy to stay behind and take care of the gîtes. He kissed her long and lovingly, and she knew in that moment that she would suffer being apart from him. But Molly was not a person who expected life to be free of suffering every second, and she was independent through and through. So she packed her bags and took a train to Aix, which she fell in love with so immediately and so violently that while she was there, she believed it to be even more magnificent than Paris (though she was unwilling to admit this to anyone because it seemed blasphemous).

Molly held onto the iron railing with both hands and closed her eyes. Someone called a cat (who says the French aren't optimists? thought Molly), and the smell of something cooking in wine drifted up to the roof along with the sound of clattering pots and pans. It was Friday night. The neighborhood was sitting down to dinner, and Molly's mouth began to water as she wondered what her friends were making in the kitchen.

The day of traveling was done, the reunion with her friends

had been joyful and instantly comfortable, her glass of wine was more than delicious, the roof garden an oasis of calm. All she had to do was wait a few more moments for her friends to return from their day of errands and cooking. Everything—even including missing Ben—should have been delightful.

But somehow, Molly could not settle. She sat down on an insanely comfortable glider with soft cushions but got right up again, back to the edge of the roof, and looked down at rue Niccolo. It was empty. She saw that the shoots on the pollarded trees were starting to sprout, which usually fascinated her, but her eyes skated past them.

I don't know, she thought. Everything is just as it should be, and yet …

Molly breathed deeply and appreciated the smell of chicken cooking in wine. Probably just some leftover stress from traveling, she thought, going back to the glider and taking another big sip from her glass. After all, feelings aren't facts … right?

"THE BIG PROBLEM, obviously, is that there is, as yet, no staircase to the roof," Adèle said, balancing a tray of food she had somehow managed to carry up the ladder with one hand, steadying the tray on one shoulder while sliding her hand along a side rail, despite having some physical challenges from having been born with a clubfoot. "We looked into installing a spiral staircase, but there is no place to tuck it where it won't ruin a room. The ladder is fine —I even like it, to be honest—it's like having a grown-up's tree-house, you know? But of course it makes dining up here something of a challenge. Michel keeps talking about putting in a dumbwaiter, but so far he's all hat and no cattle."

Molly laughed. "Are you secretly from Texas?"

Adèle grinned. "It's the perfect phrase. So many occasions to use it, I'm afraid I'll wear it out. Anyway. Here we are."

"It would kill me dead if this dinner ended up on the floor."

"And I would kill whoever dropped it!" said Adèle, somewhat fiercely. "I've been working very hard on my cooking and can't wait to show off."

"I thought you might have hired a cook, once your aunt's money came in," said Molly, and then clapped her hand over her mouth.

Adèle laughed. "No worries," she said. "You know that's one of the things we love about you, right? You say things that other people think but are too restrained to say."

"You mean I put my foot in it every five minutes."

Adèle smiled. "It is *so* good to see you. Now where is Michel?"

Molly leaned back into the soft cushions and observed her friend. Adèle was well-dressed, as she always was. Not in a flashy way—but Molly knew her beautifully-cut pants and simple-looking shirt were doubtless from some Parisian designer who Molly was unfamiliar with. Adèle's hair was pulled back into a loose chignon, a more relaxed style than she had worn when she lived in Castillac. Molly could see that, on the surface at least, Provence seemed to agree with her.

Adèle freshened Molly's glass and poured one for herself, talking amiably about the vintner who lived just outside Aix and had become a good friend. The intricacies of winemaking were still mysterious to Molly, and after some years in France, she had accepted that she was never going to understand the process as well as a native. So she listened politely but kept an ear out for Michel, finally going over to the opening for the ladder and looking down.

"These olives are super tasty, and of course I'm enjoying your friend's wine immensely. But where in the world is Michel? I'm going to faint from hunger."

Adèle looked cross. "I love my brother. No one knows that more than you," she said, affectionately. "And at the same time—

he can be quite exasperating. I thought he was right behind me with the roast chicken!"

Again Molly noticed an unsettling feeling, a twinge of anxiety in her belly, and wondered what it was about. Simply the prospect of an ambrosial chicken upside down on the floor?

The friends settled in and talked about the first time they met, at La Métairie, the best restaurant in Castillac, when Molly had discovered their not exactly well-loved aunt lying dead on the restroom floor. They talked about how nice it was to have a little money, and how it solved some big problems but hardly all of them. They talked about marriage, and decided it was much the same way.

"And you two—any romance on the horizon for either of you?" Molly asked, grinning.

Adèle waved her arms in the air and looked away. "A person can't expect ..." she started but did not finish. Molly cocked her head, waiting to see if she would continue, but Adèle stayed quiet, her eyes on the building across the street. They found some inconsequential things to talk about, which was no doubt for the best; the friends needed some time together before making their way back to the former degree of intimacy. But the intimacy had been real—how could it have been otherwise, when Molly had been privy to the complicated family secrets of the Faures, and when all their lives had been in danger as a result?

At last they heard the sound of Michel making his way up, and a roast chicken on a platter appeared through the opening, with one hand expertly guiding it to safety.

"Michel!" shouted Adèle. "Is this any way to treat a guest? What in the world have you been doing?"

With a winning smile, he pushed himself through the opening. "Sorry, sis," he said. He bowed to Molly with a wide grin. "Have I mentioned how happy I am that you're here?"

"A few times," said Molly with a laugh.

"If you're so happy, why are you intent on starving her?" asked Adèle.

"Didn't you hear all the hubbub? Down on the street?"

"We did not."

"What's going on?" asked Molly, her ears nearly pricking up like her dog Bobo's.

Michel nimbly got to his feet and brought the platter of chicken to the table. It was swimming in a thick, dark sauce, with roasted potatoes and carrots encircling it. It smelled heavenly. But even the divine aroma did not distract Molly from wanting to know more about the hubbub.

"It's Madame Trudeau. I stuck my head out the front door to see what the fuss was about and saw her being carried out on a stretcher."

"Stretcher? Is she all right?"

Michel laughed. "You're kind to ask, sis. You really are. No, she is *not* all right, she had a sheet pulled over her head."

"Yikes. I take it … this is no great friend of yours?" said Molly, watching Michel's face.

"No great friend of anyone's, I'd say," said Adèle. "Well, you'll understand what I mean: of anyone I can think of, she reminded us most of dear Aunt Josephine."

"To dear Aunt Josephine!" said Michel, merrily raising his glass.

"Ah. Not exactly a warm-hearted soul, this Madame Trudeau?"

"She was a horrible, vicious person who didn't deserve—" said Adèle, stopping herself and taking a breath. Her face was pale.

"Perhaps … let's talk about what we're going to show Molly here in Aix," said Michel.

Molly noticed Adèle's hand trembling as she reached for the salt.

"Honestly, you don't have to make any great plans for me," said Molly. "My very favorite thing, well, besides eating, is just to wander around the streets, gawking at everything and everyone. I'm not all that much for actual sightseeing. Too much pressure."

"It's a beautiful city for wandering," Adèle said, still gripping the saltshaker. "And the play we told you about—well, lured you here with," she laughed. "It's not opening for nearly two weeks. So please, *mi casa es su casa* and all that. Wander all you like."

The image of the neighbor covered with a sheet stayed on their minds, though each of them, for their own reasons, did not mention it.

Molly shook her head as though to clear her thoughts. The three were quiet for another moment, the two women watching Michel's progress carving the chicken. They heard a clatter down the street that sounded like someone had dropped a hubcap on the sidewalk.

"How did she die?" asked Molly.

Michel let out a musical laugh. "Oh, now Molly, I'm sure you're worried about being bored, here for only a social visit with no investigation to sink your teeth into. Madame Trudeau was in her eighties, wouldn't you say, Adèle? No doubt she died from natural causes."

Molly shrugged. "I wasn't hinting at anything, just curious."

"Mm hmm," said Michel, winking at her. "Sure you were."

They sipped their wine. A nightingale sang so close it seemed to be a guest of the dinner party. Each was lost in thought, and the companionable silence lasted for some time.

Michel looked seriously at his sister and nodded, then piled their plates with chicken and slices of artichoke heart, carrots, and potatoes. He refilled their glasses once more and checked to make sure they each had napkins and utensils. He was ready to scramble down the ladder for anything they'd forgotten.

"To the death of Madame Trudeau!" said Adèle, snatching up her glass and raising it for a toast. "May all tyrants meet their Maker sooner rather than later!"

It was a grisly toast, but the three friends had met in grisly circumstances after all, and they clinked glasses with enthusiasm.

The twinge of unease Molly had felt dissipated entirely with the delicious food and company, and she was nothing but glad she had decided to leave Castillac to visit her friends. Happy to be married to Ben, and also happy to have a chance to miss him. Happy to be exactly where she was, in a town new to her, on a roof listening to nightingales, a little tipsy, with two people she absolutely adored.

2

In Castillac, Ben was walking through the meadow at *La Baraque*, where he and Molly lived and ran a *gîte* business. He was on his way back from a walk in the forest with Bobo when Constance flew out of the *pigeonnier* shrieking at the top of her voice.

"*Aeiiieee!* Ben, help, *help!*"

Ben took a deep breath and walked towards her, though he was not terribly alarmed, having known Constance since she was a child and thus having heard many such outbursts. Bobo ran up and licked the young woman on the leg, which caused her to shout louder until she realized what was happening and bent down to throw her arms around the tail-wagging dog.

"Bonjour, Constance," said Ben, holding her by the shoulders and kissing her cheeks, unwilling to allow any hysteria to interrupt a proper greeting. "What is the problem, *chérie?*"

"I was cleaning in the pigeonnier. Have you forgotten? There are guests coming tomorrow, and with Molly gone I wanted to make sure everything is ship-shape. I'd already cleaned in there earlier in the week but like I said—"

"You want it ship-shape, yes," said Ben. "You've worked very hard. Thank you, Constance, you know I'm depending on you while Molly is away and you're doing beautifully."

"But so I'm running the vacuum—and let me tell you, it's way past time for Molly to invest in a new one. That thing is cantankerous like you would not believe. Some days it's okay and some days it gets in a mood and I can hardly—"

"Constance. Is it the vacuum causing you such distress?"

She heaved a sigh. "No, not the vacuum cleaner. I was only saying … okay, forget it. What happened was, the vacuum stopped working—as it *so often* does—and so I decided to wipe down the bathroom again, because sometimes if you just ignore the vacuum for a little while it gets over itself and starts working again. When I opened the cabinet under the kitchen sink to get cleaning fluid —a rat came running out. Running straight for me! An r-a-t *rat*!"

"You barely escaped with your life," said Ben.

"Oh, shush," said Constance, giving Ben a shove.

"You're so fun to tease. All right, it's ten o'clock and the new guests will arrive at, what? Around noon? What else is on our list to do before then? I will investigate the rat situation. I believe Molly puts fresh flowers and wine in all the gîtes on changeover day?"

"She does. I've already taken care of that. I want to check the cottage one more time, and then it's just sitting around waiting to greet the guests when they get here and give them keys and all that. Are you going to take care of that part or should I stick around?"

"I've got it covered," said Ben. "Finish up in the cottage and then go and enjoy this beautiful day."

Constance laughed and rolled her eyes, since the sky was dark and rain starting to fall. "*À toute à l'heure*, then," she said, scampering off and leaving Ben to find Monsieur Rat.

He ducked inside the pigeonnier and looked around. It was spotlessly clean, which was a pleasant surprise given how Molly had complained from time to time about Constance getting distracted, leaving rags lying around, and cleaning tasks only halfway finished. The downstairs was quiet and still, with no evidence of uninvited rodents. Mellow light filtered in through the small windows set into the masonry walls, and Ben thought about the mason who had done the work, his old friend Pierre Gault, who sadly had passed away nearly two years earlier.

The interior of the pigeonnier was exceptionally beautiful, and he took a moment to appreciate Molly's vision and perseverance in making it happen. Was it strange that this American had landed in Castillac, of all places, and had the vision to take a crumbling structure like the pigeonnier and turn it into a gîte that was both practical and an artistic achievement? He supposed there were people all over France doing similar things, but felt proud of her nonetheless. He ran his hands along the uneven walls, remembering a night they had spent there together, just after they were married, a ridiculously romantic night where they had splurged on a bottle of Châteauneuf-du-Pape and lit candles everywhere ...

Ben looked under the kitchen sink and saw a hole in the cabinet barely a few fingers wide. Rats are remarkable creatures, he thought, straightening up as he figured out where to get the materials for a patch, along with a few traps. A good *gîte* business depended on word of mouth, and he certainly did not want the word "rat" to be associated with La Baraque, especially not on his watch.

ACROSS THE VILLAGE, in a small and cozy apartment, Nico and Frances were considering their options for the day. The night before, Nico had managed to convince Frances to go on a bike ride plus picnic, but now the rain was coming down in sheets with no hint of stopping anytime soon.

"We could just stay in bed all day," said Nico, grinning.

"We could," said Frances, grinning back. "But I was so looking forward to our ride. I've been working too hard lately and I could have used some fresh air."

"You are the biggest, fattest, most unrepentant liar I have ever heard in my life," said Nico.

"What are you talking about?"

"I had to beg you to go on the ride."

"But now we can't go."

"I know that. You don't hear me saying we should ride in this weather, do you?"

"No, of course not. I'm only saying I regret not being able to go."

"And I'm saying you're a lying terrible horrible person and I wish I'd never met you."

Frances cackled. "And you're a hideous gnome and I wish I'd never turned over a rock and found you under it."

Nico leapt to where Frances was standing by the kitchen counter and swept her into his arms. "Then we were made for each other," he whispered into her hair.

They kissed. The kiss went on for some time, and then Frances pulled back and looked at Nico. "Okay, this may sound silly, but what Molly and I used to do in weather like this was put on slickers and take umbrellas and go for walks. We did this in college and people thought we were high."

"Were you?"

"No," Frances laughed. "It's just—it's no big deal, obviously, taking a walk in the rain. But it does something to ... elevate the spirit, not to sound all high flown. I don't know, it's just a good thing to do every once in a while. You game?"

He nodded, only a little disappointed they weren't headed back to bed. "You miss her, don't you?"

"Molly? Insanely. It goes without saying."

"Have you considered going to Provence to join her?"

"What? Absolutely not! Since when do you think I'm a party-crasher? I do have a shred of self-respect left, you know."

Nico shrugged. "I'm sure Molly wouldn't see it that way."

"It's not Molly's place I'd be going to. Besides, it's not bad to miss somebody. Just reminds you that you love them."

"Castillac's going to be a little boring without her, though."

"Eh, she won't be gone that long. And I'm sure we can stir up some trouble if we put our minds to it. Let's see ... maybe we should throw a party or something. Whose business can we put our noses into where we don't belong?"

Nico laughed. "Now that sounds like Molly! Let's get some lunch and discuss. Chez Papa?"

"Don't you want to go someplace else?"

"Why, when the bartender eats for free? And I'm in the mood for frites."

"When are you not," said Frances, pulling on some jeans, and looking at her husband with deep affection.

3

"I have one small chore to do—you can come with me, it won't take long—and then we'll be off to the market," Adèle said to Molly after they had finished their coffee.

"It's so strange to be away from La Baraque on a Saturday morning," said Molly. "I never felt this way about any other job I've had—I was always gleeful to get away, the farther away the better! But I've been doing Changeover Day at La Baraque for years now. Every Saturday like clockwork. Double-check the cleaning, then the market, then welcoming guests, that's how my Saturdays have looked since it feels like forever. Am I turning into a stagnant, boring homebody? Because I have to admit, it feels not quite right to be away. Like I'm neglecting my child. Not to mention my beloved Benjamin."

"Well, you *are* newly married, of course you're missing home. I'm sure Ben and Constance have it covered. And not to brag, but you are in for a treat with the Aix market. I hope you're hungry!"

"I'm always hungry," said Molly, patting her growling stomach. "What's your errand, shall I come along?"

Adèle reached into the refrigerator and pulled out a metal

container with a lid, then placed it carefully in a paper bag. "It's a sad case, all too common these days," she said. "My neighbor, Émile Moreau, has cancer. He's been fighting it for a while but by the looks of him, I'm afraid he's not got much time. In any case, I'm taking him some soup, we won't stay long, and then off to the market."

"I'm happy to come with you. But maybe someone that ill won't want a stranger trouping around his house?"

Adèle considered. "Perhaps you're right. I tend to think of him as he was when Michel and I first met him, so bright and curious about everyone and everything. You would have hit it off like gangbusters, I've no doubt about that. But it's true, he's gone downhill quickly and is feeling quite poorly now. How about we meet at the fountain on the far end of the Cours Mirabeau? I won't be long. It's tiring for Émile so I never stay long."

Molly agreed, and once out on rue Niccolo they separated. It was still early, but townspeople were already filling the street, carrying string bags or talking on their phones, chatting with neighbors, sweeping the sidewalk. She made her way down a narrow street, following a woman holding hands with a young girl. Out of long habit, she walked quickly to catch up to them so she could eavesdrop.

The daughter was talking rapidly about which candies she preferred and why, and the mother was kindly responding with more interest than Molly believed she actually felt. The daughter, who looked to be around eight, was holding her mother's hand tightly, and pulling on it, leaning away, and then spinning under her mother's arm as though dancing.

For Molly, these kinds of moments were bittersweet, as she had wished so deeply for a child of her own and was still getting used to the reality that it was not going to happen. Oh stop feeling sorry for yourself, she muttered half aloud, straightening her posture, and attempting to feel better by noticing how easily she understood what the mother and daughter were saying, even though their French was heavily accented in a way she was not used to. She stopped for a moment to let them disappear into the throng headed for the market.

She heard a smack. The unmistakable sound of flesh hitting flesh. Molly whirled around to see a delivery boy in a white apron holding his bare arm and hunching over.

"Do better!" a young man shouted at him. "Or there's more for you!" He raised his hand and threatened to smack the delivery boy again.

"They were out of that brand," the boy said, apparently unable to let go of the idea that this customer would see reason.

The man hit him across the face.

"What are you doing?" said Molly, running to the boy. "Get hold of yourself," she said, glaring at the man.

The delivery boy pulled away and got on his bicycle and after a shaky start, sped away. And the man, dark-haired and wearing what even fashion-failure Molly could tell was a very expensive shirt, slipped back through a door and was gone.

She was furious.

The street was placid and calm with only a few people walking by on their way to the market; it seemed that Molly was the only one to witness the assault of that poor boy, practically a child.

What in the world is wrong with people, she thought.

And then Molly turned into Cours Mirabeau, and it was impossible not to be filled with pleasure at the sight of the beautiful street, lined with grand mansions and plane trees with bright new leaves. Stalls lined the center of the long rectangle, selling everything from kitchenware to socks to salt. It wasn't crowded yet, but there was a steady hum of chatter, a dog barking, birds making a racket in the trees. The smells of strong coffee and vanilla wafted her way, and she wondered if it would be rude, or merely piggish, if she indulged in a pastry before meeting Adèle.

. . .

"I'M ABSOLUTELY FAMISHED," said Adèle to Molly at the fountain. "How about if we walk through the market without hurrying—" she glanced at her watch, heavy and expensive—"and by the time we get to the other end, we can go to this place I know, close by. Nothing fancy, but—you like pizza?"

Molly felt a surge of desperation. "Pizza?" she answered weakly. "The place wouldn't be open right now?"

Adèle laughed. "It's only ten-thirty, Molly. Come on, let's walk and talk. I haven't quite gotten over having you right here, in person, and we still have so much catching up to do!"

"Yes," said Molly, imagining some glistening bits of onion swimming in a pool of melted mozzarella, with tomato sauce peeking out on the side, atop a crust bubbled, blistered, and burnt in places. Her legs felt wobbly from desire. "All right then, lead the way," she said, her mouth watering. "I did check out some of the stalls earlier. There's quite a variety, far more than the Castillac market. And the quality is quite high, isn't it?"

Adèle nodded. She took Molly's hand and the two women walked slowly through the market, back the way Molly had come. Before long, Adèle brought up her mother, and her aunt; she and Molly spent the rest of the walk going over the events of that case, retelling the story to each other, not for the first time. It was different, having the benefit of looking back at what had happened after a longer interval of time, with a calm and objectivity impossible when the events were fresh.

"You and Michel—your lives took such a dramatic turn," said Molly, looking at a tray of silver rings and nearly asking to try one on. "How much are those traumatic events still present in your mind? I mean, do thoughts of your mother and your aunt come up a lot?" Adèle and Michel's aunt had been murdered by their mother, the sort of shock and trauma that does not dissolve overnight. Or maybe ever.

Adèle nodded. She waved at a man with a grand moustache

behind a counter of cheeses but kept walking. "I would say that in the first year, all of it was in the back of my mind nearly always. I was never free from those thoughts, not for a minute, not for a second.

And now? I would not say it is all healed, how could it ever be? I can think of my mother without agony, which is something. But ... even when I lived in Castillac and worked for the bank—holding that good job, where people depended on me and I had to hit a certain mark of competence—inside, in here—" She tapped her chest. "I was so tangled up, the rage, just ... oh Molly, it is difficult to find the words!"

"Yes. I think I understand. It must take time, is all."

"It is easier, much easier, that no one in Aix knows about our story. That Michel and I ... that we come from a poisoned ancestry of instability and violence. That our inheritance is ..." She shook her head and looked down.

"Adèle," said Molly, reaching for her friend's hand. "I understand why you feel this way, but you are phrasing it in the worst possible manner. Never forget that *you* did nothing wrong. Your aunt was cruel, your mother violent—but never you. You are blameless."

Adèle took a deep breath and then clapped her hands together. "Okay! Let's put this subject behind us for now, shall we?"

"Time for lunch?" Molly asked hopefully.

Adèle laughed. "Come with me. It's scandalous to eat at this hour, but I am friends with the proprietor and maybe they could let us in a bit early."

Molly beamed. "Oh, bless you for indulging me. I have never wanted pizza more than I do this minute. Does your friend have a specialty? You French are so much more creative with pizza than they are in America, where the idea of innovation is to put canned pineapple on top!" She shuddered. "I much prefer the

French way of drizzling cream or cracking an egg … wait—oh my heavens, look!" Molly stopped and pointed at a doorway facing on the Cours Mirabeau that had come into view as they moved past a stall.

"Ah, you like that? Imposing, isn't it? The Hôtel de Maurel de Ponteves."

"Something about those statues—they're obviously ancient and made of stone, yet it feels as though they're real giants, just pausing for a moment, who might amble on down the street if they could find someone else to watch the door. Incredible."

On either side of the heavy wooden door with its lion's-head knockers stood a statue of a man, bearded, hips draped in a loin-cloth. The men were giants, tall enough to reach to the second floor, where an ornate iron balcony rested on the tops of their heads, or perhaps they were holding the balcony with one hand while the other rubbed the top of the head. Their legs were gone —stolen, crumbled, who knew?— and Molly judged the statues to be ancient, even by France's standards.

"How old are they?"

"I believe the building dates from the mid-1600s," said Adèle.

Molly shook her head, smiling, eyes still glued to the giants.

"Has the Hôtel so distracted you that you've lost your appetite?" said Adèle, teasing.

Molly laughed. "Let's go! You can fill in the details once we've made our orders."

Adèle moved quickly down a narrow side street, motioning for Molly to follow.

It was always a thrill for Molly to meet a new city, especially a French one, even more, a French one as beautiful as Aix-en-Provence. The street wound this way and that, barely wide enough for a car.

"Sheep track," Adèle said over her shoulder.

"You read my mind! Love it."

They passed shops with postcard carousels crowding the tiny sidewalk, bakeries and butchers, shoe stores. Houses with elegant courtyards, houses with glossy lacquered doors, wrought-iron fences and balconies. Finally, Adèle stopped, grinned at Molly, and pushed through a low homely door made of rough wood, unpainted. Inside, the smell was transporting—yeast, garlic, the acid of tomatoes, the deep fragrance of aged cheese.

"Oh my," Molly murmured to herself, her eyes going straight to the back of the room to a well-used stone oven. "I can tell just from smelling it that the tomato sauce is going to be amazing. And the garlic ... oh Adèle, this is absolute heaven!"

Adèle's friend was not yet in the restaurant, but it was nearly eleven o'clock and they were grudgingly seated and given menus.

"Is it too early for a glass of wine?" asked Molly.

Adèle just laughed. "You Americans and your funny rules."

Molly ordered a bottle of Évian and perched on the edge of her chair, almost overcome with anticipation of the first bite. Adèle ordered a simple mushroom pizza and a *pichet* of rosé for them to share. That out of the way, the friends looked at each other for a moment, quiet.

"You seem happy," Adèle said, after the wine had been poured. "Happi*er*, I should say. When we first met—excuse me for being so forward—you were ... you did not quite have your feet underneath you, would you agree?"

"Yes," said Molly. "I had only been in Castillac a few months. I was a little unsteady, for sure."

"Your divorce was still raw?"

"Hm, not exactly raw ... well ... it wasn't so much that my heart was broken, more that ... my *life* was broken, and I had to figure out a way to go forward, to make something entirely different for myself."

"Ah yes." Adèle held out her glass and Molly clinked her against it. They sipped.

Molly couldn't help herself; she glanced to the back of the restaurant to see if there was any movement around the oven.

"But still," she added, "I was wounded. Hurt. And that did take some time to recover from. As I know you understand very well."

Adèle nodded. "The events ... we don't need to go over it all yet again ... I do hope you realize how grateful Michel and I are for what you did for us. Secrets are poisonous—and the secrets of the Faure family were poisoning us without our even knowing it, without our knowing they even existed." Adèle twisted her napkin in her lap. "What I wish to do, what we've been trying to do, is move forward. Not allow ourselves to be dragged down by the past."

"And what does moving forward look like to you, besides making your home in Aix?"

Adèle did not answer at first. She played with her napkin some more and sighed. "Now that we don't have to worry about money anymore," she said, and it was as though she could barely force herself to say the words, "what I would like—what Michel and I would both like, actually—is to find partners. I admit I am quite envious of you and your gendarme."

Molly flushed, not entirely comfortable with being the object of anyone's envy, and especially her friend's.

"Well, then that is what I will wish for you," said Molly. "If I had even the slightest bit of confidence I knew anything about anything, I would tell you how I managed it. But I think, in the case of Ben? I just got lucky, and that's all there was to it."

"But nevertheless, you were alert to the luck and did not push it away or ruin it somehow," said Adèle.

"True enough. Oh boy, look at that," she said, pointing to the waiter walking toward them with a large platter balanced on one hand, steam rising.

What did Adèle think she had ruined, Molly wondered. And filed that thought away for later, for all attention in the moment belonged with the glorious pie sitting in front of her, a pool of melted cheese with scattered herbs, the crust bubbled and blackened in places, the tang of tomato in her nose.

"This right here is pretty much the apex of human achievement," she murmured, and Adèle smiled, handing her the knife.

❧ 4 ❧

After lunch, Adèle went off to a meeting, saying something about paintings and a local museum, and Molly made her way back to rue Niccolo, slightly tipsy from the rosé. As Molly was jiggling the key in the lock, she heard Michel talking inside. She paused, cocking her head, the instinct for eavesdropping always at the ready. She heard footsteps, and then the voices got softer, the words not quite distinguishable, and she finished turning the key and went inside.

"Molly!" said Michel, coming into the foyer. "Come in, come in." He waved his hand graciously in the direction of younger woman who was wearing an elegant light wool suit and a strained expression.

"Molly, it is my deepest pleasure to present Apolline Cuvalier. Apolline, with great affection, I introduce you to—Molly, I'm sorry, somehow I do not know whether you took Ben's name?"

"No," said Molly.

"Molly Sutton," he said to Apolline, his face arranged in the most charming way imaginable, as though—without any discernible falsity of emotion—the fact of these two women meeting was sure to be the best moment in his day.

Molly stepped forward, even after years living in France not sure what to do next. Shake hands, kiss, nod? Just take your cue from the native, she reminded herself.

As Molly stepped forward, Apolline drew back. Her eyebrows were penciled black, darker than her hair color, and she raised them in what Molly interpreted as a mixture of alarm and condescension.

"Pleased to meet you," Molly said, trying not to react to the other woman's rebuff.

"I'm sure," said Apolline. She turned back to Michel. "As I was saying ..." she shook her head slightly as though to push away the interruption. "As I was saying, the market is practically on fire, and in my opinion, there's never been a better time to enlarge your position. Mark my words, it won't be long before word gets out and the shares will be too dear to be worth fiddling with."

Molly looked at Michel. His eyes were bright and his cheeks bloomed pink, and he seemed to hang on Apolline's every word. Was he ... was he actually interested in this woman? *Romantically* interested? To Molly it sounded as though Apolline was some kind of salesy flim-flammer trying to wheedle his money out of him. She looked Apolline over more carefully. Her dark gray suit was Chanel; she was no expert but Molly did not think it was a knock-off. Her chestnut hair was carefully done and Molly guessed the woman had been to the salon that morning. She was older than Michel by more than a few years. She was attractive enough, Molly admitted ... and, of course, who was she to judge anyway? She knew as well as anyone that love or desire weren't things you could order by ticking qualities off a list.

I should be happy for Michel, if she makes him happy, she said to herself, unconvinced.

Molly excused herself and trotted upstairs to her bedroom. She wished Ben was there, wanting to talk over her conversations and observations. And wanting simply to feel his solid body next to hers, hear him turn the pages in one of his exquisitely boring naval histories, feel him wiggle his toes under the sheet as he concentrated on his reading.

This Apolline Cuvalier, she thought, scowling ... no, she had to stop expecting bad behavior from people she did not even know. Stop thinking that people were up to no good, based on no evidence whatsoever.

Even if, so often, no good was exactly where they were steering. And unless Molly's *merde* detector had suddenly broken, she would make a grand bet that this Apolline Cuvalier was not only doing just that but trying to take Michel with her.

$\mathcal{H}$ 5 $\mathcal{H}$

Though he was certainly a competent and intelligent man, Ben Dufort had not had the most wide-ranging work experience, it must be said. As a young man, still in university, he had worked during vacations in a shop in Castillac, selling shoes.

While he didn't disgrace himself entirely, Ben did not show any particular talent for selling shoes. After graduation, his career at the *gendarmerie* began. He was promoted regularly, all the way to chief ... a satisfying trajectory all in all. However, it had ended on a bumpy note: after an especially difficult case involving the Faure family, he decided, in a moment of deep insecurity and unusual impulsiveness, to turn his back on the career at which he'd worked so hard.

There was no question Ben had high standards for himself, certainly higher than he had for everyone else. He had judged his participation in that particular case an unacceptable failure. Later on, admittedly, he regretted his hastiness and wished for his old job back—at least in moments here and there—but one did not quit the *gendarmerie* and then change one's mind. That door was closed, for good.

Afterwards, his old pal Rémy had kindly hired him to work on his organic farm, but that had, put most kindly, not been a good fit. Eventually he returned to detective work on the private side, when he and Molly formed Dufort/Sutton Investigations. It had not, so far, been the most financially successful venture, but he and Molly were dedicated to making it work and slowly gaining a good reputation.

Taken altogether, Ben's work experience was comprised of shoes, criminals, and spinach. Nothing in any of those jobs gave him any sort of preparation for running a gîte business, which was what was on his plate that particular Saturday in March.

Molly made it look easy, practically effortless. He had just assumed it was.

Oh boy.

Their next expected guests, the Sadlers, were coming from Rhode Island with their young daughter. They had emailed to ask about a car rental and Ben had briskly emailed back with recommendations and thought that was taken care of.

A young woman of nineteen, Briony Lark, was arriving sometime that day but had not said when. Ben wondered about her, since his experience with nineteen-year-olds—which was wider than one might think, since that age group got into trouble with the law the most—was that they travel in packs, rarely alone. Perhaps because Briony was British, that changed the equation? Because the British were odd ducks; all French-people knew that. Ben was unsure. He wanted to text Molly for her opinion but was resolute in wanting to take care of changeover day all on his own and not run to Molly with every idle question that passed through his head.

He had said he was happy to keep the gîte running in her absence. Which was true, at least theoretically.

Constance showed up, wanting to help, but Ben did not have Molly's management skills where Constance was concerned, and her unpredictability and occasional volatility were no comfort.

The Sadlers called from Bergerac. The car rental place where they had a reservation was inexplicably closed, and they feared they would still be charged if they tried going to a different place. Could he advise?

Ben spoke soothingly to Mrs. Sadler and then more forcefully to Mr. Sadler, but he quickly realized they were not going to take his advice to go have lunch and try the rental place in the early afternoon. They simply wanted to complain.

He was standing in the living room, having checked Molly's email in case other problems lurked there. The thought crossed his mind to pour himself a beer, though it was barely noon. Bobo nudged his leg with a hopeful look, wanting a walk.

"I can't now, Bobo, the hordes are about to descend and I need to stay right here until they're all settled. All right, well, not hordes exactly, it's only four people altogether, including the child. Hopefully they'll be installed straightaway and we can disappear into the forest together."

Bobo barked.

A bang on the front door.

"Bonjour Constance," said Ben with a sigh, opening the old door wide.

"Bonjour to you, Benjamin! Saturday! It's showtime! Are you ready? Game face on and all that?"

Ben just stared blankly.

"Ben, come *on*. You can't just give the new guests a weak greeting, throw them the keys, and Bob's your uncle. You have to make them feel *welcome*. And Americans?" She threw her head back and cackled, which Ben found ominous. "Americans like a whole brouha-ha. They like a lot of attention. Well, most of 'em anyhow."

"Attention?" said Ben, feeling a little queasy.

"Yes, *attention*. You've got to chat 'em up. Ask 'em over, give 'em a glass of local wine, and ask if there's anything they need. Talk up some of the local sights. And most of all, act like they're old friends coming for a long-awaited visit and you're just thrilled they're here."

NELL GODDIN

"Now really, I don't think Molly puts on all that."

"Molly doesn't *put on* anything. She genuinely likes meeting new people and doesn't have to fake it. She's not a secret people-hater like you and me, Benjamin," Constance said with another cackle.

People-hater? wondered Ben.

Constance shoved his shoulder playfully. "Oh come on, you know it's true. You'd much rather stay home and read a book than go to a village fête or some such, now admit it."

"Is that a crime?"

"Of course it's not! I'm just saying—it's not exactly the profile of someone in the hospitality business. And that means you, as long as Molly's away. So—when are the first guests due to arrive?"

"That moment has come and gone. Stuck in Bergerac. They got to the car rental place during lunch."

"Oh dear. Americans, no doubt?"

Ben nodded.

"They'll be complaining, you can count on it." Yet another cackle. "But with any luck, they'll be the humorous sort of complainers and not the whiny kind."

"There are different kinds?" Ben's voice was getting fainter and fainter.

Constance just laughed. "Innkeeper is not really your best job," she said. "But never fear, I came over so I could play Molly's role. You just stand there and look pretty."

They both looked to the window, hearing a car turn into the driveway. A willowy young woman got out of Christophe's cab, carrying only a carry-on suitcase and a small knapsack.

"That must be Briony Lark," said Ben. "Okay, Constance, show me what you're made of." He followed her outside. Bobo raced over and jumped up on Briony, who thankfully laughed and scratched the dog behind the ears, and that small act comforted Ben more than he would have thought possible.

36

❧ 6 ❧

Molly woke from a nap with a start, utterly disoriented. She heard a commotion somewhere close by; she sat up and yawned, then went to the window and leaned out to see what was going on.

A block away, in the direction of the Cours Mirabeau, she saw a knot of people next to a stone building with twin dark red doors. Molly felt an intensity coming from the group even though no one (as was usual in France) was raising a voice. A woman in uniform, a *gendarme*, was facing a tall man in civilian clothes who was waving his finger around and appeared to be giving her orders.

Molly hopped quickly into the en-suite bathroom, splashed water on her face and rubbed it hard with a towel, tried to run a comb through her hair. Giving up, she trotted downstairs in search of Michel. Molly found him in a sitting room, looking distractedly out of the window facing the street. Apolline Cuvalier was nowhere to be seen.

"Michel! What's going on? There's some sort of disturbance down the street. Down that way," she said, pointing.

He looked at her blankly. "What? I'm sorry, I've been sitting here daydreaming. You know, Molly, it's an odd thing, after so many years of scrabbling to get by—that I don't have to worry about making a living anymore. So many years of scheming and planning just to pay the bills heaped up on my desk. Sometimes I almost feel as though I've lost something, in a way. As though I'm ... well ... I have no usefulness any longer. No purpose to guide my days."

Molly looked at Michel. He spoke as though he had been a very hard and conscientious worker, and though she loved him dearly, Molly did not believe that characterization was entirely accurate. When she was getting to know him, his work consisted mainly of sucking up to his rich aunt and hoping for her indulgence.

"Want to give me your money?" she said. "You can go right back to scheming and worrying, if you like. I would be willing to do that for you."

He reached an arm around her shoulders and pulled her close and kissed the side of her head. "You're the best," he murmured, with a chuckle.

"Now come on, look out the window and tell me what's going on out there. There's nothing like the sight of some *gendarmes* hanging about looking somber to make my pulse quicken."

"I thought it was only the one gendarme who did that."

"Michel! Just *look!*"

Grinning, he stuck his head out of the window to placate her. The knot of people had grown to a crowd and the same man was gesticulating, pointing up at a window of the building with the red door.

Michel shrugged. "City life, what can I say? Things happen."

"But *what* things?"

He shrugged again. "If it's something terribly bad, no doubt we'll find out in due course. Patrice Jubert's out there, he's always making sure to put himself in the middle of everything. More likely, it's a bit of hubbub over nothing. You know—someone ordered a sofa to be delivered but the truck can't fit down the street, so the delivery guy is arguing with the customer, and then Jubert and anyone walking by who likes to argue—and there are always plenty of those, believe me—jumps in, and—"

"But why a gendarme?"

"Maybe someone threw a punch? Maybe there's a city ordinance being violated?"

Molly pressed her lips together. "Michel. Please. Aren't you just the tiniest bit curious?"

He cocked his head and gave her question some thought. "No."

Molly laughed. Michel could try her patience, but he had a way of being honest in unexpected moments that she found exceedingly charming. He was not one of those people who thinks others will like him if he agrees with them about everything. In fact, worrying about whether other people liked him did not seem to be on his radar at all, especially now that he was living life free of his oppressive and judgmental Aunt Josephine.

"Well, I *am* curious. If you don't mind, I'm going to wander down that way and see what I can find out."

"Come back with a good story, then," he said, smiling. "I think I'll have a drink while I await your return. It's just going to be the two of us for dinner tonight—Adèle called earlier to say she will be out."

"Out?"

"She offered no details, but reading between the lines, I believe she's going on a date."

"Oh! Well, she'll come home to get ready then?"

"One would think." He looked at his watch. "It's nearly four, I guess she'll be back before long."

Molly nodded and headed out to the street. The crowd in front of the red door had grown still further, blocking the street completely. This was not about a sofa, thought Molly, and she was not wrong.

She walked slowly down the street, observing.

An older man was putting down a saucer of food scraps in the alleyway beside a house, and a pair of stray cats zoomed over to check it out. A woman wearing a skirt and knee socks was sweeping the sidewalk with an old-fashioned broom while staring at the crowd.

"Excuse me for bothering you," Molly said to her. "Do you know what's happened?"

The gray-haired woman kept sweeping and shook her head, not making eye contact.

"Thanks anyway, have a good evening," said Molly, and kept going. She saw the gendarme talking intently to a tall man whose pants were too short. Two boys wove in and out of the crowd, laughing, one chasing the other.

The murmur of the group had an edge to it, there was no mistaking it.

A middle-aged woman wearing an apron over blue jeans broke away and walked toward Molly.

"Excuse me for bothering you," said Molly, "but can you tell me what has happened?"

The woman in the apron stopped. "I don't want to sound crotchety, I really don't, but this city is not like it was." She looked up at the sky and shook her head. "All of France is not what it was."

Molly waited for the woman to explain. But she said nothing more and took off down the street, walking quickly away, still shaking her head.

Just as Molly reached the edge of the crowd, the dark red lacquered doors swung open. A *SAMU* (*Service d'Aide Medical Urgente*) backed out, guiding a gurney. On the gurney was a body with a sheet neatly pulled up to cover it. Another *SAMU* pushed from the other end, and behind her came the gendarme Molly had seen earlier.

The crowd gasped.

"Who is it?" someone called out.

They did not answer and neither did the gendarme. "Make way," she said, walking to the edge of the crowd and putting her palms up. People stepped back, craning their necks.

"Is it a resident of the building, can you at least tell us that much?" someone asked.

The gendarme stopped. She raised one hand high in the air and the crowd quieted. "This is an ongoing investigation," she said. "No details will be forthcoming until such time as is appropriate. There is no danger to the community. Please, go on about your business."

Molly stayed until the crowd had dispersed, moving around from one small group to another, eavesdropping. It felt important to find out who had died. And *how*. But no one seemed to know anything at all.

Those dark red doors ... wasn't that the same building that the young man went into after hitting the delivery boy? She was almost positive it was.

She stopped outside the Faures's door and sighed, pressing her hand to the wood. A covered body on a gurney is not a sight to make anyone feel lighthearted, especially when it was the second one on that street in a matter of days, and it was not a sight that Molly Sutton had any intention of setting aside.

"I KNOW you're in a bit of a rush, but if you wouldn't mind, I would really appreciate it," Molly said to Adèle, as they stood in Adèle's dressing room.

"Of course I don't mind. Though I may not be able to find out anything either. We've not lived in Aix long enough to have a wide circle of acquaintances. But—Émile lives next door to that building, I can give him a call if you like."

Molly nodded. "I know I must seem like a ... a ... kind of grave-haunting monster," she said, "but I ... there was something about the way the people outside were ... it's not that I believe in spirits, exactly, or auras. I mean, not really. But it just ... well, it would surprise me very much to hear that the death of that person was due to natural causes. The gendarme did say it was an ongoing investigation, and you wouldn't say that for just any death, would you? Not that it's my business either way," she added quickly, and Adèle laughed, taking her cell from a Céline handbag.

"You just have a thing for murder," Adèle said.

Molly felt the remark as a stab between her ribs, though she knew Adèle had not intended to hurt her.

In order to give her friend some privacy while she made the call, Molly excused herself and went into her bedroom. Each time she entered it, she appreciated the simple elegance of both the room's proportions and decoration. She tried to focus her attention on the rich brocade of the green curtains, and their luxurious gold fringe, but went to the window, pushing open the shutters, and looked out. The street was empty save for a cat sitting in a doorway across the street, and an old man walking with a cane, just turning the corner at the end of the block. No activity in front of the building with the dark red doors. It was as though the dead person had fallen into a pool, the surface had been momentarily disturbed, but now was flat and serene. As though the fall, and the person, had never existed.

And that's the whole thing right there, Molly thought. The thing we are all so afraid of. The water going flat and still again, as though nothing we did in our lives, our very existence, made any kind of mark at all.

The thought opened up a kind of terror in her heart and she quickly forced her mind to go in some other direction, settling on remembering the mushroom pizza in all its glory. Which was safe and soothing enough to think about, only it made her hungry all over again.

Molly had an urge to creep down the hallway to Adèle's room and eavesdrop, but for once did not give in to the impulse. Instead, she waited for Adèle to summon her. It was forty-five minutes later when Molly finally heard a soft knock at the door.

"I'm ready," Adèle said, twirling in the hallway. "Do I look all right?"

"Smashing," said Molly with feeling. "That skirt is *so* flattering. The earrings are perfection. Oh, how I wish I could dress as well as you!"

"You're just not as narcissistic as I am," laughed Adèle as they went downstairs. "I do love nice clothes. Sometimes I think I inherited the worst qualities of Aunt Josephine."

Molly laughed. "Ha!" she said. Then, unable to stop herself, she asked if Adèle had found anything out from the friend down the street.

"I did, actually. Let's join Michel for a quick drink before I go out, and I'll tell you both at the same time."

Molly nodded. Again she had this feeling of disturbance, of something looming just out of sight.

"Bonsoir, my beauties," said Michel, opening his arms wide as they came into the salon.

"When's your date?" he asked Adèle.

"Oh, it's not anything—I'm just meeting Oscar to go to a gallery opening. It's not a date, not really."

"Who is Oscar?" asked Molly.

"Norwegian fellow," said Michel. "He's supposedly frightfully tall."

Adèle rolled her eyes. "Michel's a little obsessed with the height of other men. But if you tease him about it, he gets sullen."

"It's just that teasing about height is so old, so worn out," said Michel, not looking at all insulted. "And seriously, Adèle's Oscar is practically a giant. At least that's how she describes him, I haven't actually had the pleasure of meeting him."

"He's not *my* Oscar," said Adèle, her cheeks coloring faintly.

"I'm going to want to hear every detail about Oscar and the

gallery. But first ... please tell us, before I explode from curiosity —what did your friend from down the street tell you?" said Molly.

"Michel, you're not going to believe it," said Adèle.

"Oh, I'm not that easy to shock," he said, getting out two glasses and pouring some Lillet.

"Rosalie told me that the dead man—it's Matéo Brule!" said Adèle.

Michel's eyes open wide. "You're kidding."

"I am not."

Molly looked from one to the other. "Who's Matéo Brule?"

"And not only that," said Adèle. "Molly's intuition was spot on —he was murdered."

Knew it, thought Molly.

Michel dropped into a dark gray velvet chair. "Really?"

Adèle nodded. She was smiling rather broadly. "More good news," she said.

Molly shot her a questioning look.

Michel let out a guffaw. "It's almost too perfect, isn't it? It's been quite a week for our little block. First, we are relieved of that harpy, Madame Trudeau. And the very next day, we're rid of Matéo Brule as well. It's honestly almost too good to be true."

"Harpy?" said Molly.

"Harpy, harridan, shrew. What would you call her?"

"Monster," said Adèle.

"Who is Matéo Brule?" asked Molly.

"A different sort of monster," answered Michel. "We were warned about him the day we moved in, actually. It was the usual mess, with our moving van barely able to make the turns neces-sary to get to our street, Adèle was a bundle of nerves—"

"That is not true, Michel. I swear Molly, it's his favorite thing to accuse other people of his own frailties. Michel himself was a bundle of nerves, in fact, so worried about his precious antiques getting bumped about during the move."

"Moving is terribly stressful on everyone," said Molly. "What else did your friend tell you? Does she know how he was murdered?"

"Throat slit," said Adèle.

All three took a sip of Lillet and considered this. It was a grisly way to die, though at least fairly quick. Molly had ten million questions at the very least, but Adèle scurried off, leaving her with an unusually moody Michel and no answers at all. They chatted about this and that, neither of them especially engaged with the conversation. When he poured himself a fourth glass of wine, Molly mumbled something about needing some fresh air and made her way outside.

❧   7   ❧

Just as Molly had climbed into bed and closed her eyes, her cell vibrated. She snatched it up, expecting it to be Ben, but it was Constance on the other end.

"Mooooolllly," moaned Constance.

"What's the matter? Is something wrong?"

"Oh, where to begin? Are you having the most fabulous time ever? Because if you are, that's great, we love you and just keep on having that fabulous time and we'll see you when you get back. But if you're not? If it's just so-so? Then maybe get back here pronto before your business collapses into a burning, smoking heap and never recovers."

Molly sat up. She knew Constance was prone to exaggeration, but nevertheless a burst of adrenaline shot through her, as though a beloved child was standing in the middle of the street unaware as a huge truck bore down—and Molly needed to fly through traffic and snatch her out from under the wheels.

"What are you saying, Constance?"

"You've always, and I mean *always*, told me that word of mouth is everything. That without good word of mouth, you'd just be rattling around in a bunch of empty rooms, not making two centimes to rub together."

"And ...? Please, just tell me what's got you so upset. The specifics."

"I can sum it up in one word: *rats.*"

"*What?*"

"That's right, Molls. And a husky, well-fed fellow, too. The kind of fellow who *breeds.*"

"Where did you see it?"

"He was stretched out on a chaise under the sink in the pigeonnier. Sipping a cocktail and reading a bestseller."

"Not funny."

"Who's laughing?"

"You told Ben?"

"Of *course* I told Ben. I'd do absolutely anything for you, Molly, you know that. But rodents do not fall under the heading of 'anything.' I got Ben to hustle over to the pigeonnier and he tackled the problem. It's only that ..."

Molly squeezed her eyes closed, trying to quell impatience. "What, Constance? Couldn't Ben find the hole and plug it?"

"He said he did."

"And so? Problem solved. Rats do exist in the world, you know. It's just a matter of keeping things clean so they don't have anything to feast on if they get in, and obviously, blocking up any holes. Old houses—they get holes. It happens. It's nothing to lose your mind over."

"If I paid for a vacation and woke up to see a rat dancing on my pillow, I'd lose my mind, all right."

"Did any guests see the rat?"

"Well, no. Not *yet.*"

Molly was doing her best to talk Constance down off the ledge, and she was not terribly worried about the rat in any case, confident that Ben could manage the situation. But at the same time, in that moment? She wanted nothing more than to stuff her things into a bag and leap on the next train to Castillac.

She took a deep breath.

"So, anything else? I'm sure you've got the rooms beautifully clean. Did you help Ben with greeting the guests like we talked about?"

Constance barked a sort of laugh. "Oh, I tried, Molly, I tried."

"Let's see," Molly thought quickly to the guest list. "It's Briony Lark, right? And the Sadlers, from Providence? No one else, no last-minute reservations?"

"That's right, Briony and the Sadlers. And just thank your lucky stars that's all there is. God help us all if there was anything close to a full house. Ben would have gone totally off the deep end."

"Is ... is he ... did everything go all right?"

"Let's just say a career in hospitality would not have been a great choice for him. About the same as organic farming."

Molly couldn't help it, she laughed. Then the sound of her half-strangled laughter made her laugh even more, and finally she was able to thank Constance for the call and for helping out, and hang up. She knew Constance to be a woman of passion, a woman who felt every moment in her life deeply, and so zigged and zagged from euphoria to the depths of misery, often in a matter of seconds.

She thought about calling Ben but decided not to. She really did have confidence in him. For heaven's sake, it's not as though the job was that difficult, even with his rather halting English, which most people found quite appealing. There was nothing quite like a good laugh over a language barrier, she thought, wishing she could have been a fly on the wall when Ben greeted the guests.

La Baraque will be just fine, she said to herself, maybe more than once, as she washed her face and got ready for bed.

As she snuggled under a quilt, feeling the cool night air slipping through the window, her thoughts went not to Ben or La Baraque but to Matéo Brule, lying on the gurney as he left his apartment for the last time.

Adèle and Michel had given no solid details, but it sounded as though the neighborhood would hardly be mourning his passing. It was pure curiosity driving her, an insistence coming from deep within that she find out the circumstances of the man's death. I have no connection to local law enforcement, or stake in this, she reminded herself.

But so what? It's not as though the only murders she felt driven to solve were of people she knew and cared about. It was a question of justice, pure and simple.

Molly rolled over and tried to fall asleep. She tried thinking about Ben, even tried to work up some worry about the guests at La Baraque and whether they were happy and felt taken care of.

But her thoughts would not behave. Instead of settling on home, they darted over to Apolline Cuvalier, wondering what Adèle thought of her. And then back to Matéo, wondering what kind of man he was, what he had done to make people call him a monster.

And who had slit his throat. And why.

❧ 8 ❧

The next morning, as Molly reached the bottom of the stairs, ears cocked at the sound of talking, she heard ... not specific words, but a tone of voice that made her uneasy. Adèle was obviously upset and trying to keep her voice down. Instinctively, Molly lightened her step so as not to announce her presence. She leaned close to the door to the salon, which was closed, but still could not quite hear what her friend was saying.

I am truly a terrible person, she thought, drawing back. Eavesdropping on my good friends! What gets into me?

Making a fuss with the doorknob to alert them of her presence, Molly awkwardly entered the salon. The brother and sister greeted her with big smiles and said *bonjour*. Nonchalantly, Molly observed. They certainly recovered quickly. Were they both still upset, and only hiding it well? Did the problem have anything to do with her? Or maybe she was just inventing trouble where there was none.

Molly spied a silver tray with a coffeepot and an empty porcelain cup on a saucer. "Please tell me that's for me," she said, suddenly desperate for coffee.

"Of course it is," said Michel, his voice merry. "We know how devoted you are to your coffee."

"Isn't everyone? Yes, cream, please, and plenty of it."

Adèle sat in a gray velvet slipper chair, looking pensively out the window. Molly wondered how last night's date had gone but got the feeling it wasn't the time to bring it up.

In fact, she sensed it wasn't the time to bring anything up. Both brother and sister, while polite as ever, seemed distracted, even anxious, underneath their welcoming smiles and greetings. Were they having a fight? Had she done something rude without realizing it? Maybe she should tone down her interest in Matéo Brule—perhaps they were getting the idea she was more interested in him than in them.

"I'm not going to ask a single question about Matéo Brule," she blurted, and then clapped her hand over her mouth. "I ... I'm sorry. I really shouldn't be cleared to speak until after my first cup of coffee. I didn't mean to say that out loud."

But Adèle and Michel only laughed. "We don't mind!" said Michel. "We like having a friend who's a ghoul."

Molly grinned, knowing he was just kidding. But even so, she was reluctant to leap right in with all the questions buzzing in her head.

"So tell me, what are your favorite things about living in Aix so far?" she asked, then took a big gulp of coffee.

She did very much want to continue wandering the streets of the city with her friend and try to see it through her eyes.

"It's a lively city, with a lot going on, plenty of theater, art ... but like all cities of any size, perhaps French ones more than most, it is not a place where strangers can simply show up and be accepted right away," said Michel.

"It takes time, developing relationships," Adèle agreed.

Molly nodded. "So, about today—I don't want you to feel like you have to entertain me every second," Molly said. "If you're busy this morning, maybe we can meet up for lunch or something? Or later, if that would suit you better."

"It's Sunday," said Michel, sounding puzzled. "Of course we're not busy."

Molly laughed. "You can take the American out of America ..."

"I thought we would have Sunday lunch on the roof, if that sounds appealing? I have a spring menu planned. How does grilled lamb sound?" he said.

"Divine!" said Molly, a little too loudly, and poured herself more coffee.

They spent the next hour talking in the salon, one or the other of them sometimes getting up to stretch or glance out the window. The sentences they spoke seemed ordinary enough, the kind of sentences any guest and hosts might exchange first thing in the morning. When she had arrived in Aix only two days earlier, the warmth between them had been just as bright as when they had last seen each other. Now, although she could point to no particular word or phrase that would prove it, Molly felt more like a guest than part of the family. Someone ... not quite trusted.

Something was going on. But she did not, at this point, feel comfortable asking what it might be.

BEFORE IT GOT TOO close to lunchtime, Adèle suggested she and Molly take a stroll around the city and pick up some pastries to hold them over until Michel's lamb was ready. Feeling restless (and of course, always enthusiastic about pastry), Molly quickly agreed, and the two women headed out with a string bag.

"It's a little bit sad," Molly said, aware that she was babbling out of discomfort, "but I actually miss Edmond Nugent and Pâtisserie Bujold rather dreadfully. It's not that I don't adore Aix, and the food has been magnificent! It's just ... well, the ugly truth is: I'm a junkie and he's my dealer."

Adèle shot her a look but said nothing. They walked in silence for a few blocks, and Molly tried to pay attention to architecture and the beautiful pocket gardens tucked away between buildings, trying to give Adèle some space, and telling herself to go easy and stop being so jumpy.

They passed into a small square rimmed with shops and restaurants. It was not nearly as grand as the Cours Mirabeau, but charming in its way. In the center of the square were some bushes just leafing out, impossible to say what they were, and a series of benches. On one of the benches a man was sleeping, a blanket covering his face.

Adèle walked over to the man and bent her head down near his. Gingerly she peeled the blanket back a few inches and exposed a mat of dark hair and then his sleeping face.

"Just wanted to make sure he was still alive," said Adèle. "Now that you're here, people are dropping like flies," she said.

Molly took a sharp breath in.

"Joking," said Adèle. "Now come on, cheer up, this little hole in the wall just ahead is where we're headed. And I think it's going to rock your world, Molly Sutton."

Pâtisserie Magnifique, said the gilt-lettered sign hanging above the door. Sounds promising, thought Molly. But as she entered the shop, she noticed there was no dreamy waft of butter and vanilla, like Pâtisserie Bujold. No baskets of dense, rough sourdough rounds, or trays of napoleons and éclairs. In the glass case, instead, were neat rows of small, iced cookies. They were elegant enough, and colorful, but rather plain to Molly's eye. She looked around for something more promising.

"This is the most popular cookie of Aix-en-Provence," said Adèle, pointing at the case. "And besides being delicious, they have an interesting history."

"Indeed they do," said a woman behind the counter. She had iron-gray hair pulled into a neat bun, and a jumble of teeth going every which way. She wiped her hands on her apron. "Would you like to hear it?"

"Yes, please," said Molly.

"Well, the cookies are known as *calissons*. Back in 1454, the twenty-two-year-old Princess Jeanne de Laval was betrothed to King René, who was forty-five. As you might imagine, the young princess was not happy about marrying a man so much older than she. So the story is that the calisson was invented by a local pâtissier as a way to cheer her up. And for once—the story has a happy ending, as Jeanne and René had a long and happy marriage."

Adèle clapped her hands. "I also heard that people believed they afforded protection from the Plague," she said.

"Gullible people," said the woman behind the counter. "There are reports that priests were using calissons instead of the host, so probably people jumped to the conclusion there was something holy about them."

Molly took all this in, marveling at the way that in France, an ordinary cookie came with an extraordinary story. She laughed. "Back home, one of our favorites is the chocolate chip cookie, often called Toll House cookies. But unless I'm missing something, the only story is that they were invented at a restaurant called The Toll House. No bubonic plague, no kings and princesses ..."

"But a delicious cookie, nonetheless," said the woman behind the counter.

"Thank you," said Molly. "Indeed it is."

The woman reached into the case and drew out a pair of calissons and offered them to Molly and Adèle. "Please, have a taste. We pride ourselves on using the freshest ingredients in all of Aix."

The cookie was quite small, shaped like a thin leaf, with a white layer of hard frosting. Molly popped the entire thing in her mouth and chewed.

Then, with some effort and the fakest smile she had ever conjured, said, "Oh my! So interesting!"

Adèle glanced at her and raised an eyebrow. She bought two

baguettes, a bag of calissons, some green *navettes*, which were a specialty of nearby Marseille, and a handful of *berlingots* from Carpentras. Neither of these, to Molly's eye, looked any better than the calissons. Another dry-looking cookie and some hard candy? Where was the butter, the flaky pastry, the custard, the caramelized apricots?

Thanking the woman and making a small bow, Adèle turned to Molly and asked her to open the door as her hands were full.

Molly felt betrayed.

By Pâtisserie Magnifique, by Adèle, by all of France. She loved stories as much as anyone, but how can they have imagined that a good story was any substitute for good pastry? She wanted to call Edmond up and rant about dry-as-dust calissons and the horrid layer of candied melon that had been hiding under the frosting.

It's not that she had never before spied an unappealing sweet in a pâtisserie. You couldn't love every single thing without exception, of course not, and even Edmond had regular items that she did not favor. But at the same time, there was always an embarrassment of riches at Pâtisserie Bujold. A thousand other delectables to choose from. You were not boxed in with nothing but candied melon to choose from.

As they passed the bench with the sleeping man, Adèle stopped, wrapped some calissons in a napkin, and put the bundle just under the bench where it would not be stepped on by mistake. Then she stopped for a moment and looked up at the sky with a serious expression.

"Rain?" Molly asked.

"No, it's not the weather I'm thinking about. It's ... this man, you understand of course, is one among many. France does an admirable job of taking care of people, as we've talked about. But I fear ... there's trouble on the horizon, I'm afraid."

Molly shook her head. "What do you mean?"

"The thing people don't understand about the world is that much of it, financially speaking, is built on very precarious foundations. They go along, saving a bit from their salary possibly, or just spending like mad as though if they have a little extra right now, it will always be that way."

Molly was confused. She waited for Adèle to get to the point, still feeling bitter about the calissons.

"I believe we're in for a ... let's call it ... a financial disruption," said Adèle in a quiet voice. "Not only in France, but globally, because the systems are all intertwined. And so ... when I see a person like this, already struggling, I can't help thinking about all the others who will be joining his ranks, if I am correct."

"Is this something you figured out while you were working for the bank?"

"Not quite then, no. Of course I learned quite a lot there— though I would not say I am highly fluent, far from it—about markets and all the rest of it. Speculation is through the roof, that's one critical and obvious marker. Similar to 1929 in the States, you will recall."

Molly had heard stories from back then—one distant relative had taken a header from the roof of his office building after finding himself deep in debt. But surely there had been laws passed to keep that from happening again?

"Well, I know about the crash of '29, of course. But—you will call me an ostrich, no doubt, or worse—my feeling is that the world financial situation is far too complicated for me to wrap my head around, so I'm going to go along my merry way and cross my fingers that whatever you're seeing passes by somehow. It's not that I don't believe your analysis—only that I hope you turn out to be wrong, for this guy as well as the rest of us."

Adèle shrugged. "All right, enough about that. I thought, on our walk home, I would tell you everything I know about Matéo Brule," she said, not looking at Molly but smiling slightly.

Molly's eyes lit up. "Hooray! Please do. It's not that I ... obviously I have nothing to do with the case or anything like that, but my curiosity—"

"No need to justify a thing," said Adèle, sounding more like herself than she had all day.

Perhaps the calissons were worth it after all, Molly thought, all ears.

IN THE EARLY afternoon of that lazy Sunday, sunny with a hint of a breeze, Michel asked the women to set the table on the roof, as their lunch was nearly ready.

"I do love a man in an apron," Molly said to Adèle, as they gathered up cutlery.

"Don't say that where Michel can hear you. You know he's half in love with you."

"Wha—no, Adèle, he's totally not. He's a flirt, that's all."

Adèle shrugged the kind of shrug that says, *believe what you want to believe, I'm not going to argue*.

Molly was taken aback. All right, sure, when they were all first getting to know one another, she had been attracted to Michel—and well, who wouldn't be? He was younger and good looking as well as utterly charming, with a flop of hair always dropping into his eyes, a sly smile and twinkling eyes, sort of a French Hugh Grant. But she didn't believe the attraction was romantic, on either of their parts. She and Michel liked each other. She would even say they liked each other profoundly, but the feelings stopped at *like* and did not go anywhere near *crush,* much less *love*. Not to mention she was newly and *quite* happily married, thank you very much.

"Hello?" said Adèle. "You wandering in the cabbages again?"

Molly had been standing like a statue, holding a fork in the air. "Oh, sorry," she mumbled. "I just want to say—and this will come out wrong, I'm sure—I heard what you said about wishing for a partner the other day. And believe me, I know the feeling. I know the kind of hollowness that being alone can bring, and also—I know how easy it is to look around you and see all these happy couples and feel left out. You forget, in those moments, that all relationships have problems, even the good ones.

And you know—it's not like being in a couple is the only way to have a good life. There are a million ways to skin a cat, as my grandmother used to say!"

Adèle was looking at her feet. Molly saw her take a deep breath, but she kept her head down and said nothing.

"But, even so—I have absolutely one hundred percent faith that if that is what you want, you will find someone," said Molly. "It was just chance that I was walking down rue de Chêne on that particular afternoon when Ben came running the other way. And something like that will happen for you, too. It's a matter of patience, that's all, and being open."

"Thank you, Molly," Adèle said softly, still not meeting her eyes.

"It's really frustrating that there's not really a way to force it. I really do understand."

Adèle reached her hand out and squeezed Molly's arm. "I'm fine, really I am. I don't mean to sound ungrateful. We have this beautiful house, live in this beautiful city, have a new life after everything ... everything that happened. I only meant ... it would be nice to have someone in my daily life besides my brother. I sometimes wonder if my past ... if all that happened with Maman ... has wrecked my chances somehow. Has ... warped me, in some way that people—that men—can see."

Molly shook her head. "Oh no. Please, Adèle, do not tell that story about yourself. You were blameless, absolutely blameless. Of course you have feelings about it, of course. But warped? No. I don't believe that for one fraction of a second."

Adèle looked away to hide the tears filling her eyes.

Michel's jaunty curses came up through the opening. The women ran over to the ladder. "One of you—take the platter, quickly!" A beautiful porcelain platter heaped high with slices of succulent lamb and decorated with branches of rosemary appeared, balanced on one hand. The platter trembled and shook as Michel tried to push it up within their reach.

"Got it!" said Adèle, firmly grasping each side and standing up. "Oh Molly, just inhale!"

Molly leaned close and breathed in, the aroma of rosemary, garlic, and lamb so fragrant and exquisite she felt weak in the knees, especially after that disappointing breakfast.

"That little tang of lemon," she murmured. "Exquisite."

The three of them bustled about getting the food served and settling into chairs, with a nice rosé to wash it all down. For a few moments they did not speak, though Molly let a moan escape when she tasted the first bite of lamb, perfectly cooked and flavorful, with a hint of char on the edge of the slice.

"On the way home from Pâtisserie Magnifique, I started to tell Molly about Matéo Brule," Adèle said to Michel, once they had eaten for a few minutes and complimented his cooking. "People here love to gossip—perhaps not quite as much as the Castillacois—and so I've heard a rumor or two. He was a horrible man, that much is clear. I'm hoping you might be able to fill in more detail, Michel."

Molly appreciated a lack of detail to start with. That only meant there was investigation just begging to be done. "So far, what Adèle has told me is that Matéo was maybe or maybe not arrested for doing something, but she's not sure what, to a young woman whose father is somebody or other, she can't remember who. So, uh … plenty of gaps to fill."

Michel nodded. "Um. Let's see. The young woman—she's quite young, seventeen or eighteen, I believe. From Aix, though had spent some time in Paris just before the attack. I believe she was doing some sort of filmmaking course? I can't recall. What I heard was that Brule was nearly arrested for sexual assault—I never heard any details either of what that meant exactly—but was quickly let go on some sort of technicality. Perhaps he has friends in high places, or at least high enough to get him out of trouble? Thankfully, the young woman was rescued before he could ... well, I suppose we can't claim to know what he intended to do. But in any case, whatever it was, it was an attempt and not a success because the woman screamed bloody murder, a *flic* happened to be passing by, and she was rescued."

"Thank heavens," said Molly. "Where did this happen?"

"His apartment."

"You mean just down the block," said Molly.

"Yes. As I said, he was taken in and charged, but Matéo must have had a good lawyer and I don't think he spent more than a night in jail before being let go. An interesting side bit of the story is that the victim also had friends in high places—her father is Victor Chopin, a well-connected businessman, the sort of fellow who knows everybody and can make things happen behind the scenes. So whatever did happen, I suppose we'll never know. Perhaps the young woman insisted the case be dropped and her father acquiesced to her wishes? Or perhaps Matéo's connections turned out to be more powerful than hers."

"When was this? Any details on what Matéo's version of the story was? What did Mademoiselle Chopin have to say about it?"

Michel shrugged. "Last month? Not much. It was a big flap when it happened but seemed to be forgotten quickly. Do you remember, Adèle? The young woman did not want to bring charges, refused to testify, and went off to school in Toulouse, is what Berenice told me. And that was the end of it."

"Berenice?" asked Molly.

"She lives in Brule's building. The sort of woman who keeps an ear out for what everyone's up to."

"Sounds like my kind of gal," Molly said. She drummed her fingers on her thigh. "It's curious, isn't it, though I understand quite common—when a person who is attacked does not want to do anything to help bring the attacker to justice."

"A million reasons for it," said Adèle. "Probably most of all, they just want to move on and forget the whole thing."

"But—"

"Not everyone is as concerned with justice as you are. Or at least, the kind of justice that is out in the open and requires public declarations. Some people ... they want normal lives. They just want to enjoy their dinner, their cat, take a trip now and again, laugh with their family. Maybe the attack was so traumatic that the desire for these simple things, for some measure of safety, feels close to desperate. They don't want the police grilling them and going to court and on and on, reliving the terrible thing over and over," said Adèle.

"And also, sad to say, they may worry they won't be believed. Or that they will be believed, but nobody will much care," she added. "And—this is the last thing I will say on it—perhaps people come up with their own ways of justice. Not every solution has to go through the courts, after all."

Molly laughed. "I never knew you were a closet anarchist," she said. "And so that's it, that's all you remember?"

"Well, with the victim being unwilling to testify, and no longer in town, like I said, the whole thing blew over," said Michel.

"Matéo went on living in the same apartment without a care in the world, as far as I could see," said Adèle. "Not that we seemed to keep the same hours. He was something of a party-boy, stayed out late at clubs, that sort of thing. Enjoying himself. No thought for the damage he nearly inflicted on that poor girl, and I think you'll agree that she was without doubt not the first woman Matéo attacked. It's never just one. Blithely he went on without a care in the world."

"Until he was murdered," said Molly.

"Well, there's that," said Adèle, and all three of them laughed darkly.

They were scraping the last bits of the very delicious potatoes Anna off their plates when they heard banging from the street below.

Michel went to the edge of the roof and looked down. "Coo-coo!" he called out to someone standing by the front door.

A man stepped back into the street so he could see up. "Michel! Come down, I'm sorry to bother you, but it's important!"

All three of them hustled down the ladder, Molly giving the plate of potatoes a parting glance as she went.

❧ II ❧

❧ 9 ❧

"Tommaso!" exclaimed Michel, grasping the man's shoulders and kissing him on both cheeks. "So good to see you, where have you been lately?"

"India," said Tommaso. He was tall, dark, with a broad chest. His hair was slicked away from his face, showing a noble hairline.

"Bonsoir, Adèle," said Tommaso, kissing her with feeling on both cheeks.

Michel introduced him to Molly, but Tommaso was impatient. "Lovely to meet you, Madame Sutton, and I'm sorry to be rude—" he glanced at Molly in apology—"but I just heard something you must know. It's about Madame Trudeau."

"Dear, departed Madame Trudeau," said Michel, putting his palms together in mock prayer.

"Yes. Well. Apparently she had a little help with that departure."

The Faures and Molly stood staring.

"What are you saying?" said Michel.

"I just got back into town three seconds ago so I'm afraid I don't have a lot of details. Ran into Patrice Jubert on my way home from the train station. He stopped me, quite excited, saying

I ought to know there are now officially two murders on rue Niccolo—"

"In less than a week," murmured Molly.

"Patrice says the coroner has ruled Madame Trudeau's death suspicious," said Tommaso. "Not a heart attack as first thought. Perhaps 'heart attack' was just off the top of his head, and apparently the guess didn't hold up. Suffocated, is what the coroner is saying now. You know how Patrice is, he probably camped out on the poor coroner's front step until he got the information he wanted."

Adèle, Michel, and Molly did not speak at first.

"But we were so happy Madame Trudeau died," complained Michel finally. "You're spoiling it for us."

"Sorry!" said Tommaso, with a grim smile. "Patrice is a bossy sort, isn't he? He asked me to go house to house on this side of the block, letting everyone know about the latest developments. He's going up the other side of the street, knocking on doors. I do agree with him on this, people need to be informed since we have no way of knowing ..."

Molly was all a-tingle but did her best to keep that to herself. Tommaso excused himself, leaving the Faures and Molly standing in the street, trying to process this latest news.

"What difference does it make, really," said Adèle. "Madame Trudeau was horrible and now she's dead. I'm not going to rend my garments and weep over her."

Molly blinked. "But murder ..."

"Oh, of course, I mean, it's unthinkable," interrupted Adèle.

"Well, obviously not to someone," said Michel. "We should know better than most that murder is plenty thinkable to all kinds of people you wouldn't expect. Many more people think of doing it than is generally understood. And perhaps—many more get away with it than we know."

"The very block we have moved to, where we are attempting to make our lives anew, is set upon by this ... by this ... dark force.

EYE FOR AN EYE

It feels almost ... as though it has followed us here." Adèle paused. "Though I cannot help saying—perhaps she deserved what she got."

Michel looked as though he were about to make a crack, then thought better of it. "I'm sure murders are happening all over the place, all the time, and we're just a little more ... attuned to them, shall we say, because of our history. When you consider how many big cities there are, and whatever number of drug and organized crime murders there are, France comes out quite creditably," said Michel.

"I don't care about any of that," said Adèle. "But I will say this: maybe this is what happens when you treat people so abominably. Maybe Madame Trudeau might have regretted it, if she could have seen she would pay with her life."

She scowled at Michel and Molly as though they too were horrible, and went inside, slamming the door behind her.

"What exactly did the woman do?" asked Molly. "To listen to Adèle, she must have been torturing babies and puppies en masse."

"I'm so sorry," Michel said softly. "I don't know what's gotten into Adèle lately."

69

M olly and Michel cleared the dishes from the terrace and washed up in silence. After sharing a short nightcap with Michel during which they silently agreed to keep the conversation light, Molly was glad to go up to her room and be alone.

At bedtime she washed her face, and for once, took a little time with her hair so as to get in bed with the red curls more or less untangled. Slowly she washed her hands and put on her nightgown, all the while going over everything Tommaso had said.

She reached over to the small nightstand and picked up her cell to call Ben.

"Hey you," he said, his voice softening when he realized who it was.

"Missing you like crazy," she murmured, the sound of his voice almost chasing thoughts of murder out of her head. They didn't speak, phones pressed to their ears, just breathing and being together quietly for a few moments.

"So how is everything?" Ben said finally.

"It's been … you know … great, not so great, and everything in between. Like stuff usually is," she said. "But right now, part of the reason I called, something's going on, and I'd like to hear what you think."

"I'm all ears."

"It's not a case—or what I mean is, I'm obviously not *on* the case—but in the last week, two people have been killed. In this neighborhood. This exact street, to be precise."

She heard Ben suck in some air.

"So," Molly continued, "the first night I was here, a woman was found dead in her house. In her eighties, everyone figured she'd had a heart attack or something."

"But she didn't."

"Suffocated, says the coroner."

Ben flinched. "Were you able to find out anything about her?" he asked.

"A little. Before there was any indication of murder, Adèle and Michel were practically giddy when they heard she'd died. She was not well liked, to put it mildly. She was mean, and it was a little like ding-dong, the witch is dead."

"But *murdered*—that's a different story."

"Indeed. But there's more. The very next day—yesterday—a man who lived in an apartment down the block was found with his throat slit."

A pause, in which each listened to the other breathe.

"Molly? I don't want to sound ... of course, absolutely I know you can take care of yourself and please don't take this as talking down your abilities in any way. But please ... keep a sharp eye out, will you? Maybe sharper than usual?"

"I'm fine, Ben, truly. Nobody has any reason to hurt me. Nobody has any connection to me at all, besides Adèle and Michel. So, unless the murderer turns out to be one of them, I'm good."

"Just keep in mind—you don't have any idea what you're dealing with. Those people might have been murdered by someone who had no connection to them. I know, I know," he said quickly, "that's far less likely. But it *does* happen. Just please—don't go wandering around alone, will you? Especially at night?"

"Sure, all right," said Molly. "I might see if I can get any of the other neighbors to talk a little bit. Just for something to do."

"Of course you will."

"So tell me about La Baraque. I miss it so much—and *you*."

Ben talked for a few minutes about the Sadlers and Briony Lark, to bring Molly up to date on all goings-on at the gîte, and then, the distance between them pressing him to speak more directly than he usually did, he offered some detail on just how much he missed her, and how delighted he would be to see her again. And just how long was she planning to stay away?

Molly didn't know. She had thought her trip would only last a week or so, and she did miss Ben so much it physically hurt ... but with these intriguing developments right on the very block where the Faures lived, how could she think of leaving?

❧ 11 ❧

Adèle was up, showered, immaculately dressed, and out of the house before eight o'clock the following morning. Molly and Michel were sound asleep and did not hear her leave; Adèle was careful not to put on her sleek alligator heels until she had left the house, closing the heavy front door carefully so it did not bang.

Once on the street, she took a deep breath and squared her shoulders. She stood still for a moment, appearing to be considering her next move, patting the large and expensive leather bag hanging on an elbow. First, she turned toward the Cours Mirabeau, passing the house of Madame Trudeau. But then she slowed, rubbing one of her temples with her forefinger, and then stopped altogether. A few pedestrians headed to work moved around her. A small truck made its way down the narrow street and Adèle pushed herself against the stone wall of a house to stay out of the way.

"I don't have any choice," she said out loud, and jerked, as though startled by the sound of her own voice. Abruptly she turned in the opposite direction and walked quickly past her own house, eyes straight ahead, mouth set.

. . .

MICHEL WAS in the salon having coffee when Molly wandered in. She rubbed her eyes as they said bonjour and kissed cheeks.

"Did you have a good sleep?" he asked.

"Not really. It's ... well, it's these murders. I couldn't get them off my mind."

"Of course you can't," Michel said, grinning. "It's what you do."

"Honestly, I wish people would stop talking about me like I'm squatting over graves, delightedly licking my chops. It's not like that at all."

"Molly! I'm only teasing. And not in that way some people do where the teasing is meant to be a quick sharp stab between the ribs either. Nothing but goodwill coming from me. Surely, after everything, you know that?" He reached his hand toward her but she did not take it, and awkwardly, he let it drop.

She drank half a cup of coffee, barely tasting it, her mind still occupied by Madame Trudeau and Matéo Brule.

"It's a question of justice," she answered eventually. "I don't mean to sound defensive. But the reason these situations make me so crazy is that I cannot stand the idea of some random person deciding who lives and who dies. I'm not about retribution or making murderers suffer. I only believe they should be stopped, and pay the consequences of their actions, which are always, and I mean always, selfish in nature."

"That's quite a speech, and I second every bit of it. But Molly, surely you know when I am only joking around? I suppose I do it too often."

Let me ask you this," she said, switching gears. "Are you at all ... frightened? I'm not insulting your manhood. I'm only wondering—do the murders on rue Niccolo worry you at all, in terms of the safety of the neighborhood? Do you think your neighbor Patrice is right to be alarmed?"

Michel shrugged. "Don't you always say it's a grave mistake to make assumptions? So all I can say is: I have no idea."

"I've been trying to understand whether the two murders are related, and obviously—it's a question I can't answer. There aren't enough facts. So instead of facts, let's talk about intuition, about what our guts say, just for fun. Not making assumptions, just trying to feel our way along and see what comes up. Let's say ... you wake in the middle of the night, you hear a creak on the stair. Are you more worried about what that might mean than you would have been last week? Do you imagine a stealthy intruder with a knife in his fist creeping towards your bedroom? Or do you just think, ah, the old house is breathing, and don't give it another thought?"

"There is a creak on, I believe, the eleventh step going from the second floor to the third. Did you hear it last night?" He raised his eyebrows comically.

"You think I'm silly. And listen, you absolute heathen, may I have another cup of coffee before you tease me to death?"

"Oh, how I forget myself," he said, horrified. "Back in a second."

While he was gone, Molly put off thinking more about the murders—she had covered the ground enough times the night before, *ad nauseum*—and looked around at the room. It was beautifully decorated, just as elegant as she would expect, knowing the high taste level of the Faures. The wallpaper was an artistically faded damask in blue-green and muted gold. The furniture would doubtless have delighted her friend Lapin, who sold antiques (and plenty of junk) at his shop in Castillac.

Briefly, Molly wondered how the Faures's money was holding out. Not that it was any of her business. But neither one was working, they both very much liked nice things, and of course, nice things do not come cheap.

"I should be flogged for being so distracted," said Michel, coming back into the salon with an extra-large porcelain cup of steaming coffee. "But at last, here you go. I did remember you take cream, no sugar."

"Thank you," said Molly, gratefully taking the cup. "Sometimes I worry that I am too dependent on caffeine, but then—"

"Oh, you Americans worry too much. It's that Puritan blood," he laughed. "You want to take away everything in life that's enjoyable."

"I may worry, but I don't ever actually give anything up."

"Not a true Puritan, then," he said softly.

"Hardly."

Their eyes met. In Michel's was a question. Molly looked up at the ceiling and asked him whether the chandelier had come with the house or whether they had managed to find it themselves, as it fit the room so perfectly it seemed to have been made for it.

Michel sighed. He told the story of how they had stumbled on the tiny shop in Marseille where they had bought the chandelier, and all the ten thousand things that had gone wrong during the installation. Molly listened politely, enjoying Michel's talents as a storyteller and at the same time racking her brain for how she could uncover some evidence pertaining to either murder.

She came up with exactly nothing.

AFTER BREAKFAST, Michel sat in the wing-chair with silk upholstery (a bright, candy-colored stripe that Adèle had picked out) and listened to Molly go upstairs. He heard the creak on the eleventh stair between the second and third floors. His brow furrowed.

Abruptly he jerked out of the chair, drank off the last of his coffee, and hurried outside. He turned in the same direction Adèle had, hours earlier, but after a few blocks turned a different way, toward the business section of town. Before long he crossed through Cours Sexius to rue Victor Leydet, and stood looking across the street at a bank, a BNP Paribas.

He stood for some time. He put his hands into the pocket of his trousers and then took them out. He was short of breath as though he had just sprinted up a steep hill.

The bank was unassuming, a small branch, tucked between a café on the corner and a clothing shop. As Michel stood across the street, no one went in or came out.

He looked furtively in each direction. And then, lifting his chin as though in defiance to someone, he jaywalked to the thick glass door of the bank and pushed his way inside.

❧ 12 ❧

Ben faced Monday morning with the slightly sinking feeling that always came with having no cases to work on nor any idea where to find one. It was all very well for the income from La Baraque to keep him and Molly afloat during the slack times, and heaven knows he was not a workaholic who needed to be busy every second of the day, but he would very much like a little something to turn his investigative skill towards.

First, I will make the rounds of the gîtes, and see if anyone needs anything, he thought. Then perhaps go for a run, followed by breakfast at Café de la Place, where I can find out the village news. If there is any.

"Come, Bobo!" he called, though Bobo did not have to come because she was already sitting almost under his feet, having spied the running shorts with tremendous hope. They went first to the pigeonnier to check on the Sadlers. Bobo accomplished her usual zooming through the meadow, leaping up at various points for reasons unspecified, and waited, panting, at the door of the gîte.

Ben cocked an ear but heard nothing. He wasn't entirely sure of the protocol, now that he was standing on the doorstep of the pigeonnier. Was it better to ignore the guests and wait until they came to him with any problems or questions? Are they sleeping in, only to be annoyed if he knocks this early in the morning? Or not?

Well, what is early? Now that he was thinking about it, "early" was obviously different for different people. The range of "early" was enormous, actually.

This running of a gîte—it was so much more complicated than it looked.

He took in a quick breath and went ahead and knocked, figuring the Sadlers could always ignore him if they wanted to.

No answer.

Backing away, relieved, Ben said, "All right Bobo, that's one down. Let's see about Briony Lark and then we'll hit the road."

Briony was staying in the cottage. Ben had not seen her since she arrived. She was young and British, and to Ben, practiced at assessing people, she seemed to be a bit wild, still in the rebellious time of life during university, still figuring out who she was and what her path in life was going to be. Castillac seemed rather a surprising choice for someone her age, traveling alone; Ben was mildly curious about what had brought her to La Baraque.

Briony's hair was short on one side and long on the other, a style he found disconcerting—which he understood was a mark of middle-aged stodginess, which amused him.

He knocked. Bobo gave a quick yip and sat in front of the door, wagging her tail, which brushed leaves from side to side.

Ben heard a noise from inside, then footsteps. The door swung open, making a creak.

"Bonjour," said Briony Lark, looking at Ben with a muted smile. She was entirely undressed, standing in the doorway, one hand resting high on the doorjamb, without a stitch on. "What can I do for you?" she asked, eyes twinkling.

Ben's mouth hung open for a moment before he closed it. Oh Molly, please come home soon, he thought, with an edge of pleading.

But Ben Dufort was French, after all, and not one to find the female form shocking or off-putting, whatever the situation. He collected himself and smiled back. "I was just making the morning rounds, seeing if any of our guests need anything," he said.

"Ah," said Briony, with a rather penetrating stare that made Ben bite the side of his mouth so as not to smile. It was not easy being nineteen, he thought.

"Well then, have a lovely day, Briony. I hope you enjoy it." He turned back to the house. Briony frowned.

Let's hope the Café de la Place is busy this morning, he thought, tying up his running shoes and motioning to Bobo to follow. I need a case to sink my teeth into before I go stark raving mad.

It was a dead hour at Chez Papa, neither breakfast nor lunch, and Nico Bartolucci stood at the bar, leaning on his elbows, looking into the eyes of his wife and grinning.

"You know, it was at this exact spot that I first noticed you," Frances said.

"Now you're just making stuff up. It was at that funeral and you know it."

"Funeral? Whose funeral? Are you saying I was flirting at a funeral? Who do you think I am?"

"A giant, adorable nut?"

Frances laughed and pretend-smacked his cheek, then ruffled his hair. "I miss Molly," she blurted, and Nico nodded. "The village just feels so blah without her."

"Thanks."

"Oh, stop it," said Frances, pretend-swatting him again.

"It is sort of nice that no one has been murdered lately."

Frances guffawed. "Ben must be at such loose ends. Somehow,

without having heard any details, I imagine that running La Baraque is not exactly something he's cut out for."

"Work is strange," said Nico, polishing the last cognac glass and putting it away. "When you're young, you have all these grand ideas of what you might do, and then ..."

"You end up writing jingles," she said, shaking her head.

"Making drinks and wiping down a bar, day after day."

"Are you unhappy about that?" Frances leaned forward a bit, watching his face.

Nico took a few moments to answer. He pulled a freshly laundered rag from under the bar and began to rub the wood, which was already nicely buffed. "I had a fancy education," he said. "And there is a sense ... I couldn't say this to anyone but you ... a sense that having been born into such a privileged family, I should go out into the world and ... what exactly? I'm not sure. Make something of myself. Do something important."

"Not tend bar."

He laughed. "Definitely not tend bar. But the thing is, when I started really thinking about it, those so-called important things turned out mostly to be about making lots of money."

"I like money."

"Who doesn't? I'm only saying that at a certain point I realized my life belonged to me and I wasn't going to start using it up trying to meet other people's expectations. Especially—and this is sort of the hilarious part—people who were already dead! It seems ridiculous now, looking back on it, because when I was just becoming an adult, I spent so much time worrying about what my parents thought of me. And they weren't even alive."

Frances opened her arms out for him and he bent toward her. They kissed lightly, then deeply. Then Nico went back to leaning on his elbows. He looked at Frances, his eyes wet. "I will tell you something," he said, his voice slightly breaking, "nothing so far in my life has made me happier than this." He reached his hand across the bar and patted her belly.

"I know," Frances whispered. "And it's the weirdest thing—I didn't have the slightest idea it was what I wanted until it happened."

The bar was still. A beam of March sunlight came slanting in, showing dust motes. They heard no one walking down the sidewalk, no cars driving by, just the quiet and calm of the village, the barely-leafed-out tree outside not moving because there was no breeze.

"I worry—just a little—over how to tell Molly," said Frances.

Nico nodded.

"Having children has always been her deepest desire. Of course she's still trying to get used to the hand she's been dealt."

"Meanwhile you ..."

"I know. Never had any interest at all."

"Until you met me," said Nico, and made a fart sound on the side of her neck.

Frances laughed, a pure and joyful laugh, never imagining she could be this happy.

❧ 13 ❧

I t was after ten o'clock, a placid time of day on the streets of
Aix, most people having already arrived at work and students
safely in school. Quiet enough to hear some warblers in a linden
tree arguing about something. Quiet enough to hear the scrape of
a chair through an open window, the murmur of music playing, an
old-fashioned song, something American.

Molly walked toward the music, cocking her ear. It was—yes,
it was Ella Fitzgerald, one of her very favorites, singing *Night and
Day*. When she reached the window where the music was coming
from, she stopped to listen, smiling broadly, feeling—and enjoying
—a little pang of homesickness for the States.

Ella segued into another song and Molly moved on, unable to
shake the sight of Matéo Brule being carried from his building
from her mind.

Halfway down the block, an old woman stepped onto the tiny
sidewalk with a broom and began to sweep vigorously. She wore
knee socks and Molly remembered asking her what was going on
the night Brule was murdered. Could this be Berenice? She
watched the woman sweep for just a moment, then walked up,

armed with the one sentence guaranteed to melt any French person anywhere.

"*Excusez-moi de vous déranger, mais j'ai une problème,*" said Molly. Excuse me for bothering you, but I have a problem. And I *do* have a problem, Molly thought. Two dead bodies and friends who are acting strangely.

The woman drew back and did not look up or pause in her sweeping. Molly had the clear impression that she was using the broom as a way to be on the street and keep an eye on what was going on, rather than from a deep desire for keeping the sidewalk free of dirt. But perhaps I'm projecting, Molly thought.

The woman looked Molly up and down, scowling, her face not having lit up as faces usually did when Molly uttered the magic sentence asking for help.

"Who are *you?*" the old woman said finally. She swept faster.

"*Pardon,*" said Molly. "I am so sorry to interrupt you. My name is Molly Sutton, I live in Castillac, in the Dordogne. I am here in Aix to visit friends who live down the block."

The woman's expression did not soften. She made a face and looked away, the swish-swish of the broom even faster.

Molly was nothing if not dogged. "It's certainly upsetting, losing two neighbors in the space of a week," she said.

"I'll say it is," she snapped. "It's just one more thing. One more thing on the list."

"The list?"

At last the woman stopped sweeping. She put one hand on a hip and narrowed her eyes at Molly. Her dark gray hair was cropped short; it looked as though she cut it herself, and the uneven choppiness gave her a sort of punk look. "The list of all the ways this city, in fact the entire country, to say it plainly, is falling down around our ears. There's no morality anymore. It's all going to go up in smoke, you know. They can't keep on like this."

"They?"

"The powers that be," the woman said darkly. "And all the witless citizens who do their bidding."

Molly nodded sympathetically. The woman stayed silent. "Did you know Matéo?" Molly asked softly.

The woman shrugged and then glared. "What are you, some kind of spy? What business is it of yours whether I knew him or not? You think I can't hear that American accent of yours? People think once you get to a certain age that you can't think straight anymore. Well, listen to me, Madame Sutton, if that's actually your name: I can think, I can see, I can hear. What business is Matéo Brule of yours? I'll answer that question, thank you. *None.* It's none of your business, and that's it."

Molly let the woman's words flow past, not taking offense. "Again, sorry to bother you," she said. "I'm no spy—but it's true, I *am* interested in what is happening on rue Niccolo. Two violent deaths in such a short time is, at the very least, unusual. I'm rather worried about the safety of my friends, who live right there." Molly half-turned and pointed to the Faures's building. "Madame, respectfully, I don't usually say this to people I have just met, but I will tell you: I have a business, back home in Castillac. My partner and I are private investigators and we have seen our share of murders and solved them. I very much apologize if you find my questions nosy or impertinent—and they *are* nosy and impertinent, no argument there—but as I hope you understand, I do have some experience in situations like this."

The woman rolled her eyes and began sweeping again.

Molly was annoyed at herself for not figuring out a way to get the woman on her side, but it was clear she had pressed as far as she could. "*Au revoir,*" she said, waving to the woman's back, and walking toward the Cours Mirabeau.

Suddenly she wanted an almond croissant with a desperation that verged on mania. Surely she could find a shop that offered something besides calissons? Walking quickly, she scanned the storefronts looking for a pâtisserie, while reviewing the older woman's remarks. It was almost never true that a bit of information stood out right away. You had to comb back over conversations, listening to the words over and over, and finally—with a great deal of luck—you might see a faint glint among the rubble, and, when you pick up the dusty pebble, it turns into a diamond once you rub off all the dust.

At least, she thought, her mouth watering as visions of almond croissants crowded into her thoughts, that was how it went when she was very, very lucky.

AFTER A FEW HOURS OF WALKING, finding herself far from rue Niccolo, she stopped at a café for a coffee, not intending to linger. The place only had three tables on the sidewalk, the inside just a counter. But the coffee-making equipment behind the counter looked serious enough, and so Molly took a seat and prepared to people-watch.

With a polite nod, a lanky young man took her order and returned with an espresso. Molly stretched out her legs and then raised her arms over her head and stretched some more, in between sips. The young man stood in the doorway. He spoke but his accent threw her and she could not quite follow. Though maybe she caught the word "yoga"?

Molly laughed. "I'm afraid I don't do yoga, though I'm sure I should," she said.

He disappeared inside the shop and returned with a flyer.

"Ah," said Molly, reading the ad for a local yoga studio. "I'm afraid this is one fad I'm going to let pass me by. My idea of exercise is walking my dog."

The young man pretended to look around for the dog and appear confused.

"I am here visiting friends," Molly said. "My other favorite exercise is walking through cities new to me. Maybe you could point me in an interesting direction? I'm not looking for tourist sites, necessarily, but just any part of the city you think is interesting or worth seeing?"

Usually, when you ask locals about their city, they have a million ideas of where you absolutely must go and things you cannot miss, and they're proud to tell you about them. But the lanky yogi simply shrugged. "Your path is yours to find," he said, and went back inside.

Molly sat blinking. Well. Of course, he's correct, she thought. But isn't it funny that we're surprised when someone simply says the truth?

Unfortunately an espresso takes only a few gulps to drink, and she left, waving to the young man and continuing down the street with no idea whether she was heading towards the Faures's apartment or away from it. Eventually, she figured, she would see a traffic sign that pointed her toward *Centre Ville*, so in the meantime she enjoyed feeling a little bit lost.

Several bistros looked fine but rather ordinary. One was packed with workers in blue shirts, drinking red wine and smoking. A few were nearly empty, which at half past noon seemed ominous. Then up ahead, in the next block, she saw a sign with no words, just a blue and green pattern, vaguely Indian. I could really dig into a pile of samosas, she thought, her suddenly starving.

Molly walked faster. She glanced at a menu posted outside and had her hand on the door, ready to push inside, when she pulled back with a start. She stepped out of sight and tapped her fingers on her forehead, trying to think.

She was almost sure that Michel and Apolline Cuvalier were inside. She couldn't have imagined it. What in the world were they doing in such an out-of-the-way spot, in this tiny Indian restaurant?

Wait, was it really them? Molly tried to look nonchalant as she moved back in front of the door and peered through the glass. It was them all right. Michel's back was to the door but she had no doubt—it was his hair, his jacket, even the color of his shirt she remembered from that morning.

And Apolline, no matter what you thought of her, was not a woman who blended in with a crowd. She was striking, with her extra-dark eyebrows and theatrical manner. Molly saw her smile intimately at Michel. She watched as Apolline reached across the small table and take Michel's hand. Michel did not draw back but let her take it.

Molly moved away from the door before anyone could notice her. She had a momentary and childish wish for an invisibility cloak, so that she could slip inside and stand beside Michel's table and listen to their conversation.

Forgetting all about lunch, she turned and headed back toward Adèle and Michel's—or at least what she believed was that direction—her brow furrowed, trying to come up with some reason why a woman would reach for a man's hand in an out-of-the-way restaurant in an out-of-the-way part of town and it didn't mean anything.

Molly figured she knew perfectly well what it meant. She just didn't like it.

14

That night, the three friends were going out to dinner. Nothing fancy, Adèle said, just a neighborhood place with hearty peasant food. "You're going to love this place," said Adèle, slipping her arm through Molly's as they went out. "I know how fond you are of a good stew. And this place has a *daube* that will make you weak in the knees."

Molly smiled, suddenly starving, having remarkably skipped lunch.

The place was just around the corner. It had low ceilings and dark rafters. The walls were smudged with smoke and a grill was visible in the back, an aproned man at the helm, flames shooting up.

The hostess chatted with Adèle and Michel, who were regulars, and seated them not far from the grill. Michel had a private word with her and she smiled and nodded at his instruction.

"Did you have a good day?" Adèle asked Molly.

"I walked and walked. In my opinion you've chosen one of the most beautiful cities in the world for your home. I don't know what it is exactly—it's just a feeling, really, a *vibe*, as we used to say —but there's something absolutely magical about Aix. The back streets are just as lovely as Cours Mirabeau. I have the sense there is a tremendous amount of mystery here, and no, I'm not referring to the current murders, but more ... there's a feeling of depth, as though, I don't know, the people who live here are more complicated than people who live in other places, silly as that sounds. More layers. More *mystery*.

"Maybe that's ridiculously romantic," Molly said, her cheeks getting a tinge of pink. "It's just ... I have the feeling that in Aix, there's more to the truth than what's on the surface."

She managed not to look at Michel as she spoke, but just barely. Had he told Adèle about his lunch with Apolline? Molly doubted it.

"Just to get it out of the way, I have a bit of bad news," said Michel with a nod as the hostess returned to their table with a bottle on ice. "I saw Patrice Jubert this morning, as I was running off for an appointment. Thankfully, no more deaths—but he told me there have been two burglaries recently, one on rue Niccolo and the other just down a side street, a block away. They were rather high-end affairs, the burglars knowledgeable and selective in what they stole. So that's just another wrinkle to add to our neighborhood crime spree."

Adèle shook her head and her mouth looked tense. She did not say anything.

"I was thinking, Adèle," Michel continued. "We really should throw a little money at our security system."

"What security system?" asked Molly.

"Our front door lock," said Michel with a laugh. He sipped the champagne the hostess had poured for him and nodded to her.

"When I was just talking dreamily about mystery, this is not what I was going for."

Michel shrugged. "To city life," he said, raising his glass.

They clinked and said "*Santé!*" in unison. Molly mustered a mostly genuine expression of pleasure—the champagne certainly went down easily, though she felt as though there was a tickle not only in her throat but in the base of her brain, an itch she couldn't quite scratch, a thought she couldn't quite bring to the surface.

"I am concerned about the silver bowl with strawberries around the edge," Michel said to Adèle. "It's worth quite a lot, far more than what I paid. It would break my heart if it were stolen."

"Usually thieves on that level have specialties," said Molly. "Did Patrice say what was stolen?"

"A sapphire necklace was taken from the Boisettes, and apparently it was kept in a safe. The burglars did not pry the safe out of the wall, if that would even be possible without dynamite. They managed, somehow, to open it."

"Patrice and his safe-crackers," said Molly with a smirk. "Maybe it was an inside job, and the Boisettes want the insurance money? Sorry, I don't mean to insult your neighbors. But this Patrice character—it sounds like he enjoys being in the middle of everything and relishes telling people a lot of bad news."

"Well, of course, Castillac has not cornered the market on gossip, *or* bad behavior," said Adèle. "Now listen, I was picturing a nice, easy dinner—let's talk about something else. I'll call the locksmith in the morning, Michel. Better yet, I'll go see him. I want to get out early again tomorrow and go see poor Émile first thing. Would you like to come this time, Molly? Or do you have sight-seeing plans?"

Molly agreed to go, figuring that if the man did not look happy to have a new visitor, she could always make an excuse and leave. They drank another glass of champagne while Molly regaled them with some choice tales from her and Ben's honeymoon, and at last, big steaming bowls of *daube* appeared, the vegetables glistening on top like jewels in a sea of rich, brown broth.

❧ 1 5 ❧

"Are we still going over to Émile's?" Molly asked, after they had kissed cheeks the next morning.

"I think he would like to meet you," said Adèle. "At least, he most certainly would have before his illness. I admit, there's a sort of ... there's a divide, isn't there, between sick people and healthy people. There's this vast difference of experience getting in the way that you just can't understand, no matter how much sympathy you have."

Molly nodded.

"It feels like my relationship with him has deepened in some ways, because since getting ill, he is more *direct*, I guess you could say. He doesn't default to evasive politeness, not anymore."

"It makes sense. Why waste time?"

"Indeed," said Adèle. "So, have you had enough coffee? Shall we go?"

Thinking to herself that there might never at any point be quite enough coffee, Molly nodded and they set off. She did notice, as Adèle locked the front door behind them, that the lock seemed old and not terribly trustworthy, the ground-floor windows had no bars, and the Faure house would probably be a

97

snap to break into—by a bumbling teenager, by the looks of things, not to mention any burglar worth his salt.

Émile's house was just down the block. Adèle rapped hard on his door and Molly cocked her head, listening. Adèle rapped again, and eventually they heard slow, shuffling footsteps approach, and the door cracked open.

"Bonjour, Émile, how good to see you up and about!" said Adèle, kissing him on both cheeks.

"Ma chérie," he said, and slowly turned his gaze to Molly.

Adèle made introductions and then disappeared down the hallway to the kitchen to put a wedge of cheese into the refrigerator while Molly and Émile went into the salon and sat down. Molly watched him lower himself slowly into an armchair, pressing much of his weight through his hands. His legs, in a pair of light wool trousers, looked very thin. His skin was gray with a tinge of yellow.

Adèle returned with what Molly recognized as an artificial smile. "All right then," said Adèle, clapping her hands together. "Your cheese selection is robust, I can say at least that much. I found a bit of the Banon you like so much, and put it on the second shelf next to that hunk of Parmesan I brought you last time."

"It's one of the things I love about Adèle," said Émile to Molly. "You know, there are French women who would never buy an Italian cheese. Just on principle. But our Adèle is not so rule-bound."

Molly grinned. She could listen to French people talk about cheese all day long.

"So, Madame Sutton, tell me what brings you to Aix?"

"Call me Molly, please. What a lovely city you live in," she started, but noticed a look of impatience on Émile's face. "I made friends with Adèle and Michel a few years ago, and it had been too long since seeing them. Email and the telephone are all fine and well, but of course no replacement for seeing their faces."

"And sharing some of Michel's roast lamb."

Molly nodded, grinning.

Émile smiled too though Molly could see it took some effort. She glanced at Adèle, who gave a quick nod.

"All right then, we're off," Adèle said, standing up. "I'm going to drag Molly all over the city today, it's my duty as hostess. If we hear anything interesting, we'll stop by soon and give you a report."

"Thank you for coming, my darlings. And ... be careful, will you please? I may be a shut-in, but news does reach me. Stay on your guard a bit more than usual?"

"She may be short of stature, but believe me, you wouldn't want to find yourself caught in a dark alley with this one," said Adèle, pointing at Molly.

Molly beamed.

"Do not joke," said Émile. "It is true we have not known each other very long. I have not even laid eyes on Madame Sutton until today. But it would grieve me sorely if anything happened to either of you. Now, I'm going to lie down on the daybed for a nap. And dream, if you will allow the impertinence, of a trip to the beach with the two of you once I am finished with this treatment. There's a small secluded place I am thinking of, with a fine view of Marseille but never crowded. The beach is a bit stony but protected from the wind, and the water, of course, is magnificent: clear and as blue as can be."

Adèle and Molly kissed him on both cheeks. Molly was surprised to feel tears spring to her eyes, sensing that Émile did not for one moment believe he would ever see the beach again, and was only trying to protect their feelings.

Back on the street, Adèle and Molly walked in silence to the Cours Mirabeau.

"I'm going to leave you now," said Adèle.

Molly looked surprised. "Oh! Do you have ... well, no worries,

I can amuse myself." She waited to see if Adèle was going to explain.

Adèle opened her mouth then closed it again. She looked up to the sky and then to the ground, avoiding Molly's eye. "I ... well, Oscar called and asked me to lunch. I hope you don't mind."

"Of course not!"

"I'm off then!" Adèle looked grateful and walked quickly away.

Molly was happy for Adèle and hoped eventually her friend would feel like sharing more about Oscar. And the truth was, she didn't mind having a chunk of free time to see if she could make any progress on the murders. She turned back to rue Niccolo, walking slowly, forehead wrinkled in thought. The knee-sock-wearing sweeper was nowhere to be seen.

Just for intellectual curiosity, let's assume the murders were performed by the same person, she thought. A suffocation and a cut throat. For the first, a killer needed nothing but a pillow. And, I suppose, a bit of strength because presumably the victim would struggle. Though perhaps Madame Trudeau might have been too old and infirm to put up much of a fight? But some eighty-five-year-olds are tough and hearty, Molly thought.

Without really meaning to, at least not really, she found herself standing outside the gendarmerie, which was not far from Adèle and Michel's house. Three stone steps led to the massive wooden door that was studded with ancient iron nails. She put her foot on the first step, then took it back down. She had no business going inside—she knew no one and had no legitimate reason to ask any questions. She wasn't even French.

She walked around the side of the building, searching for another door. She looked up at the windows on the second and third floors as though contemplating what would be required to scale the wall and climb in a window.

Molly waited. She *loitered*. But no one came out, not one single person over the course of nearly an hour. You would think there were no criminal activity in the entire city and the gendarmes were all taking the day off.

FOR LUNCH, Molly wanted something local, something luxurious and indulgent. And as she turned a corner onto a lovely street, with the sun coming through bright green leaves caught in the act of opening, she caught a whiff of the sea coming from a restaurant that made her grin.

Bouillabaisse. Of course. It was luxurious, expensive, Provençal, and the most delicious thing she could imagine, though she had never actually had the pleasure of tasting it, as it was not a dish of the Dordogne and Castillac. It would be sensible to make a plan to have it with her friends, or at least to wait, to ask for recommendations for the best place to get it. But Molly was feeling peckish and impulsive, not prudent, and besides, something with her friends felt a little off—was it her imagination that Adèle was avoiding her? At any rate, she walked straight in and ordered it without hesitation.

Even anticipating its glory as much as she did, Molly was stunned and thrilled when the large porcelain bowl arrived and was put in front of her with a flourish. Chunks of fish stood in a heap in the center of a small lake of fragrant broth. A jumble of clams and unfamiliar crustaceans decorated the heap. A few octopus tentacles peeked out from the broth. She leaned in and breathed in the deep oceanic smell, grinning some more.

The waiter had stepped back after placing the bowl in front of her, and he was smiling then too, watching his customer's immense pleasure before she had even taken one bite.

Molly glanced up at him. "You know," she said, "I've never actually eaten bouillabaisse before."

"Madame," said the waiter, still smiling. "Congratulations. Your next moments are going to be something you will always remember. You may spread the *rouille* on the toasts, or spoon it into the broth, as you like."

Molly's eyes were wide and her mouth watering as she dipped a bit of *rouille*—a mayonnaise made of olive oil, saffron, garlic, and cayenne—into the broth, and watched the broth change color to a light orange. Then she scooped up a bite of fish with some of the liquid and ate it.

"Oh my!"

"I know. It's simply one of the world's best dishes." The waiter looked as proud as if they were discussing his first-born child.

The waiter went off to other tables and left Molly to wallow in delight alone. She managed to keep her attention on the succulent hunks of seafood, and plowed through the bowl with such enthusiasm it took her barely thirty minutes.

Fortified and deeply satisfied, Molly paid her bill and headed back to the Faures. She was remembering the fun of swimming with Ben while on their honeymoon as she turned into rue Niccolo, and enjoying the memory so much she nearly missed the knee-sock woman sweeping in front of her building.

Molly stopped, observing the woman as she swept. It amused her that she had seen her sweeping several times before, and there were distinct variations—sometimes she swept with such ferocity it was as though the dirt were making her angry. Sometimes the woman's pressure on the broom was light, as though she were merely trying to give the sidewalk a tickle. She was a sweeper of many moods.

The broom was one of those old-fashioned implements that looked as though it had been made in the Middle Ages—a handful of twigs tied to a stick with a bit of twine, or perhaps wire.

"Did you buy that broom somewhere, or make it yourself?" Molly blurted out.

The knee-sock woman startled. She stopped sweeping and glared at Molly.

"I mean, um, *pardon*. I'm terribly rude. Bonjour, Madame."

"Bonjour Madame," the old woman answered with notable frost.

"I'm just so curious about your broom. It's really quite beautiful, and obviously wasn't made in a factory. I'm wondering—have you tried a more modern broom and you like this one better? Maybe it's a family heirloom or something you have a personal attachment to?"

The woman was not glaring but she stared at Molly as though she were an extremely odd creature.

"I'm sorry, I ask too many questions!" Molly grinned at her, and the old woman's eyes softened just a teeny tiny bit. "My name's Molly Sutton, I introduced myself yesterday? I'm visiting your beautiful city, staying with your neighbors, Adèle and Michel Faure. That building over there," she added, pointing down the street.

The woman leaned her broom against the wall and took her time pulling up her socks before speaking. "I am Berenice Verette. I have lived on rue Niccolo for sixty-three years." She peered at Molly. "You're not interested in my broom."

"I—well, truly, I *am*, Berenice. It's fascinating, these objects that humans have been using for so many centuries. You can just picture a caveman using a broom just like that to sweep out his cave after a party."

Berenice glowered. She grabbed the broom, turned her back, and continued sweeping. Forcefully.

"Wait," said Molly, "I didn't mean it like that. I'm just, oh I'm one of those people who finds a way to put her foot in her mouth every single day!"

Berenice did not pause in her sweeping.

"And yes, to be perfectly honest, though I honestly am interested in your broom, what I'm also interested in is ... your building, it's where poor Matéo Brule lived, isn't it?"

Berenice stopped sweeping. "Poor Matéo Brule? You don't know what you're talking about."

"You're absolutely right, I don't! Please, do fill me in."

Berenice sniffed. "Has no one told you anything? Brule lived above me. Heavy foot, let me tell you. He clomped around all times of the day or night, he didn't care about an old woman needing her sleep. And the riff-raff he let into the building—it was ... it makes the bile rise up in my throat just thinking about it, I will tell you! That girl—young too and looked even younger than she was—it was terrible she got mixed up with the lot of them."

Them?

"Which girl?" Molly asked.

Berenice looked up, trying to remember. "Mmm. Her name is ... her father is some important—head of something or other—at any rate, she got away." She smiled slyly. "Never told anyone this, but I was the one who let the *flic* into the building. And just in time, I don't mind saying."

"You heard something?"

"I'm not going to tell anyone what I heard. I put those sounds into a box in my mind and nailed the lid shut."

"It was that bad?"

Berenice nodded. "You ever heard someone being ... being ..." She turned away. "Anyway, the brute is gone now, and those lowlife women who used to come around, they're gone too, at least from my building. Brute Brule, that's what I called him. And I'm not sorry about what happened to him either. My view is, if you're a terrible person on this earth, there are consequences. Either in the afterlife or here, and probably both. I don't know who did the deed but I am nothing but grateful to him. If I had the courage, I'd have done it myself. With Brute Brule gone, I sleep like a baby."

"You wouldn't happen to remember the name of the girl?"

Berenice narrowed her eyes at Molly. "What, you're going to call her up and ask her out for a coffee?" The woman laughed and then looked serious. "She has a beautiful name, have some patience, it will come to me. Ha! There it is: Liliane Chopin. Like the composer. A suitable name for a pretty, rich girl, and that's exactly what she was. Or *is*. I have no idea how she got mixed up with the likes of Brule."

Molly nodded, her face turning a bit pink with excitement over this small progress. She talked about the weather for a few minutes, asked a question about local vegetables. And then, casually, Molly said, "I wonder if Madame Trudeau lived on rue Niccolo a long time as well? You must have known her?"

"Of course I knew her. She moved next door in 1983, in the summer."

"Was she married, did she have a family?"

Berenice glared again and Molly reminded herself to move more slowly.

"I'm just wondering," said Molly, "... about her history. I'm thinking—I don't mean to state the obvious—but when someone is murdered, the story of how that event comes to be is a long one. At least, often it is. Maybe Madame Trudeau's story began the day she moved into her apartment on this street."

"It was an unusually hot day," said Berenice. She seemed to be weighing whether to say more.

Molly struggled to keep quiet.

"You've heard she was a piano teacher?" said Berenice.

Molly nodded.

"And that she was mean—downright cruel—to at least one of her students?"

Molly waited, holding her breath.

"Probably more," said Berenice. "Where there's one, there's usually a hundred, that's what I always say. You must understand, French schools were not always the soft, easy places they are today. Back in my day, children were hit with regularity, sometimes with ferocity. I had a geography teacher who used to bang my knuckles every day until they were split and bleeding! And I can tell you, I did not run home to Maman and complain about it. It was just how things were." She got quiet and looked down at her shoes.

Molly held her breath, feeling that little buzzing tingle in her chest as she anticipated a useful bit of information being dropped.

"But Madame Trudeau ... she certainly had plenty of success as a teacher, early on. But eventually ... she took things too far." She looked at Molly. "Who can say why some people turn like that? Was she bitter over not being a star? Over not having a husband or children of her own?"

Molly swallowed hard and shrugged.

"We'll never know now. To state the obvious. Well, I can't tell you anything special about the history of brooms, but I can tell you—since you're like a dog with a bone and I can see you're going to be hanging around my doorway into eternity if I don't throw you a scrap—" Berenice nearly smiled but held it back. "Look into the Plouffes. Monsieur Antoine Plouffe, to be exact."

Molly gathered all her patience, giving Berenice time to elaborate, but the woman said no more. "The Plouffes?" asked Molly. "They have a connection to Madame Trudeau?"

Berenice nodded, her mouth turned down. She looked at Molly and squinted at her, then held her broom to her chest, shaking her head, and went inside her building.

The door banged shut and Molly stood on the sidewalk for a long moment, eyes unfocused, thinking.

Two names, she thought, her heart thumping in her chest so hard she put her hand there and patted herself. A pretty, rich girl and an angry father.

And one of them might be a killer.

❧ 16 ❧

That night, no one felt much like eating, or saying much. Molly, Adèle, and Michel shared an aperitif at six, ate a few handfuls of potato chips and some peanuts, and called it a night. Molly wanted to ask them about the Plouffes and Liliane Chopin but did not think it was the right moment.

Molly burrowed into her comfortable bed, the shutters angled so that the cool evening breeze swept into her room. There's no point obsessing about Antoine Plouffe before I even meet him, she told herself, picking up her book and snuggling further under the covers.

An hour passed while Molly transported herself to Ukraine, traveling with a false passport, trying to save a renowned scientist who had secrets that could save the world. Ah, nothing like a good thriller, she thought, finally closing the book and rolling over on her back, though she was not sleepy.

Antoine Plouffe. His name rattled around and around in her mind, with no image or even the tiniest detail attached to it. She considered how it would feel to find out you had sent your child off to be alone with an abuser, week after week, possibly even years. How the child might have begged: *please, no more piano*, and you brushed off her pleas and lectured about the importance of cultivating discipline or the joys of playing a musical instrument, so secure that you knew what was best.

It did not take any imagination at all to feel how a consuming desire for revenge might be kindled in such a circumstance.

Berenice had surely seen plenty over the years, in her role as habitual sweeper of the street, and Molly was sure that the name she had passed along was going to end up being extremely useful, one way or the other.

Her cell buzzed and Molly dug it out from under the covers.

"Bonsoir, chérie," said Ben, and the sound of his voice made Molly grin.

"Bonsoir to you," she said.

"Tell me how your day went."

"Oh," Molly said, stalling for a moment. She wanted to keep Antoine Plouffe to herself for a moment longer, thinking how satisfying it would be to tell Ben how she had solved the mystery of rue Niccolo all by herself. "Well," she said, feeling torn. "I've already told you about the murders, but now what everyone's talking about is the burglaries." She laughed.

"What?"

"Fancy burglars too, not your basic low-rent break-and-enter types. They're even *safe-cracking*," she added, with relish.

Ben did not answer for a moment. Molly smoothed out the duvet while struggling to decide whether to talk to him about the conversation with Berenice.

"Molly," he said finally. "I know you—"

She grinned. "Listen, no worries, I'm being careful! I can hear the worry in your voice and just ... don't be. I'm not ... I don't have anything to do with what's going on. That's the whole problem, I don't know anyone here, there's just not any way for me to ..."

"... for you to get in the middle of murders and burglaries? Molly, please, I'm not going to lecture you. I just know ... look, your safety ...."

Molly grinned again. He wanted to lecture her so badly, she could hear the words he was struggling so hard not to say, and she loved him for it.

"So tell me, what's going on at home? What juicy events have I missed out on?" she said, imagining La Baraque, and feeling a longing for it and her friends and Bobo. Even the orange cat, just a little.

"Hmm. Well, I don't have much to report. People have been remarkably well behaved in your absence. I stopped by Chez Papa last night—there were plenty of people there, but it was quiet, no communists jumping on tables and giving speeches, no one airing any dirty laundry."

"Disappointing."

Ben laughed. "I'm not sure what, but something ... I don't know, it was probably nothing. But Nico and Frances were acting a little funny."

"Funny how?"

"Oh, let's see. Distant, I guess you could say?"

"Sometimes they act like they just fell in love yesterday. So ga-ga it's a little hard to take."

"Maybe that's it."

"How's my sweet girl?"

"Bobo? She misses you terribly. I've been giving her liver every morning for consolation. You remember Madame Dubois, who sells chickens at the market? She gave me a container of chicken livers the other day and now Bobo sits by the refrigerator when I make coffee in the morning, with an air of expectation and entitlement."

Molly laughed and pulled the covers up to her chin. "I miss her. And you. So much."

"Chérie, I cannot even tell you ..."

HER FRIENDS WERE STILL LOUNGING in their bathrobes when Molly came down in the morning. She spied the silver coffeepot with an empty cup and saucer at the ready, and a platter of pastries alongside. She cut a hunk of butter from a softened slab and eyed a pot of dark red strawberry jam. "Is it ... would it be considered bad form to put jam on an almond croissant?"

"If only that were the most pressing issue of the day," said Michel, his tone unusually serious. He snapped a newspaper open and began to read. "'Monsieur and Madame Longchamps reported the theft of two pearl necklaces and a Bulgari watch, which they claimed were kept in a safe in the attic of their house on Avenue Saint-Jérôme. The gendarmerie has declined to comment on the case. This is the fourth such burglary reported in the last week.'"

Adèle looked stricken.

Molly took a sip of coffee and bit into a croissant, thinking.

"Shall I go on? There's plenty more bad news where that came from."

"Michel, I'm not used to you sounding so cynical."

"Perhaps there is more to me than you have discovered," he said.

"Well, all right, let's think about this logically," said Molly. "First of all, let's assess your risk and see what we can do to lower it. It sounds as though the burglars are after small things—jewelry is easy to make off with, just slip it in your pocket and no one on the street's any the wiser. Do you two have valuable jewelry here at the house?"

Silence from the Faures. Adèle got up, looking agitated, and poured herself another cup of coffee. Michel looked out of the window, making no sign that he had heard Molly's question.

"Umm, I'll take that as a yes?" she said, pressing on. "Here's some unasked-for advice then. Even if the jewelry is in a safe, obviously that's not going to be enough protection. I would take the stuff to a bank and get a safety-deposit box, at least until the burglar is caught. You have those here in France, I presume?"

A short pause. Molly saw Adèle shoot Michel a look, but he was still turned towards the window. What in the world is going on between them? Molly wondered.

"At least getting stolen from is better than being killed," said Michel.

Again, Molly stared at her friend. "I know you're joking," she said. "But ... are you really ... I mean, do you not take this threat seriously? Did you arrange to get the door locks changed?"

"Oh, Molly," said Michel, looking more like his usual jocular self. "I don't mean to be one of those people who always jokes at everything as a way to deny reality. It's just that, in the grand scheme of things, the jewelry we have is not really such great shakes. We did go a little crazy when we inherited Aunt Josephine's money, I suppose anyone would have, right? So we were, perhaps, less conservative in our spending than was wise."

"'Less conservative,'" repeated Adèle with an edge of sarcasm, and almost-but-not-quite glaring at her brother.

Molly looked warily from one to the other.

"Just get back on the murder beat," Michel said to Molly. "Adèle and I will sort out how to foil the burglars. And who knows, they may be across the border by now and no longer bothering anyone in Aix."

"That sounds like wishful thinking," said Molly. "And as for the murders, well ..." She paused, tried to restrain herself, then plunged on. "I wonder if either of you know the Plouffes? I've heard their daughter was singled out by Madame Trudeau. Or ... how about Victor Chopin, and his daughter Liliane?"

Adèle looked as though she were trying to recall, but her facial expression looked false to Molly, as though her friend was trying to seem interested but was actually thinking about something else.

"Michel?" said Molly. "Can you give me any more detail on exactly what Madame Trudeau did?"

"It was cruelty, plain and simple." said Adèle. "Just like Aunt Josephine. Only Madame Trudeau chose a child as her victim. So —a coward, on top of it all."

"She had quite a good reputation, and many children in Aix studied with her. But just recently, what was it Adèle, just two or three weeks ago? She was accused by one of her students of all kinds of terrible things."

"What kinds?" asked Molly, always wanting the details.

"Oh, telling the girl—we're talking about an eight-year-old— that she is talentless and will never amount to anything. That her playing was so dreadful it brought shame upon the entire family, shame that could never be washed off."

"Ah," said Molly. "The poor kid."

"I don't think anyone objects to a strict teacher. But Madame Trudeau was ... more than that. Also—I would say worse, but how do you even measure?—apparently she started out rapping the poor girl's knuckles with some sort of stick and then graduated to pulling down her pants and spanking her with it. Hard enough to make the poor child bleed. Celeste, the young girl, kept it to herself for a while, feeling so embarrassed. But finally she did tell her parents, who went straight to the gendarmerie to report that awful witch."

"And?" said Molly. "I hope they threw the book at her. How anyone could hurt a child ..."

"I know," said Michel. "Well, all this happened just last week. Madame Trudeau retired immediately, and I assume the wheels of justice were turning, but I hadn't heard anything about an arrest. She was in her eighties. I guess no one was worried about her running away, and as long as she wasn't seeing students any longer, maybe the gendarmes figured they could take their time, or just forget the whole thing. Who knows? Do any of us really believe justice is usually served? I certainly don't."

"So this was Celeste Plouffe? Was she the only one who was mistreated?" asked Molly. "It seems as though there would have been some clues this was going on. But you're saying for many years, parents felt fine about leaving their children alone with her?"

"Well, Madame Trudeau had something of a brilliant career in music—she was at Fontainebleau, after all—and, well, perhaps her bad temper seemed like part of being a real artist. You know how people have kooky ideas like that. I suppose we don't absolutely know if she hurt any other children—just following Molly's advice not to make assumptions," said Michel.

"Well, it's all over now," he added. "Celeste and whoever else Madame Trudeau hurt won't be getting any justice now. At least not in court."

Molly shook her head. "I suppose smothering has the benefit of not needing to carry a weapon," said Molly, thinking out loud. "But it has a feeling of ... as though the killer was trying to say 'shut up!' Does it seem that way to you?"

Michel shrugged and Adèle looked away with a glazed expression. They were worn out, as though they had not slept.

"Why are people so terrible to one another?" said Molly quietly.

"A question for the ages," said Adèle. "As you might imagine, given our family history, I've given it a great deal of thought. All I've been able to come up with is that people are wounded, and what so many of them seem to do in response is try, unthinkingly, to repeat that hurt on someone else, as quickly as they can and as often as they can." She glared at Michel.

I don't know what in the world is going on, but something is rotten in the state of the Faure household, Molly thought to herself. She stuffed the rest of her croissant into her mouth and gulped down the rest of her coffee.

"We thought we'd have people over tomorrow night," Michel

said, making an attempt at a cheerful tone of voice. "An *apéro*, to introduce you to the neighbors?"

"Sounds great, thank you!" said Molly. She suggested inviting the Plouffes and Chopins, which Michel agreed to.

But the tension remained, and Molly made up an excuse to leave the salon. She had the distinct feeling they were relieved to see her go.

Preparations for the *apéro* involved typical last-minute revelations: the champagne glasses needed polishing, as did the silver serving bowl for the candied walnuts, and they did not have nearly enough ice (at least according to Molly, who had an American appetite for it). The hors d'oeuvres delivered by the caterer were being readied for the oven or brought to room temperature. For an hour or so, Molly hung around in the kitchen watching Michel and a helper from the caterer's get everything ready, chatting and joking while pinching tastes of the walnuts and foie gras when no one was looking.

Generally speaking, and perhaps unexpectedly, the point of a French apéro is not so much food but rather socializing and alcohol. Countless times, Molly had arrived at a friend's and been given a kir (her very favorite), but nothing more to eat than a few plain potato chips and a handful of peanuts. From the French point of view, dinner was right around the corner and heaven forbid one show up to the table with an appetite ruined by stuffing oneself with tidbits. From Molly's point of view, stuffing oneself with tidbits was one of life's absolute best pleasures. In any case, she saw with delight that Adèle and Michel had chosen to go all out, the caterer having tempted them with an array of deliciousness to equal the foie gras, such as salmon mousse and a glistening tapenade.

It was too bad that the Faures had not been able to figure out a way to invite the Chopins, but perhaps it was better not to be spinning too many plates at once anyway.

As Molly was dressing, guests began to arrive. The living room was already filling up as she came down. Conversation was animated, and Molly stood for a moment on the stair, listening:

"—quite an enormous sapphire, that's what I heard—"

"—don't think for one second anyone is the least bit sorry—"

"—yes, we need rain, it goes without saying, my poor peonies are just fading away before my eyes—"

"—stands to make an absolutely disgusting amount of money! Are you—"

"—oh darling, if I only could just take it back—"

Molly leaned over the railing, trying to zero in on that last snippet. In the world of eavesdropping, people expressing regret was almost always a prize, as it hinted at an authentic moment with the added benefit of an interesting backstory. But the thread of the conversation was lost as another couple came in through the door and everyone standing in the hallway offered greetings and bustled over for kisses.

Feeling a sudden rush of shyness, Molly stood on the stairs for one more moment, peeking into the living room as though she were a child who has sneaked out of bed to observe her parents' party. She saw Michel pour a drink for an old man with a cane. Adèle whispered into the ear of a chic woman dressed in black, and the two leaned their heads back and roared with laughter. Curious about what was so funny, Molly trotted the rest of the way downstairs and pushed into the crowd towards Adèle.

"I have to tell you, I had no idea you knew so many people already! Your social circle is wider than I thought."

Adèle shrugged. "It's not, actually—when we made invitations,

EYE FOR AN EYE

we asked people to bring any neighbors who might like to come. So now we're swamped."

"Ah," said Molly. "No doubt people are curious about the 'new' people and want to get a look inside your house. Is Oscar coming?"

Adèle shrugged again. "It's a stressful time, with everything going on. People want to share a drink and be together. Everyone just wants to feel safe. Our little street has had more than its share of excitement lately."

"Well," said Molly, about to mention the possibility of either of the killers being right there in the Faure salon. But for once, she managed to keep her thoughts to herself. "It's ... I mean ... yes indeed, a very stressful time." Molly tried to smile. The last thing Adèle and Michel needed was to be triggered by the prospect of a murderer (or murderers) right under their own roof, drinking their champagne, and possibly, Molly thought, even scoping out prospective victims. The killer (or killers!) may even have developed a taste for killing; it was known to happen, after all.

That's probably going a little far, she said to herself, imagining Ben's expression of affectionate head shaking.

But is it?

Quickly she moved across the salon towards the bar, and asked Michel for a glass of champagne. Molly loved champagne—who didn't?—but that evening she would make sure not to overdo it. She may not have been hired by anyone but nevertheless considered herself on the job.

"Anything suspicious yet?" Michel said, *sotto voce*, as he handed her a delicately etched flute overfilled with champagne.

"Not yet. But this party's just getting started."

"I'm going to be very disappointed in you if we don't have at least one arrest by dinner time," he said, deadpan.

"Apolline! Dearest darling!" a woman cried, and Molly turned to see Apolline Cuvalier making a grand entrance, standing in the doorway to the salon with her chin lifted, head in profile, as though the room were filled with clamoring photographers and adoring fans. Her dress was tight, showing off her figure, and Molly wanted to say the outfit was in poor taste, but admitted to herself that perhaps some envy was coloring her judgment. It was not the dress itself, really, it was more that one did not expect a woman of Apolline's age to wear anything so immodest—but then Molly chastised herself for being so puritanical and judgmental. Maybe if I had her figure, I'd wear a dress like that myself. And anyway, surely women can wear whatever the hell they want, no matter how old they are, she muttered to herself, and she's younger than I am, then pressed her lips together, as talking out loud to oneself in the midst of a cocktail party is not really a good look.

She glanced at Michel and saw him watching Apolline with an inscrutable expression.

She took a long sip of champagne and glanced up at the dangling crystals of the chandelier, trying to clear her head. I've got other fish to fry right now, she said to herself. Where are the Plouffes, anyway? Were they already there?

"I will tell say this," a woman behind Molly said, her voice like acid. "If I had had the slightest inkling about what was taking place, I would not only have yanked Lilou out of piano lessons, I would have gone over to have a private word with Madame Trudeau myself, and she would not have been well pleased, I can tell you that."

"Oh, Marianne. It's easy to sound fierce now that she's dead and gone. But we have to face reality. Even after the news was out —even after little Celeste was so brave and told Antoine, and Madame Trudeau lost every single student—even then, how many people confronted her in person? Almost none."

Marianne opened her mouth to argue but shut it again. "Well, I suppose you've got a point. What I mean," she said in a softer voice, "is that I *wish* I had gone over there and given her a piece of my mind. We were lucky: she was rather horrible to Lilou but in the sort of way we were used to, back when we were children. A few raps across the knuckles, a few insults, that sort of thing. Lilou did complain about her, and sad to say, I shrugged it off. I ... I feel quite terrible about that now. It's the worst, most damaging thing about what happened, isn't it? That we didn't believe our children. And then I felt a different kind of terrible that once the news was out, I did not march over to Madame Trudeau's house straightaway and tell her exactly what I and everyone else thought of her."

"It almost seems unfair, that she would be simply smothered in her sleep, doesn't it? It's an odd thing to say. But the suffering seems so slight, so momentary. Oh my, I sound so vindictive."

"Yes. It's decidedly not good for our mental health to dwell on thoughts of revenge, yet here we are. It's hard not to want that witch to suffer, and in the most dreadful ways. I honestly don't know how Antoine and Margot can stand it. Their dear, sweet Celeste ..."

The women shuddered. Molly leaned closer.

"Bonsoir," she said, turning after a moment and smiling at the two women. "My name is Molly Sutton, I'm staying with Adèle and Michel for a few weeks."

The women introduced themselves politely, then made excuses about needing a drink freshener or the *toilette*, and Molly was quickly standing by herself again. Slowly she squeezed through the crowd, ready for a fresh glass herself.

"One problem is, so often there's just no way to prove anything," a woman standing near the bar said.

The older man next to her shrugged. "Do you want every flirtation to be recorded on videotape or some such? In my opinion, it's all being blown way out of proportion."

"Blown out of proportion?" the woman said, with gritted teeth. "You think attempted rape is what, no big deal? Just a little miscommunication?"

"Calm down, Juliette. I said nothing of the sort. I only—"

NELL GODDIN

"Why Victor Chopin didn't pull every string he had to keep that man in prison, I do not understand. He had plenty of strings to pull, so why not pull them? It's incomprehensible. Unless ... maybe *he's* the one who got rid of Brule? The upstanding and well-connected Monsieur Chopin wanted to take care of the situation by himself?"

He laughed. "No one can fault you for lack of imagination."

"Well, if there were any actual justice in this world, Matéo Brule would have been in prison, and then wouldn't have had his throat cut."

"I'm surprised you aren't cheering about the throat-cutting, chérie, as an efficient and unambiguous sort of fairness," he answered.

Molly stopped. She wished she were wearing shoes with laces so she could stoop down and pretend to be tying them. It is not all that easy to stop short in the middle of a crowd to eavesdrop, and not look as though eavesdropping is exactly what you are doing. But Molly was no amateur. She waved at a pretend stranger across the room and then mouthed something unintelligible, while listening intently to the people she stood next to.

"Listen," Juliette said, lowering her voice so that Molly could barely hear her, "if anyone did that to someone I love, and got away with it like Brule did, I'd absolutely consider cutting his throat. I might even enjoy it."

Molly forced herself not to stare. She made another wave across the crowd and nodded theatrically.

"I don't mind saying," the older man said, even more quietly, "that I find your passion to be quite ... inspiring. It's not often that I run across a woman willing—not only willing, but eager—to act in such a way. So forcefully. According to her deepest principles."

Molly saw him put a hand on the woman's shoulder and let it drift down her arm. He grasped her by the wrist.

"If you think I was just trying to seduce you," she said, with a choking laugh, "you've misunderstood in a rather grand fashion. Lionel, take your hand away. I mean, *really*. You're acting as though you're fifteen.

"I feel fifteen," Lionel growled.

Molly put her hand over her mouth and laughed. She looked at the woman to remember her face: a long, narrow nose, a high forehead, confident posture. Ash blonde hair gracefully swept into a high bun. Then Molly continued on her way to Michel, who was opening another bottle and laughing with a woman in a yellow dress with a swirly skirt. Molly glanced around for Apolline but did not see her.

Was it too much to hope that Victor Chopin might drop by? And where were the Plouffes?

Apolline Cuvalier leaned against a doorframe, talking to a young man with a scruffy beard wearing an expensive suit.

"Bonsoir!" Molly said to Apolline, a broad smile on her face. "Nice to see you again. Lovely champagne, isn't it?"

Apolline looked as though she'd just eaten something spoiled.

"I am Richard de Coumaine," the young man said, holding out a limp hand for Molly to shake.

"Very pleased to meet you," said Molly.

The three of them stood in silence, the awkwardness growing every second.

"I'm wondering—just out of curiosity—did you happen to know Matéo Brule or Madame Trudeau?" Molly said at last, with no clear idea why.

Apolline cocked her head. "Who have you been taking to?"

Molly shrugged, keeping her expression pleasant. "Oh, you know. People. It's just … it's quite a situation, wouldn't you agree? I'm trying to get an idea of how widely known the unfortunate victims were."

"I hear you've done some work as a private detective," said Apolline.

"Tongues do wag, don't they?" Molly smiled. "There's a string of murderers in prison thanks to that work," Molly said, making her smile broader.

"Oh my," said Apolline, the mocking tone intensifying. "Don't put a foot wrong with this one around," she said to Richard, who smirked.

"What kind of man was Matéo?" Molly asked, telling herself not to take the bait.

"A useless waster, to be honest," said Richard. "But good-looking, eh Apolline?"

Apolline shrugged. "We had some business interests in common," she said. "May he rest in peace," she added, raising her glass.

"I don't think there's much chance of that," Richard mumbled, making her laugh.

Apolline looked disapprovingly at Richard. "I have some people I absolutely must see tonight," she said, and disappeared into the crowd.

"Tough cookie," said Molly.

"You have no idea," said Richard, and melted into the crowd before Molly could ask anything further.

ABOUT FORTY PEOPLE were jammed into the salon and hallway. "Tommaso," Molly said. "So nice to see you again."

He kissed both her cheeks and Molly got a whiff of an expensive-smelling cologne. "What have you been up to?" he asked. "It must seem like great good fortune, as a private investigator, to find yourself in the middle of a crime wave."

"I wouldn't exactly say that," she said. "But for sure, two murders on the same street—it does seem unusual."

"And don't forget the burglaries! It's a wonder any of us in the neighborhood can get a wink of sleep." Tommaso said this, eyes merry, as though he himself had not the slightest anxiety over any of it. "It wouldn't surprise me to hear that all of it goes back to money, one way or another. People these days—the greed is unimaginable."

"Are you talking about the stock market? I've heard—"

"Oh certainly, yes, but that's not the end of it. People are hawking these 'opportunities,' as they call them. Nothing but thievery, if you ask me." Tommaso leaned in close to Molly's ear. "That Apolline Cuvalier," he said, nodding his head in her direction. "If someone doesn't stop her, she's going to fleece every single well-off person in Aix!"

Molly felt a spike of cold settle in her chest. "Stop her from doing what, if I may ask?"

"She's peddling some so-called 'financial instruments,' some supposedly new thing that guarantees enormous profits with low risk. Who needs to hear the details? Anyone with half a brain can see that's a scam. It may be dressed up in new clothes but it's an age-old way to separate fools from their money."

Molly's throat was suddenly insufferably dry. "And—" she tried unsuccessfully to swallow, "she was mixed up with Matéo Brule, yes?"

Tommaso nodded slowly. "Do you think—"

"I don't know," she said softly.

Out of the corner of her eye, she saw Adèle wave, and motion her over.

Reluctantly she excused herself from Tommaso and made her way to her friend. "It's so crowded!" said Molly.

"And apparently everyone is starving," said Adèle with a dry expression, gesturing at the food table where a young woman in black pants and shirt was replenishing the prunes stuffed with foie gras. "Listen, the Plouffes just arrived. As I said, I've never met them, but I just heard someone call out 'Antoine!'"

"Which way?"

"Front door," said Adèle.

Molly needed no urging. She scooted past Michel, still talking to the man with the cane. In the hallway was another knot of people and she pushed her way through until she was facing a short man wearing a pair of wire-rimmed glasses that had been fashionable several decades ago. An even shorter woman stood next to him, looking a little overwhelmed.

"Bonsoir," said Molly, with a warm smile. "I am Molly Sutton, houseguest of Adèle and Michel. I've been given the job of door greeter for the moment, so please allow me to welcome you!"

The woman slipped her arm through her husband's. He stared at Molly without changing expression. "I am Antoine Plouffe," he said finally. "Allow me to present my wife, Margot."

"Very pleased to make your acquaintance. What may I get you to drink? I'm afraid the entire neighborhood has shown up and it's not easy to move around. I'd be happy to bring you—" Molly stopped, seeing the distress on the Plouffe's faces.

Margot leaned into her husband, then whispered in his ear.

"Don't you think …" he said softly. "Just allow Madame Sutton to get us a glass of champagne. We'll only stay for a moment. We talked about this. It will be good for us, Margot."

Margot's face was pale. She looked a little unsteady and Molly wondered if she were about to faint.

"Are you all right?" she asked, reaching to touch Margot on the arm.

"We heard about the vintage, and it's exceptional," said Antoine, trying to smile. "It would be tragic to miss it. So thank you, Madame Sutton, it would be very kind of you to get glasses for us. I think … I think it would be best if we wait just outside, on the street, if it's all right. It's just so crowded inside, and Margot needs some air."

"Of course!" said Molly. It *was* awfully crowded, and she could understand that being in the crowd might seem daunting for any number of reasons. She would much rather speak to the Plouffes outside where there were fewer distractions and less noise.

Finally Michel handed her two glasses of champagne and she made her way back through the press of people to the front door, introducing and excusing herself along the way.

"Oh my!" she said, heaving a great breath as she reached the outside air. She looked down the street, one way and then the other, but Antoine and Margot Plouffe were nowhere to be seen.

Crestfallen, Molly sipped champagne from one of the glasses. It was very, very good champagne. And Antoine Plouffe knew it, so why had he taken off when he knew Molly was delivering glasses to them outside so that he and Margot wouldn't have had to go inside if they didn't want to?

She took another sip, the bubbles tickling her throat in the most refined and expensive way, and peered down the street in both directions.

A teenaged boy was leaning up against the wall of the house, his expression so typical of his age that Molly felt almost moved to tears: a scattering of acne on one cheek and forehead, and so glum his face could be in a pictorial dictionary to define the word.

"Bonjour," Molly said to him, offhand.

The boy looked up, in agony at being noticed and expected to respond.

"I brought these glasses out for some people who've disappeared," she said. "You want one? It's extremely good, I'll say that much. I promise I've only taken sips from this one," she laughed.

The boy cracked a small smile and reached out for the other glass.

"Your parents inside?"

The boy nodded and sighed. "I don't know why they drag me to these things. I don't know anybody."

"Me neither," said Molly. She leaned against the wall next to him, and they both drank, appreciatively. "You gotta admit, this is some fine champagne. I'm from the US and you'd have to take out a loan from the bank to afford anything this good."

"Champagne is elitist and I don't support it," said the boy.

Molly grinned. "You're a socialist, then?"

The boy laughed darkly. "Archano-nihilist. Socialists are scum-sucking moderates."

"Ah. Well, you can't blame the champagne itself just because rich people like it. Anyway, your glass is poured and it will only be wasted if you don't drink up. Politically speaking, how do you feel about wastefulness?"

The boy looked the tiniest bit amused but did not answer. Molly looked straight ahead but could see out of the corner of her eye that he raised his glass and drank off the rest.

"I'm Molly," she said, holding out her hand. "Very pleased to meet you."

"Aleron," said the boy, shaking her hand with seriousness.

"Are you going to be out here for a while? Would it be okay if I came back, when mingling with a lot of strangers gets to be too much?"

Aleron nodded his head once. He handed Molly his glass and jammed his hands in his pockets.

"Thanks. I expect I'll be back sooner rather than later," she said, and stepped back inside, into the fray, wondering what had happened to the Plouffes and whether their disappearance indicated guilt, social anxiety, or simply that someone had forgotten to turn off the stove.

❧ 18 ❧

It was well past dinner time when the last guests left. Adèle, Michel, and Molly gathered by the front door waving and saying goodbye. The man with the cane, who moved achingly slowly, was the final one to go; Michel closed the door gently after him and leaned his back against it.

"Oh," he said, his shoulders sagging. "Is it just me, or was that something of an ordeal?"

"Not just you," said Adèle and Molly in unison.

"Well, in the future we will not suggest that people bring friends. Never again."

"Who knew so many people would be desperate for a glass of champagne?"

"It was the vintage. Once word got out ..." said Molly.

Adèle laughed. "It *was* extraordinary, wasn't it? And the salmon mousse?"

"Why don't I box up some leftovers and take them over to Émile?" asked Molly.

"Oh Molly, how thoughtful of you. Thanks. I would go with you but I'm just exhausted. I'll pack up the box," said Adèle, going off to the kitchen.

"So?" said Michel, cocking his head and looking at Molly.

"Yes?"

"You just met at least half the people who live on our block. Surely you've got some information you did not have earlier?"

"Well, I wouldn't go that far." Molly shook her head. "To be honest, I was hoping ... but it's not like I can push people up against a wall and demand they talk."

"No?" Michel laughed. "You have your ways, Molly Sutton, you have your ways." He leaned over and gave her a kiss on the cheek, lingering, but only a fraction of a fraction. Without making eye contact, he went off to pack up the bar and make sure all the dirty glasses had gotten to the kitchen.

Molly stood in the hallway, grateful for a minute alone. Though the party had gone on for hours, she had not talked to everyone she wanted to talk to. She wondered again about the Plouffes. Had Margot taken ill? Antoine had seemed to be such a polite fellow, not at all the sort to run off like that without a word. Were his good manners hiding another side of him?

"Here you are!" said Adèle. "I called Émile to let him know to expect you. He does get tired easily so I expect he won't want to talk for long. You're an absolute dear to do this. I can't face another conversation tonight, not even with him."

Molly took the brown paper bag with two covered metal boxes inside and went out. Rue Niccolo was quiet as usual. It was toward the end of dinnertime, and most of the city was at the table just then. Molly listened to a car revving in the distance, its muffler broken, and then a thrush singing in a scraggly tree in the front yard of an ancient stone house.

She blinked and shook her head, and moved on down the street toward Émile's house, and rapped loudly.

Before too long the door opened a crack, then wide, and a smiling Émile gestured for her to come inside.

"Bonsoir, Émile," said Molly. "Adèle and Michel send their love. And perhaps even better—this bag of hors d'oeuvres. I can speak as something of an expert, having tried them all more than once, and I predict you're about to be a very happy man."

Émile chuckled. "I'm afraid they will be wasted on me just now. Chemotherapy has slowed my cancer, and it goes without saying I'm tremendously grateful for that. But alas, it has completely ruined my taste buds. I could eat the most magnificent hors d'oeuvres in the world, and they would be as flavorful as sawdust."

Molly shook her head. "That's so unfair, isn't it? Talk about being kicked when you're down."

Émile smiled. "Ah, that's one way to look at it. Another way is for me to experience what it is like to be freed from certain appetites. When I was healthy, I spent much of my time and money, like any self-respecting Frenchman, on food and drink. I don't say that regretfully—there are distinct and valuable pleasures, including life-force, to be gotten from them. Yet still, it is a particular kind of pleasure now—'pleasure' is not the precise word, but I hope you take my meaning—to do without."

Émile slowly rubbed his hand over his belly and looked up at the ceiling.

"Heavens, Madame Sutton, I did not intend to sweep you off into my philosophical ramblings this way! Come sit, and talk with me a moment about everyday things. Perhaps you can tell the story of the apéro so I will be able to imagine I was there. I know we have not had time to get to know one another, but I sense you are a decent storyteller."

Molly was pleased by the compliment. She reminded him to call her Molly, then ducked into the kitchen to put the bag of food into the refrigerator. Quickly she was back and took her place across from Émile on a tufted chair upholstered in a masculine pattern of chintz.

"How is your treatment going, if it's not too personal to ask?"

Émile looked very small once he was sitting down; he had lost so much muscle and flesh that he seemed no bigger than a child.

Molly felt a complicated emotion even though she had just met him.

"Well," Émile began, "The treatment ... ah well, honestly, that's not a very interesting subject. I'm sure you've known enough people who have gone through it? My doctor brought me back from the brink of death, I will say that for him, though as I'm sure you know, chemotherapy is a sort of torture. Carpet-bombing, you know. A few months ago, things were bad enough that I got my affairs in order, such as they are, so that's done. I sometimes feel as though—this is not easy to describe ..." He looked up at the ceiling, head cocked to one side. "As though I am still alive but can see a little bit into the next world. Peeking over the fence, as it were."

"And what do you see?

Émile looked at Molly. They sat gazing into each other's eyes for a moment without speaking or moving. "I don't believe I can describe it," he whispered. "But I will say: I am not afraid."

Molly felt an urge to make a dark joke but stopped herself. Instead, she reached for Émile's hand and held it for a moment. He squeezed back, then put his hand in his lap, still looking deeply into her eyes.

"You know, it's perhaps contrary to what one might think, but it's reassuring, my understanding that none of this matters," he said.

"None of what?"

"Life!" he threw his arms out. "All the details that we get so attached to! From the perspective of the universe, we are nothing."

"Well, I don't suppose I can argue the point. But at the same time, we aren't the universe. Our details matter to *us*. Very much so."

Émile simply smiled a rather Buddha smile and did not argue back. He closed his eyes and took a long, deep breath, and Molly could see he was tired.

Hopping up from the chair, her voice bright, she said, "I've got to run off and help Adèle and Michel with the cleanup. Maybe I can come back soon to tell you about the party? Though there isn't that much to tell, at least nothing very juicy. People behaved themselves, more or less."

"Ah, that's too bad."

"It *is*," laughed Molly, liking Émile more than ever.

❧ 19 ❧

On Saturday morning, Ben woke with a start, realizing it was Changeover Day already and he was not free to take Bobo on a long ramble through the woods, spend the morning at Café de la Place, and read naval histories all the rest of the day. No, he needed to make sure Constance carried out her cleaning duties, go to the market, and greet—who was he supposed to greet again?

How did Molly keep all these details in her head?

Blessedly, the Sadlers had turned out to be no trouble at all, and they left before Ben was even up and about. He heard the sound of a car and just caught Christophe's taxi pulling out of the driveway with the Sadlers inside, and waved goodbye. After a cup of coffee, he went to the pigeonnier to see what shape it was in, noticing that he felt some trepidation at opening the door, even though the Sadlers had given no reason for worry. The place was ship-shape. They had left the key on the kitchen table along with an appreciative note, and Ben tucked it into a pocket to save for Molly.

That left Briony Lark. He started toward the cottage, Bobo darting underfoot as she chased the orange cat under a shrub.

Was he supposed to find out the guests' arrangements for leaving or did Molly even involve herself with that? Maybe he would knock at the cottage and find Briony gone, just like the Sadlers.

He stood at the door with his hands in his pockets. For a moment he closed his eyes and let the industrious chatter of birds enter his consciousness while breathing in the first waft of warm springtime air. He was suddenly hungry and wanted to finish up the rest of the gîte business and get to Café de la Place for the breakfast special. Surely he would have time if he didn't dally.

I am a coward, and that's the stone-cold truth, Ben said to himself, after raising a hand to knock on the cottage door but then letting it drop. He put Bobo in the main house and took off for the village on foot, hoping to pass Christophe's taxi coming back for Briony, and thought about Molly.

He trusted his wife, that went without saying, but at the same time, he noted an increasing anxiety over her being in Aix, in a neighborhood that was unstable at best and quite dangerous at worst. He also trusted Michel and Adèle ... though when he considered them objectively, all he could really say was that he knew they would never intentionally do anything to hurt Molly. Which was, to Ben's mind, not one hundred percent reassuring.

Should he make a quick trip down to Aix and take stock? Would Molly be glad to see him or feel as though it was a vote of no confidence?

He settled at a table outside though it was still a bit brisk out. Pascal came running out with a placemat and tableware. "We're not serving out here, but I'll make an exception for you," he said, flashing his movie star smile. "We'll just pretend you're on a stake-out or something."

Ben smiled wryly. "If only," he said. "Appreciate it. I'll have the usual. The streets look awfully quiet this morning. Is something going on I don't know about?"

"Not that I know of," said Pascal. "Inside, we've got a typical number of customers. It's this cold breeze, Ben—I expect people are avoiding that and aren't strange like you." He grinned and took off for the kitchen.

Ben leaned back in his chair and tipped his face up to the sun. He closed his eyes and a vision of naked Briony Lark jumped into his mind. Opening his eyes again, he rubbed them and muttered under his breath, then pulled out his cell to call Constance and ask her to find out when and how Briony was leaving.

"COME ON," said Nico, grinning at Frances, who was lounging in bed in something of a glamor movie star pose. "I've got a couple hours before going in to Chez Papa, we could take that bike ride."

"Mmm," said Frances, rolling to one side and caressing her belly, which was beginning to swell, though not enough to show when she was dressed. "Mmmmm."

"Mmm to you too," he laughed. "Seriously. Get up!"

"The baby needs a bit more sleep."

"Oh, he's talking to you already?"

"Indeed. She would like another cup of coffee and ... um ... a grilled sausage and a baked apple."

Nico leapt onto the bed and began tickling. He knew all the right spots and she wriggled and laughed uproariously. Finally Frances begged for mercy and promised to arise.

"But how about let's go for a walk, instead of a bike ride. Maybe just out rue de Chêne and see how things look at La Baraque."

"If you like. You're not actually concerned, are you?"

"Nah. Ben's ... well, he's probably just awful at that job, but he does have a certain charm. I'm sure he's muddling along okay. It's just ... I do miss that redhead something fierce. So I want to walk out there and just soak up her spirit."

"You're a kook, you know that?" He kissed her cheek, then put his hand on her belly.

"I do."

"And I know your secret," he whispered into her ear. "You don't know how to ride a bike."

Frances shrieked and leapt up, much more quickly than one might guess a pregnant woman might be capable of, and chased Nico around the apartment, whacking him with a pillow.

🕊 20 🕊

T he next morning, Molly came downstairs to find Michel alone in the salon.

"I didn't think I had that much champagne," she confessed, "but my head feels a little big this morning."

Michel grinned at her. "I thought you were magnificent."

Molly looked askance. "At drinking champagne?"

"No, little goose. At doing your work. I watched you move through the crowd, listening, paying close attention to everything. I saw you pretend to wave at someone so you could eavesdrop on Juliette and Lionel. I can't imagine he had anything interesting to say, but maybe my interactions with him haven't given the whole story? Anyway, tell me, I'm dying to hear! What did you find out?"

"Not much, to be honest."

"Could it be that you did uncover something but just don't know it yet?"

"It would be nice to think so. But maybe a tad optimistic." She shrugged. "I'll say this much: people are definitely upset at how Madame Trudeau treated poor Celeste Plouffe. I suppose that's hardly a surprise, since it's all still fresh. And Juliette was quite angry at Matéo Brule's not being arrested and in jail." Molly shrugged again. "Tommaso is not a fan of Apolline's, as I learned last night. Everything else I heard, at least on the surface, was ... more or less what one might expect."

"Do you think the murderer—or at least one of them—was here, in the salon?" Michel looked at her seriously.

"You were wondering about that?"

"Of course. Weren't you?"

"Well, yes, but I didn't want ..."

Michel got up and poured himself more coffee from the silver pot. "I wish you would speak more freely to me," he said, his voice full of feeling.

"What do you mean?" she said.

Their eyes met and neither looked away.

"Only that ... I like it very much when you are open with me, when you tell me what you are really thinking. On the other hand, if you're trying to protect me, or hide things, feelings, whatever—I like that a great deal less."

Molly made a long, slow inhalation. There was something a little reckless about Michel, and it was appealing, there was no denying it.

"I did a bit of detective work myself," he said, walking to the window and looking out to the street.

"Really? And was it productive?"

"The detective on both murder cases is Yves Dupont. The general opinion is that one detective should not be expected to manage both investigations, but apparently the gendarmerie is operating a bit light at the moment: one detective recently retired and another was moved to Toulouse, so that's how it is."

"What's Detective Dupont's reputation?"

"Stern. No nonsense."

"All right. But wait— 'stern' as in all business, or 'stern' as in brutal, or close-minded, or egotistical?"

"You ask questions I know not the answers to," said Michel, and Molly smiled in spite of herself.

"He doesn't sound very approachable."

"You mean by you? Probably not. I mean, of course it would be his loss, the city's loss—but your reputation hasn't made it to Aix. Yet."

"Not sure it would be much help," said Molly. "Our chief in Castillac now, Chantal Charlot—I'd say on a good day she's ambivalent about me."

They both poured more coffee and sat in silence.

"I wonder if *you* could talk to Dupont," Molly said finally.

"Me? And say what exactly?"

"I don't know. Not so much specific questions I can give you in advance. It's ... well ... you just start talking, you know, about whatever comes into your head. You don't go in with a preconceived goal, necessarily. All you're trying to do is get the person talking. And then you listen for anything they might let drop. Either on purpose or not."

Michel shook his head. "That's a few levels above my pay grade, I'm afraid."

"Oh come on, Michel! You have gobs of charm, and that's all you need."

"You think so?" he asked, meeting her eyes.

"Of course!"

"I mean about the charm," he said softly.

THE PRETEXT WAS THIN, Molly didn't pretend otherwise. But sometimes you have to use whatever scrap is at hand rather than wait for something better that may never appear. How was she going to get anywhere with the Trudeau case if she had no opportunity to talk to the person who had the biggest motive for killing her?

She stood at the door to the Plouffes's house and took a moment to compose herself before knocking. She ran her fingers through her tangled curls and brushed a few crumbs of almond croissant from her shirt. Then she banged the brass lion's head knocker hard, three times.

Ten o'clock on Saturday morning. The Plouffes might be at the market, running errands, out on a walk before the expected rain came later that day. It was too much to expect that they would be home, simply waiting for her to arrive with a long list of intrusive questions. Nevertheless, Molly was disappointed when no one answered. She started to turn away but decided what the heck, and gave the lion's head three more bangs, this time so fiercely it rather hurt her ears.

Footsteps inside. Not purposeful, not striding towards the door, but tentative, halting.

"Madame, Monsieur Plouffe?" she called out, stepping away from the door where they could see her in case they were peeking through the curtains at the front window.

The door opened. Antoine Plouffe smiled a perfectly pleasant smile, said bonjour, and politely ushered her inside. He did not look alarmed or discomfited by the American's appearance on his doorstep as far as Molly could tell.

"I'm—well, I do apologize for knocking on your door like this without calling first, but had no idea how to reach you," she said. "Berenice pointed out your house the other day when she was telling me the story of—but I—well, listen, Antoine, I'll just say it plainly—last night, I was worried about you and Margot. I understand that the party at the Faures may have been somewhat overwhelming—it was for me, too, honestly—and so when I came out with your glasses of champagne and you were gone—"

"It's all right," said Antoine softly. "It is kind of you to check up on us. Please come in." He led her down a short hallway to the salon and gestured for her to sit down. "May I get you something to drink? A coffee, perhaps?"

"Always!" said Molly with a grin.

Antoine nodded and excused himself. Molly had started to sit but jumped right up, wanting to use every moment he was gone to see what she could see. Under a window was a low bookshelf with tchotchkes arranged on it: a porcelain bear, a small glass ballerina that looked as though it might have been a souvenir from the glassworks in Murano, a nest made of real twigs with some tiny blue eggs nestled inside.

The lower shelf was packed with books. Molly ran her eyes over the titles—they were mostly history, biography, a spy thriller, and then—

Psychological and Physical Trauma and Their Effects on Children. A second book, same topic. Thick and academic-looking.

Well. Not unexpected, she thought. Of course the Plouffes would want to do the responsible thing and read up on the subject to try to see how to help their little Celeste. People were allowed to read whatever they liked; in any case, she hadn't found *How To Suffocate Your Neighbor in Three Easy Steps.*

Molly cocked an ear, listening for Antoine, but the house was quiet. She thought she could hear the hiss of a coffee machine at the back of the house.

A small desk was tucked in the far corner of the room and quickly she went to it, nearly opening the top drawer but too afraid of being caught. It wasn't as though she were going to find smothering weapons hidden in there. She had a silly flash of announcing to the stern French detective that she had caught the murderer red-handed with a pillow.

She jiggled the mouse to make the computer screen come alive. And there, in the glowing blue light, she saw a scholarly article titled *Criminal and Psychological Consequences of Revenge.* Quickly she tried to scan it, but the French was academic and jargony and she failed to get more than the most surface understanding.

But the title itself—it told a story. And that story was precisely what she needed somehow to entice Antoine Plouffe into telling her.

❧ 21 ❧

"Look," Molly said. "Let me lay it out for you, step by step. Maybe I've left something out, or my telling of the story has been too disjointed or something."

"All right," said Ben.

His patient voice was calming to hear. "Ok," she said, collecting her thoughts. "My hands are tied, I can't run around interrogating people, and so far I haven't succeeded in connecting with local law enforcement. I don't know how good they are or what they're doing. It's monumentally frustrating."

"Understood."

"So, end result, I have to approach the murders by motive. There's no other choice, unless you've got some other idea?"

"Just tell me what you've got."

"Start with Madame Trudeau. The parents of the child she abused have a strong motive. You can try to minimize that by saying the abuse was on the milder side, that yes, the woman hit Celeste's bare behind and said nasty things to her but on a spectrum of abuse this is on the less severe end. Do you think that?"

"I don't think it matters," said Ben. "There is always someone who suffers more, so these sorts of comparisons aren't fruitful. What matters is: how did the Plouffes react? Was their instinct to brush it off, or to think that their daughter was the victim of an assault that was psychologically as well as physically damaging?"

"Just what I was thinking, thank you for that. So let's say, just ruminating here, that they fall on the side of its being a terrible assault, and they are filled with a degree of rage they have never felt before. Indeed, a murderous rage."

For a short moment, Molly and Ben considered this.

"But whether they would be willing and able to act on it, obviously, is a different question."

"Molly—"

"I know what you're going to say, that an angry parent, even an angry, furious-to-the-point-of-insanity parent isn't necessarily a murderer. I know that. And thank heavens that is true. But all the same, it is indisputable that the motive exists, it's the only one we have, and it is *possible* that Antoine Plouffe, or his wife, chose to act on it. They even have books in their house on how trauma affects children, so they are aware of the possibly serious damage Madame Trudeau may have caused their daughter. And what really hit me hard—on their computer, I saw an article that was so on point it would seem planted, if there were any chance the true murderer somehow managed to get into their house to frame them. Which idea there is zero evidence to support, I know. I haven't gone completely off the deep end."

Molly stopped to take a breath. She realized she had raised her voice a little too much and ducked down a side street with no pedestrians.

"The article was about revenge, Ben. The psychological—and criminal—consequences of acting on revenge."

Ben stayed silent.

"Hello?

"Are you giving me the green flag to speak?" said Ben. "Do you have anything more? Did they mention the article on the computer?"

"I only talked to Antoine. No sign of Margot. And no, he didn't bring it up. He appears to be the most mild-mannered man, practically like Mr. Rogers."

"Mr. Rogers?"

"Oh, sorry. He was the host of an American TV show for kids, famously mild-mannered and kind-hearted—listen, Mr. Rogers is beside the point. You know as well as I do that you can't make any sort of guess about what someone has done or is capable of doing just on the basis of their temperament. Their *public* temperament."

"Actually, Molly—"

"Well, all right, you can make *some* assessment, sure, but it's not proof, is all I'm saying. Just because Plouffe has good manners and self-control and might have been a very nice man before this tragedy happened to his little girl—all of that doesn't mean he didn't knock on Madame Trudeau's door, perhaps pretending or even intending to come in peace, and then at some point becoming overcome with fury and out comes the pillow.

"Okay, I don't mean to suggest he brought the pillow with him, that's just silly. And like I said, maybe he did go in peace, maybe he only wanted Madame Trudeau to explain herself, and he was hoping to find a way to let it go and forgive her. But let's say she was unrepentant, even nasty ... and in a moment unlike any other in his life, Antoine Plouffe lost every shred of self-control and propriety and all the rest, he looked wildly around and snatched up a throw pillow—"

"Every time you say 'pillow,' it feels like you are describing a slapstick comedy and not the end of a woman's life."

Molly laughed in spite of herself. "I know. Here I am laughing too, and I promise you, the entire thing is not funny to me in the least. Perhaps I've been affected by Michel and Adèle, who were unashamedly giddy when they heard of her death. Back when we all thought it was nothing more than an unpleasant woman who died quietly in her bed."

Molly switched the phone to her other ear as she turned a corner and spied an empty bench to sit on. The street was more crowded than on a weekday; people carried string bags full of vegetables from the market, paper sacks with bottles of wine poking out the top, and children raced back and forth like border collies as their parents trudged along far too slowly for their taste.

"Here's the thing, Ben. I know the situation as I've described it thus far is not especially convincing. But I think seeing it that way ignores what was going on under the surface. If Antoine did indeed kill Madame Trudeau, my guess is that it was not only revenge that spurred him on, but something far more powerful."

Ben waited but Molly did not continue. "Like what?" he said finally.

"Just imagine for a moment that you find out your most precious, beloved child has been shamed and hit, behind your back, and how infuriating that would be," she said, her voice barely audible over the street noise.

"Yes. Of course. And you're arguing, leading to murder from revenge."

"Revenge is part of it. And from what I understand, acting out of revenge can have a real sweetness to it. But I believe something even more potent might be the real reason. Keep imagining—and turn your feelings away from Madame Trudeau and towards yourself. Think of how it would feel to know that not only had this witch hurt your child, but that it was *you* who opened the door and pushed your sweet girl into that house. *You* who paid the fees, arranged the dates. *You* who brushed aside any hint of complaint from your suffering daughter."

Ben grimaced, as anyone would. "Unspeakably bad," he said.

"I can't swear to what Antoine Plouffe did or didn't do, but I can say this with assurance: he feels tremendous, crippling guilt," said Molly. "For being an accessory to the abuse. He must have gone over it in his mind a million times, seeing images of bringing Celeste to Madame Trudeau's door and leaving her there, playing them over and over. And with every image, he feels his own complicity. I doubt that when he tries himself in his private, internal court of law, ignorance of what Trudeau was doing gains him much lenience. I imagine that he—and Margot too—lash themselves almost constantly with the thought that they should have known, they should have realized far sooner, they should have done a better job of protecting Celeste. They should have *listened* to her, even if the girl was not telling them everything.

"Apologies for being so insufferably long-winded—I'm trying to suggest that Plouffe could have killed Madame Trudeau not only for retribution but also to assuage his own guilt. He did not listen to his child, and that is *his* crime, not Madame Trudeau's. I believe that if circumstances had somehow been different and there was no possibility of his feeling complicit, Madame Trudeau might still be alive."

Ben nodded. "But ma chérie, as you would be the first to tell me—beliefs do not make a case."

"I know, I know. Obviously an article on a computer doesn't amount to much in the way of evidence. It did serve to help me understand the whole picture, however. Another bit of information to illuminate their mildly odd behavior last night. I had been wondering ... Antoine and Margot did not want to face their neighbors. Why?"

"Perhaps they do not like being on the receiving end of sympathy. Many do not."

"Or—perhaps they are worried that people who know them well will be able to see through them. Worried that the mask will slip. Or, more directly, worried that others blame them."

"Or maybe it is embarrassment, and only that," said Ben.

Molly made a face and heaved a sigh. "Maybe," she allowed, but she did not believe it.

. . .

Just as Molly was turning to go back to the Faures's, Adèle called and asked her to lunch. They agreed to meet on Cours Mirabeau. Once Adèle caught up with her, they saw that every restaurant terrace was packed, as the Saturday shoppers flooded the tables under the warm spring sunshine and dappled light of the tall plane trees.

"Um, can I suggest ... I found this restaurant with the most amazing bouillabaisse," Molly said. "I had it for the first time just the other day but boy, I am more than ready for round two."

Adèle laughed, ever amused and pleased by how much Molly appreciated food. "I'm game," she said. "I haven't had it in ages and ages. You don't mind repeating so soon?"

"Never!" said Molly fervently. "In fact, I'm hoping we can revisit that pizza place soon. I've been having daydreams about that bubbly, charred crust. And those mushrooms!"

They cut across Cours Mirabeau, dodging the crowd, and Molly managed to find the narrow side street with the seafood restaurant tucked a few blocks down. The same waiter greeted Molly with a grin and seated them by the window.

"No need for menus," Molly said. "Two kirs. And two bowls of that glorious soup, please!"

The waiter's face fell.

"Oh no, is it—you don't call it soup? I did not mean to diminish its glory by calling it by the wrong name!"

The waiter nodded a bit curtly and walked briskly to the kitchen.

"I will tell you one difference between America and France," Molly said to Adèle. "Your servers are quite a bit more invested in the reputation of the food. He and I were old friends by the end of my lunch here, and now I fear I have fatally insulted him."

Adèle laughed. "Soup is not a bad thing, of course, we love

soup. But you will admit, it is rather more pedestrian than a tureen of bouillabaisse."

"Well, sure. The last thing I meant to do was to insult that magnificent dish. I wonder if I will ever be truly fluent? Way too much of the time, the wrong word leaps out of my mouth before I can stop it."

Adèle reached for Molly's hand. "No worries, chérie. I can see enormous improvement in your French since we met."

"Really?" Molly's face brightened. "I can't tell you how that cheers me up. Now if I can only get back on the waiter's right side."

She watched him lead two older women to the table behind her, swiveling around to get a good look at them and to try to catch the waiter's eye, but he did not glance in Molly's direction.

Out of habit, Molly eavesdropped as the two women got settled at their table. They too had come for the bouillabaisse. The woman closer to Molly began talking in (thankfully) clearly enunciated French about a niece who lived in Germany who was going to have a baby next month, and Molly turned her attention back to Adèle, who looked fretful as she spoke. "I can't help wishing things were different. I looked forward to your visit for so long, and now the city is in the grip of something terrible, and I—"

"Adèle. It's me, remember? This is the world I choose to live in. Well, I just surprised myself by saying that, but I guess it's true. I could have stayed in Boston writing grants, but that's not the decision I made."

"No regrets?"

"Absolutely not. Of course, I still get homesick sometimes. It helped a lot when Frances came for a visit and never left. And of course, making friends with you and Michel. So please, no apologies! I only hope that these cases get resolved soon, the murderers and burglars get caught, and your neighborhood returns to normal."

Adèle smiled but her eyes were flat. Molly tuned back into the conversation behind her, now concerning which shop had the freshest oysters.

Adèle had an expression of expectation and Molly realized it was her turn to speak. Just as she was opening her mouth, her ears pricked up and her face turned hot—because one of the women behind her, remarkably and unmistakably, had murmured the name *Antoine Plouffe*. Giving Adèle a distracted smile, Molly scooted her chair back half a foot and turned her head so as not to miss a word.

"So," said Adèle, "if you don't mind, I'd like to ask your advice about something. But I'll tell you right up front—not that you'll be surprised—that I feel shy about it. I'm ... as you know very well ... I'm a very private person. And it's very hard to change those sorts of habits, even when one is motivated to do so."

Molly tried to smile encouragingly to Adèle while straining to hear the women behind her.

Adèle continued, "It's about the lunch with Oscar. I believe, at least I very much hope, that it went quite well. We talked easily, and that by itself is no small thing, don't you agree?"

Molly startled. "Agree? Oh, of course. Yes," she said, having no idea what Adèle had just said.

"... so it was a question of her history grade, you see. I am nothing if not fair, and I think most parents would back me up on that. I certainly do not mark students down for no reason, or some arbitrary whim. But oh, that Monsieur Plouffe—"

"—but he never, I mean, we kissed cheeks when we greeted each other, but you know, cheek kisses are for great-uncles and hardly any sort of—"

"—I thought his eyes were going to burst right out of his head, he was so furious—"

"—do you think?"

Molly felt sweat prickling her forehead and only stopped herself from using the napkin to wipe herself down because, on top of managing two conversations at once, she didn't want to make the situation with the waiter even worse.

"Molly?"

"I'm so sorry," Molly said. Her eyes were unfocused with the effort of eavesdropping.

"—and the nerve of him to imagine that he would be able to intimidate me that way! That I would simply cross out the grade Celeste deserved and pencil in what he wished! I do not cave to pressure, he learned that quickly enough!"

"The absolute nerve!" said the other woman.

"What do you mean, sorry?" Adèle was asking.

Molly inhaled sharply. "I'm—ugh, again, apologies," She paused but the women had moved on to discussing whether or not a friend was having an affair, and with whom. Molly leaned toward Adèle and whispered, "Sorry for being so distracted. The people behind me were talking about something important. I'll tell you later."

Adèle's smile was tight. She nodded and fiddled with her napkin.

"So you enjoyed the lunch with Oscar, this is good!" said Molly, but Adèle did not look up.

They sat in silence until the waiter came with white porcelain bowls of bouillabaisse, and they both, with gusto and relief, had something else to pay attention to. The waiter smiled in spite of himself at Molly's enthusiastic expostulations. She hovered her soup spoon above the glistening pool and looked seriously at Adèle.

"Please," she said. "I know I was just terribly rude and I offer no excuse. Tell me more about your lunch with Oscar. And your feelings about him."

Adèle smeared some rouille on a round of perfectly toasted baguette. "Well, my own feelings? Honestly, it's going to make me sound like a schoolgirl. My heart literally races when I'm with him."

"Uh oh," said Molly, grinning. "Go on."

As they ate, Adèle told the entire story of the lunch, sparing no detail. She talked and listened to Molly's comments, though her friend's head was always half-turned to the side as Molly managed to listen to her story and also, apparently, to every word that was spoken at the next table.

22

Molly had fallen asleep with the light on, her face pressed into a book.

She startled awake. Sighing, she peeled the book off her face and put it on the bedside table, but slowly, placing it carefully so as not to make a sound, a habit from not wanting to wake Ben.

Molly had a feeling, sleepy as she was, that something was not right. She sat up, wincing as the bedsprings creaked. She cocked an ear.

Silence.

Must have been having a bad dream, she said to herself, and settled back down, reaching to turn the lamp off.

A sound of metal scraping metal.

Molly sat back up, her eyes wide, no longer groggy. Quietly she slipped out of bed and went to the window, and leaned out, thinking the sound had come from outside. A window box of geraniums blocked her view. She stood still and listened again.

She heard a low voice, male. Then again, the sound of metal on metal, a sort of clinking and scraping.

Should she wake Michel and Adèle? Was there time for that? Quickly she put on slippers, left her bedroom, and headed downstairs as quietly as she could, remembering to skip the eleventh step. On the second floor, she paused to listen.

Again, men talking in low voices, on the street just outside the front door. Again, the sound of metal on metal.

It occurred to her, heart pounding, that there was no Bobo or Ben to defend her, and perhaps she should not fling the door open standing there in her nightgown and ask the men what they were about. Michel's bedroom was on the second floor. Quietly she headed to the kitchen.

Hmm, she thought, peering into the knife drawer. She ended up going with a paring knife so she could sort of hide it in her palm. Less showy, but perhaps more business-like in the end.

She crept back to the front hallway. Heart still pounding but feeling a strange calm.

But now … all was quiet. Molly got to the front door, listening hard. But there were no more sounds of metal, no low murmuring voices, and no sound from the street at all.

After waiting another few minutes, she flung the front door open suddenly and looked up and down the block. It was empty. Or at least it was as far as she could tell, since there was no moon and apparently the streetlamps were not working; the street was as dark as the driveway at La Baraque on a stormy night.

Satisfied that whoever had been there was gone, Molly turned back inside. Because of the dark, she missed the gouges in both the lock and the beautiful lacquered paint of the door.

23

"Molly!" Adèle called the next morning. "Can you come downstairs right away?"

Discombobulated, Molly had not slept well after the disturbance of the night before. She swung her legs over the side of the bed, sat up, and the paring knife bounced to the floor. Gracious, she thought, was that a dream? And what has got Adèle upset?

Molly splashed some water on her face, dressed, and staggered downstairs, wondering if the Faures were about to tell her about another break-in. It must be about the burglars last night, she thought.

"Bonjour," said Molly, entering the salon. Michel jumped up and kissed her. "Adèle called, is something the matter?"

"Indeed," said Michel, and Molly could see that he looked troubled and not his usual sunny, flirtatious self.

"It's Louise Boulay," said Adèle, coming in from the kitchen with a tray holding the coffeepot. "I just spoke to her yesterday. Yesterday!" She dropped into a chair and put her face in her hands.

Molly rushed to her side. "Oh! I'm so sorry! Who is Louise Boulay? What happened? You were friends?"

"Not exactly," said Michel.

"What do you know about it?" snapped Adèle.

Molly had the impression Michel had more to say but was holding back.

"And so ... did something happen? Is Madame Boulay all right?"

"She's been found dead in her garden," said Michel. "The ever-conscientious Patrice has already paid us a visit this morning."

"Was she ... was she elderly? In poor health?" asked Molly.

"Neither. Fifties, or thereabouts," said Michel. "Seemed to be quite robust."

Molly dropped into a chair, forgetting even about coffee. "It can't be ..." she murmured.

The three friends were quiet. Adèle had picked up a napkin and was twisting it in her hands, staring at the rug. Michel walked to the window and looked out.

"A pair of gendarmes just went by," he reported. "In a bit of a hurry."

"Which way?" asked Molly, jumping from her chair and heading for the door.

Towards Cours Mirabeau, Molly could see Berenice with her broom, sweeping and looking up and down the street. Some workmen in blue shirts were taking a ladder from a truck. In the other direction, craning her neck to see past a family of four strolling hand in hand and spilling into the street, Molly caught a glimpse of a gendarme ducking into a small stone building a few blocks down. Quickly she walked towards it, trying to come up with some reason that she should be allowed into Louise Boulay's house.

A second gendarme approached from the other direction. She was compact and fit, her uniform neat and tidy, hair pulled into a tight bun under the blue cap. Molly smiled. The gendarme did not smile back but looked away, pushed through the door, and left Molly standing on the sidewalk. The family of four walked past, laughing together, and Molly shrugged off a pang of wishing she were the one laughing and holding hands with a child on either side instead of standing alone with her head full of murder and death.

Taking a deep breath, she crossed the street and observed the house. It was quite humble, tucked in between its grander neighbors, the stone walls and terracotta roof very old and in good repair. One story with an attic, and a chimney rising from the back. Two square windows on either side of the unpainted wooden door. A terracotta pot of pansies to the left of the door. Curtains were drawn at the two windows and she could see nothing inside. She wondered if three gendarmes coming to the scene indicated that the death was not natural but suspicious. Probably depends, she thought. Was Yves Dupont, the lead detective on the other cases, one of the men whom Michel had seen through the window walking toward the Boulay house?

What pretext might get her inside?

Molly waited.

She considered walking up the block to talk to Berenice but the sweeper had disappeared. A half hour passed, then an hour, the shadows on the street moving with the sun. Molly worried that it might look shady for her to be standing outside the house so long with no cover story to explain why, yet she did not leave. I'm spending half the morning waiting—and for what? What am I hoping for? That the gendarme who ignored me will have a change of heart on her way out?

That is never going to happen.

She wasn't in Castillac, after all. It was such a wonderful thing, this French idea and practice of community. In her beloved Castillac, she was part of that fabric. Even when a gendarme or even the Chief would rather not talk to her, they did anyway, because she was known there, inside the circle, whether they liked it or not. But here in the beautiful city of Aix-en-Provence, Molly had no claim to be part of anything.

Just because there had been two murders on rue Niccolo, she reminded herself, did not mean that this was the third. It was probable that Louise Boulay had died of natural causes. Most likely she had been out enjoying a spring morning in her garden and been struck down by a heart attack or something equally commonplace. It wasn't as though you had to be old for such things to happen; she remembered a childhood friend whose father had died suddenly, seemingly the picture of health, in his early forties. Murder is the unlikeliest possibility, no question about it, ninety-nine point nine times out of a hundred.

Molly told herself these things; she tried to pretend to herself she believed them, but ... she did not. She also told herself she didn't believe in instinct or gut feelings, yet that was what guided her.

The door to the little house opened at last and the same female gendarme came out with a short, round man. The man was tearful. He spoke too quietly for Molly to hear, his hands moving through the air as though painting a picture with his fluttering fingers. The gendarme kept nodding, looking down at the street, and then walked briskly away.

Squaring her shoulders, Molly walked just as briskly towards him. Nothing to do but take the chance, she thought.

"Bonjour, Monsieur," she said softly. "I'm very sorry to intrude. I am a friend of your neighbors, the Faures. Molly Sutton," she said, offering a hand.

The man took her hand and held it. He looked into Molly's eyes but did not speak. He pressed his lips tightly together and shook his head.

"Monsieur Boulay?"

"Yes," he whispered. "They will say it is I. I know this to be true."

"'It is I?'" Molly leaned closer. "What do you mean?"

Monsieur Boulay looked into the sky and held his head tilted up for a long moment. When he lowered it, tears spilled down his cheeks.

"I'm so sorry," said Molly, squeezing his hand since he had not let go.

"Even if by God's grace I'm not arrested, people will—but I tell you—" he took Molly's hand in both his hands and shook it emphatically "—I tell you it was *not*. I would never. Never *ever*. No matter what."

"Of course not," Molly murmured. "You loved her."

He bowed his head. Molly saw tears splash onto the slate of the sidewalk and darken it. His shoulders shook. She squeezed his hand again. "What can I do? Is there anyone you would like me to call?"

Slowly Monsieur Boulay raised his head. "There was no one but Louise." He blinked hard several times and dropped Molly's hand. "I'm—what am I doing, I'm embarrassing myself. I don't even know you. Please forgive me." He glanced down the street both ways, then stepped back into his house and closed the door.

Well, thought Molly.

They will say it is I. She pondered. Perhaps Berenice might have something to say about the Boulays.

She turned back toward the Faures's and saw a white van moving slowly down the street. Just like Florian Nagrand's, Molly thought, thinking of the coroner in Castillac. The van rode up on the sidewalk in the way the French often did, which always thrilled Molly's rule-breaking heart. A small decal on the door showed it to be property of the city of Aix-en-Provence. A lanky man with close-cropped hair slid out and trotted around to the back. Molly followed.

She watched him take a leather case out of the back while an associate was getting out of the passenger side, but before she could think up a way to accost them, they were inside the small house and the door closed once more.

❧ 24 ❧

"Molly's doing fine—well, more than fine, actually, since there seems to have been a spate of murders in the neighborhood," said Ben, sitting at the bar of Chez Papa.

"Ha," said Lawrence. "Is it something genetic, do you think, that causes such bloodshed and mayhem wherever Molly goes? Or some sort of aura she has, a power field that attracts the worst of humanity?"

Ben grinned and clinked his glass of beer with Lawrence's Negroni. "You think she's a witch, then?" He sighed. "I do miss her," he said, so quietly Lawrence barely heard him.

"As do I. All right then, what have *you* got going on? Some projects at La Baraque? Any deliciously scandalous cases you would like an opinion on? I do love giving opinions."

"Afraid not. It's gotten so I only check my bank account once every couple of weeks, so as not to have to watch it sink daily, bit by bit. Molly's still taking care of bookings but they're a bit thin this month. Yet if you read *Le Monde* it looks like people are making money hand over fist!" He shrugged. "There's no investigative work at all. If we had any sense we'd move to a much larger town, with better prospects."

"I've worked freelance many times over the years," said Lawrence. "Interior decorating—that lasted nearly six years. Never knew whether the month was going to be glorious or utter garbage. Just to say—I do understand. No doubt something will come along."

Ben nodded and they drank.

"Someone will cheat on someone and that second someone will get absolutely deranged and bash the first someone's head in. Or old Madame So-and-So will have had it up to here with her husband's idiotic remarks at the breakfast table and start spooning a bit of arsenic into his oatmeal ..."

Ben tried to laugh and drank some more beer.

"So tell me," said Lawrence. "What would you say are the main reasons people get murdered? Money has got to be right up near the top."

Ben nodded. "Yes. That's probably the biggest, and we can agree that it doesn't say anything very good about humanity."

"Jealousy? How does that rank?"

"Mm, not as high as you'd think. For beatings, absolutely yes, it's an enormous driver of that. But for murder ... a much larger category would have a label like ... how about Last Straw? Your example of the woman at the breakfast table. What her husband said that particular morning isn't necessarily so terrible, all by itself. It's the accretion of fifty years of similar remarks, fifty years of her keeping quiet when she wants to tell him to shut the hell up. So finally, she snaps."

They drank again, not speaking.

"It must feel ... rather good, snapping like that," said Lawrence finally.

Ben laughed. "The going-to-prison part, maybe less good. All right, now that we've delved into the darkness, let's move on to brighter subjects. What have *you* been up to?"

Lawrence waved his hand in the air and made a dismissive noise. "Not a whole lot, I have to say. I've been reading Trollope, which I've been meaning to get around to for years. Obviously not the most scintillating tidbit, next I'll be telling you which television shows I'm watching, and giving you plot summaries," he said, shaking his head. "Not to be dramatic, but it does feel as though Castillac is unbearably boring without Molly. How soon is she coming back?"

Ben shrugged. "She's not saying. It was supposed to be a couple of weeks, but now … no estimated time of return. I don't think she's having an especially good time, but you know her, she can't drag herself away from these murders even though she has no chance of getting involved in a professional capacity."

Lawrence sighed. "And the everyday running of La Baraque? How's that going?" He couldn't help making the smallest smirk.

It was time for Ben to wave away the question. "Fine, fine," he said. "I suppose it's never a bad thing to have an opportunity to miss someone," he said, feeling some emotion bubble up in his throat that he pushed back down.

Lawrence nodded. He leaned forward to try to get Nico's attention and saw him whispering to Frances at the end of the bar. Nico stood up, with an expression of what Lawrence could only describe as profound happiness.

Now what has got our Nico so very pleased? Lawrence wondered, waggling a forefinger at him for another Negroni.

❦ 2 5 ❧

"I do apologize, Molly. We're treating you abominably, asking you to stand in the kitchen on Sunday night and have nothing but scraps for dinner. And not for the first time. We're absolute heathens." Adèle's expression was strained as Michel took another cheese out of the refrigerator.

Molly laughed. "Are you kidding? Goat cheese and wild boar salami with a sparkling rosé to wash it down—what could be better? And these olives, oh my! This right here," she said, gesturing to the table with a grand flourish, "is one of the reasons I moved to France. Add a plate of almond croissants and that's grandeur beyond anyone's wildest dreams."

"Please add oysters and bouillabaisse to that list. And—I hope now that you're settled in France, you've found some other redeeming qualities to our country besides food?" said Michel.

"That goes without saying," said Molly with a grin.

Adèle's eyes were downcast, and Molly noticed that the sleeve of her shirt was more than a little wrinkled, the sort of messy detail Adèle never allowed. Molly was about to ask if anything was wrong, but something stopped her.

There was plenty wrong, as Molly already knew. And plenty more that Molly did not dream of, not yet.

The friends ate in silence. Michel topped up their glasses, and the silence stretched out and then out some more.

"Is—I mean—are you two all right?" Oh, she had meant to stay quiet a bit longer, but her mouth sometimes had a mind of its own. "I don't mean to pry. But if either of you would like to talk? About ... anything that's bothering you? I'm all ears."

Neither Adèle nor Michel met her eye. The silence began to grow, and Molly tried not to grimace.

"Something concerns me," said Adèle finally, as Michel began wrapping the cheese and putting dishes in the dishwasher, "Even frightens me. It's that—I don't want to sound so doom and gloom, but sometimes that's just what's real—I believe we are headed to dark times, financially speaking. I don't mean us specifically, but worldwide: the metrics look very bad to me indeed."

"The glass is always half empty with you," said Michel lightly.

"No, Michel. I'm talking about numbers, not feelings. Of course my prediction is an opinion, but it is not based on something I am making up in my head, a manifestation of my glass-half-empty spirit, as you might call it. It's a prediction, yes, but based on *data*. This level of reckless investment we've been seeing, not only in France but the UK, the rest of the EU, and the United States especially, well, it's an absolute frenzy! It's not organic, not based in actual value, do you see what I'm saying? It's *speculation*. And it isn't healthy."

"I understand that it's a frenzy of people making a lot of money," said Michel. "I see this as a good thing. An opportunity. A time to invest. That's what some experts are saying, at any rate."

Adèle shook her head. "These sorts of trends—the 'opportunities,' as you call them, only last for a short while. They're built on sand, Michel, not solid fundamentals. You remember what happened to the Dutch with tulipomania, don't you? And there have been many other examples of this as well. Greed can take over people's brains as much as a drug. Bottom line, if you don't nail the correct moment to pull out of such a market, you can be ruined. Easily. In the blink of an eye."

Michel flicked his fingers in the air and shook his head. Adèle scowled.

Molly had expected Adèle's worries to be more personal and did not really believe she was getting the whole story, or even a fraction of it. But all right, if Adèle wanted to talk about world finance, Molly would try to meet her there. She debated whether to mention what Tommaso had told her at the apéro, about Apolline Cuvalier and her shady investment scheme. And decided to go for it. "I have no idea whether this is just gossip. But at the apéro, Tommaso told me that Apolline Cuvalier is running around town sucking people into some kind of new investment. He seemed to think it was baloney and people would lose their shirts." She peeked at Michel, trying to keep her expression blank.

Adèle rolled her eyes. "This is exactly what I've been warning about. The economy is like a piece of meat that's been left out too long and the flies are swarming around it."

"Not sure you could have come up with a more disgusting image," said Michel. "Listen, people have their problems with Apolline because she's a strong woman who has real presence. A lot of men can't handle that in my opinion. So they talk her down." He shrugged and picked up another slice of salami. Adèle rolled her eyes again and crossed her arms over her chest.

Another uncomfortable silence.

"I guess I should be glad I have no assets to lose!" said Molly, trying to lighten the mood.

"Excuse me?" said Adèle. "You have La Baraque. If there is a global financial meltdown, you will see quite a falling-off of business that might endanger everything for you. Can you get by without any gîte income whatsoever?"

"Oh dear!" said Molly, picturing an empty cottage and pigeon-nier, and no calls or emails whatsoever. "I hadn't thought of that. I mean, sort of? But only vaguely."

"At least you have the investigative work too, it's always a good thing to have multiple sources of income," said Adèle. "Perhaps you'll be fine, since financial struggles tend to lift the crime rate."

Molly wasn't sure if her friend was joking. "Do you think—I'm not trying to tell you your business, you obviously know far more about such matters than I do—but is it possible that the ... the instability in the neighborhood might be coloring your judgment? It would be understandable—"

Adèle stood up as tall as she could and glared at Molly. "I didn't have all those years of training at the bank for nothing, you know. I was an analyst, it was my job to study this very thing."

"Yes, of course, I do know," said Molly. Adèle was touchy and Michel was distant and friendly, by turns. These days she never quite knew what she was going to get from either of them.

"Has Patrice stopped by again?" she asked. "Just wondering if there's any news about Madame Boulay."

Michel shook his head. Adèle continued to glare. After savoring a chocolate *pot de crème* (not homemade but from the supermarket, and completely delicious) Molly said goodnight.

Though she did not hop into bed and go to sleep, but lay on her back looking at the ceiling while she thought about the murders.

Top of the list for the moment: was Monsieur Boulay's show of emotion genuine? Someone should be able to answer that question, but who?

❧ 2 6 ❧

Early the next morning, Molly slipped out of the house and got coffee on the Cours Mirabeau instead of waiting for Adèle and Michel to wake up. She fortified herself with an almond croissant from Pâtisserie P and then took up her post, watching and waiting for Berenice.

She didn't have to wait long. Soon the old woman stepped outside, broom in hand, and after taking a careful look in each direction, began to sweep with her accustomed vigor. Molly could hear tuneless humming, equally vigorous. She ate up the late bite and approached.

"Bonjour, Berenice," said Molly, cursing herself for not bringing an extra croissant to offer.

Berenice stopped sweeping and looked at Molly, her eyes lively. "Bonjour, Madame Sutton. I thought you might be along," she said, taking another few strokes with the broom. "Another day, another person croaking here on our little street, eh?"

"At least Madame Boulay died naturally."

Berenice stopped sweeping and leaned on her broom. "It must nearly kill you to be the last to find things out," she said.

"What have I missed?"

"Louise Boulay was strangled. The official report isn't out yet, of course. But that's what I heard."

"Oh no," said Molly. "That's terrible news."

Berenice shrugged. "Depends on how you look at things. Sometimes the good Lord takes out the trash, is one way to look at it."

"Huh?"

Berenice half-turned away and kept sweeping, her lips pursed.

"Have you heard anything else? Do you know something?" asked Molly.

Berenice looked Molly up and down, as though trying to decide once again whether to trust her. She squinted and did not answer.

Finally, unable to stay quiet, Berenice said, "Awful lot of people going in and out of the Faures's lately. Wasn't like that before you came."

"Is that right? Like who?"

"Well, that tall woman, for one. Dresses a size too small. In and out of the house, all times of day or night."

Apolline. But in and out at night? What had Molly been missing, right under her very nose?

"Speaking personally," said Berenice, "I wouldn't trust that woman as far as I could throw her. You tell that nice Michel to steer clear if he doesn't want a big load of trouble parked on his doorstep, that's what I have to say about it." Berenice stopped sweeping. "Now it's the Boulays you're interested in, eh?" She put a hand on her hip and narrowed her eyes at Molly, but she was obviously enjoying herself and Molly wasn't put off by her scowling.

"Well, there might be a few things to talk about," said Molly. "We don't know how she died, for one thing, at least I haven't heard anything … I met Monsieur Boulay yesterday."

"Mm? And? Did he show you the marks?"

"Marks?"

"I'm not one to cast aspersions, you should know that about me. I'm not one to repeat all manner of things just because it's what people are saying, like some. I'll just tell you this: Delano Boulay has been a long-suffering man, Madame Sutton. For many, many years. I happen to know this for a fact, and I don't believe anyone who's lived in this neighborhood would step in to say otherwise. Or if they tried, they couldn't prove it. That kind of behavior, thanks be to the Lord, doesn't go unnoticed. I am surely glad he has found some respite at last."

Molly cocked her head. "Long-suffering …? What are you … are you saying … she *beat* him? And everyone knew about this? It's common knowledge?"

Berenice just shook her head and started sweeping again. Molly had the agonizing sense she might be done talking when the older woman spoke in a rush.

"Do you live in some fantasy world, Madame Sutton? Do you think that such things are unusual, shocking? A woman beats up her husband over the course of years—oh, it may be far more common for a man to do the beating. But believe me, some women get their knocks in. It barely rises to the level of noteworthy."

"His wife has just died. He seemed quite undone by it."

Berenice laughed while reaching down to pull up her socks. "Delano is always undone by something. That's his way. He's not what you'd call a stiff-upper-lip sort, know what I mean?"

After silence and more sweeping, Berenice gave Molly a side-long glance. "So you met Delano, eh? Just strolled up and knocked on his door? You really don't mind poking your nose in, do you?"

Molly's face reddened. "I didn't knock. He came outside where I …"

"… just happened to be loitering around? Right outside the poor man's door the day his wife died. That it?" She cackled.

"Berenice—"

"I'm joking with you, Madame Sutton."

"You do a fair bit of loitering yourself, seems like," Molly said.

The old woman leaned her head back and cackled again, eyes merry. "Indeed," she said, looking down the block toward the Boulays and taking a few robust sweeps. "Indeed. So ask me. I know you've got questions. Can feel them hanging in the air like a bunch of spiders on webs, dangling down in front of my face."

Molly's face felt hot again. It was a little uncomfortable, two curious women who knew pretty well what the other was about. "Well—Monsieur Boulay—Delano—said something that struck me a little funny. '"They will say it is I,"' he said. More than once."

"He's a teacher, you know. That's why he talks so fancy. And sure, Delano thinks he's gonna get nabbed for it. His motive is right out in plain sight for all the world to see."

"Murder? Really? Are you guessing, or have you heard something?"

"If you were any kind of actual investigator, you might have caught on to the fact that these murder victims are not exactly the cream of the crop, not exactly the most upstanding citizens. Cruel bastards, the lot of them."

"You think … the cases are related? It's one murderer?"

Berenice shrugged.

"What else do you know about their relationship? So they fought a lot?"

Berenice looked at Molly with wide, disbelieving eyes. Then she leaned her head back again and laughed until tears flowed down her wrinkled, sunburnt cheeks and she was gasping for breath. When she had collected herself, she leaned on the broom and looked at Molly. "You say you're some kind of detective," she said, shaking her head. "But to say what's what: you're not much of a listener. I asked you not five minutes ago if Delano had shown you the marks. I told you exactly who Louise Boulay was— a woman capable of hurting her husband in the most vicious way. Yes, they *fought a lot*. I can't decide—is it that your French is that bad or are you just slow-witted?"

Molly opened her mouth to answer, but Berenice had made it back to her door and closed it behind her before Molly could get the words out.

BACK AT THE FAURES'S, Molly was in her bedroom considering what Berenice had said and thinking about lunch when there was a knock on the door.

"Yes? Come in," said Molly.

"So how did the morning's work go?" Michel asked, walking over to the window and looking out, as was his habit.

"Work?" Molly laughed. "I wouldn't quite dignify it as that." She shrugged. "I had a little gab with Berenice. She's a funny one."

"How so?"

"She pretends like I'm annoying her, but she loves telling me stuff. She likes to pay it out, not give me everything at once. And insult me along the way," Molly laughed.

"Anything good today?"

She shrugged.

"Oh, come on, Molly."

"Louise beat her husband. Badly enough to leave marks. And ... everyone knew it."

Michel's eyes got very wide. "Well, not everyone, I certainly had no idea. I guess that goes to show we are not considered real locals yet, and not clued into half of what's going on." Michel scowled. "But ... Delano ... I mean, why wouldn't he defend himself? Louise was a petite little thing. I mean, I understand that these situations are complicated, but still, just on the face of it, it seems almost ridiculous, a hefty man like that getting beaten up by a sparrow."

Molly was chewing the side of her mouth while imagining the scene: the wife gets enraged over something, and tries to expunge her rage by beating the nearest target, who happened to be poor Delano, who did not want to fight back against a woman. A woman whom he actually loved, despite everything. She wondered if Louise had been repentant afterwards, and whether that moment of contrition was so precious to Delano that he had allowed the beatings in order to receive the apology.

"Trying to decipher what drives people—it's endlessly fascinating, isn't it? But so often, a fruitless endeavor. Just off the top of my head—a lot of men have a real aversion to hitting women, and thank heavens for that. Anyway, whatever was going on between them, it sounds like a terrible trap they were both stuck in, and neither could find a way out," said Molly. "It might be the sort of thing people on the outside can never fully understand or explain."

"Unless her death was exactly that, a way out," said Michel. "Perhaps the prey became the predator?"

Molly nodded slowly. "Delano fears people will think exactly that. I wish the coroner would move along!"

"To be fair, his office has been rather jammed up of late," said Michel. "Anyway, I came up to ask if you have plans or if you'd like to go to lunch? Adèle is off on one of her mysterious errands—she pointedly did not tell me where she was going—and I thought I would grab this chance to have you all to myself." He smiled his merry smile, a hank of hair flopping down into his eyes as though on cue.

"Sure, I'm starving. Lead on!"

Once on the street, Molly looked both ways but there was no one on the street, no cars, no pedestrians, not even a cat.

"Shall we have some oysters?" said Michel, and Molly beamed at the idea.

"I wanted to tell you—I got a call from Stéphane Boisette this morning. They were, remarkably enough, robbed once again. Quite a valuable antique clock plucked right off the mantel, and yet more jewelry."

"The Boisettes *again*?" Molly hurried to keep up with Michel's pace. "Honestly—do you know them at all? Because getting robbed again so soon ... frankly, that sounds a little fishy. Don't you think? Could they be running an insurance scam or something like that?"

"No idea," said Michel. "Though apparently it wasn't only their house. The man next door to them, Marius Latour, also had some things stolen. A window in back broken, the thieves helped themselves to all the silver flatware Monsieur Latour had inherited from his great-aunt."

She asked which houses belonged to Latour and the Boisettes; Michel gave her descriptions of the buildings since he didn't know the exact addresses. "Ready for oysters? This is the place," he added, stopping in front of a tiny building at the end of one of Aix's shabbier blocks.

They ducked inside and inhaled the lovely smell of extremely fresh seafood, as though they had magically been transported to the edge of the sea. Michel guided Molly to the bar, on which stood an impressive display of oysters, mussels, clams, and a few shellfish Molly could not identify.

They settled in at the bar and Michel ordered them Pernods. Not Molly's absolute favorite but the first sip did taste refreshing, she had to admit. People in Castillac only rarely drank Pernod. For a moment she pictured a map of French apéritifs and the places they were popular, and planned a trip someday with Ben to drive through France and try all of them, province by province.

"Is it death, as usual?"

"What?" said Molly, feeling alarmed.

"You were so lost in thought. I wondered if you were thinking about Louise Boulay and the rest. And—what a world, that I just said 'and the rest' because the number of victims on my street has become so unmanageably large."

"Actually, I was just thinking about Pernod," Molly said. "Which, okay, is one of the few moments when I was not thinking about the recent victims, so point taken. It's just ... very hard ... to sit idly by, with everything that's happening."

"You're not idle. Anyone can see that."

"There's not much for me to do if I can't talk to Yves Dupont or the coroner or anyone else who might be working on the investigation."

Michel shook his head. "Oh come on, Molly. Since when have you depended on the authorities for everything?"

"Maybe I've gotten a little soft," she agreed. "I mean, way back —when your aunt was killed, for example—it's not like I had any inside information. Ben and I barely knew each other. Remember Gilles Maron, the detective on the case?"

"Indeed. Good man. Does he keep in touch? I seem to remember he was quite smitten with you."

Molly laughed. "Oh no, not in that way. But we did have a sort of … professional regard, I guess you could say. I was sorry when he was transferred."

Michel had ordered a large plate of oysters to share and the harried bartender placed it between them. Molly breathed in the salty smell of the ocean and grinned. Michel picked one up and slurped it down.

"A question for you. It may seem far-fetched. But is it possible —could the burglaries be connected to the murders?" Molly blurted out.

Michel cocked his head and gestured for Molly to eat. "Um. Hadn't thought of that. How would that work?"

"I didn't realize I was thinking it until the words came out of my mouth," she said. "It seems unlikely, simply because … too many moving parts, too complicated, and for what reasons would they be connected? You know, there are sayings in many disciplines that make the point that the simplest explanation is usually the correct one.

"But I just can't help wondering … are the burglaries a way to … take up the attention of gendarmes that might otherwise be focused on the murders? Distract—or frighten—the residents of the neighborhood, so they feel they're the target of a widespread crime wave rather that something more ... specific? More particular?" Molly shrugged. "Now that I try to flesh out the idea, it doesn't seem any good at all."

Michel sipped his Pernod and observed Molly.

"It's just that—I'm no mathematician, but all these people being killed, every one of whom has at least one plump and juicy suspect, someone with strong motives for killing them—how possible is it that three such murders would take place within a few blocks and in a matter of days?"

"It doesn't seem plausible."

"It does not. Yet here we are." Molly tapped her chin, thinking. "I wonder if having a murder occur right down the street from you acts as a sort of ... *normalizer*, almost. Like 'Oh look, someone else followed through with the impulse, why not me too?'"

Michel shrugged and ate another oyster.

"But whatever, I should just let this whole topic go. Because if the murders *are* connected, the cops will certainly know. No one could barge into that many homes without leaving DNA behind."

"But matching that DNA to the person who dropped it—that could be the tricky part," said Michel, as he watched the oyster-shucker at work. "The flics can't just work their way down the street asking for samples from just anyone. And the murderer might not even be someone who lives here, or maybe someone with no criminal record, no collected DNA to match to."

The oysters were wasted on Molly, and the marinated octopus as well. Michel bought a very nice bottle of champagne and persisted in trying to entice her to talk of something else. But throughout the lunch, it was only Madame Trudeau, Matéo Brule, and Louise Boulay that had her attention.

✦ 27 ✦

That night the three friends had a brief nightcap in the salon and went to bed early. The sense of strain continued, Molly wondering once again whether it was her presence, the events in the neighborhood, or some other mystery that was causing the ill feeling. Though it wasn't exactly ill feeling—more an atmosphere of cautiousness, where there used to be freedom. A touch of prickliness, where there used to be playfulness. Molly dreaded that walking-on-eggshells feeling whenever she was with both of them. Was it simply a matter of staying too long? The play—the whole impetus for the invitation—wasn't until next week. But she couldn't help wondering if she should make up an excuse and skedaddle back to Castillac.

With a sigh, she decided to open her laptop and do a bit of research before calling it a night.

She googled Madame Trudeau and read a bit about her early music career and what a sensation she had been: concerts all over southern France, and Paris, even a tour to America. She searched for Antoine Plouffe and found next to nothing, the same for Brule and Boulay. She put Yves Dupont in the search bar, just because why not, but all she found was his name listed as detective at the gendarmerie.

Are all these people experts at digital privacy, she wondered, disbelieving. Or do they simply lead quiet, unremarkable lives?

Finally she put her laptop away, rolled over in bed, and tried to quiet her thoughts and go to sleep.

But sleep did not come, no matter how many sheep she counted. Rolling over for the tenth time, she thought she heard a creak on the stair and sat up in bed, listening hard.

If only Bobo were here, she thought, with a great and sudden pang of missing her dog.

The old house made another creak, a shutter downstairs banged lightly, and Molly got out of bed and went to the window. The street was quiet and moonlit, the stones of the street glimmering, only a few branches of a tree waving a bit in a nighttime breeze. It was sometimes handy that French windows generally had no screens, and Molly leaned out and looked in each direction but saw no one.

Everything happens during the night, she thought. The burglaries, the murders—never during the day. Which was probably typical for criminal activities, but nevertheless, the idea took root that if she had any desire to find out who was responsible, lying in bed asleep while the crimes were being committed was not going to get her anywhere at all.

Molly threw on a pair of jeans and a dark shirt, and sneakers with no socks. She crept into the hallway and closed her bedroom door quietly.

Then down the stairs, moving quickly, she took a housekey from the small drawer in the console table in the front hall and went out.

Her heart was racing although the street appeared just as quiet as it had looked from her bedroom. She locked the front door and took off in the direction away from Cours Mirabeau with no specific aim in mind, her eyes wide and other senses alert.

The crimes had been concentrated in this one neighborhood, and the area was not large. She could cover the whole thing on foot easily, probably in half an hour. If anyone was out on the streets, she had a decent chance of seeing who it was.

It was three in the morning. A Tuesday morning. Bars and restaurants were long closed, no tourists roamed about, and the streets and sidewalks were empty.

Her sneakers occasionally squeaked if she changed direction too abruptly, but for the most part Molly moved along with admirable quiet, eyes scanning alleyways and spaces between buildings. From time to time she stopped to listen, straining to hear any sound of confrontation or break-in, or just someone walking. She stuck to the perimeter of the Faures's neighborhood, bordered by the Cours Mirabeau on one side, a small park on another, and a busy street to the south side. The neighborhood was comprised of some apartment buildings, many private homes, and some shops: she passed a tailor's, a pâtisserie she had somehow missed, a luggage and handbag shop.

All quiet. Nothing stirring.

As she walked, her mind was filled with images of Madame Trudeau brandishing a cane and Louise Boulay beating Delano with a stick she picked up in the garden. Of Matéo Brule looming over the frightened film student before the flic showed up and she was saved from worse.

Maybe it's a good thing I'm not a parent after all, she thought, turning down another dark, unfamiliar street. Wandering around at three in the morning actively trying to stumble across thieves and murderers doesn't seem like optimal parental behavior.

She was about to turn back to the Faures's when she heard footsteps. She stopped, ear cocked, then stepped into the shadowy space between two houses, listening, heart in her throat. The footsteps got faster and closer. It sounded like only one person. Molly regretted not bringing the paring knife with her.

The person had a heavy foot. Not quite running but walking

fairly quickly, clomp clomp clomp. Molly desperately wanted to poke her head out for a good look but did not dare. The steps got closer. She pressed herself against the side of the building in case whoever it was glanced her way.

She saw a figure go by, the briefest flash, a tall, dark body. Almost certainly male, and slim.

Molly leaned out and saw him clomp down to the end of the block and around a corner. She followed. He was wearing jeans and a sweatshirt, and basketball sneakers. He walked quickly but a bit awkwardly.

He could be anybody, she told herself, not necessarily somebody up to no good. A baker on his way to work. A college student going home after studying with a friend. A man scurrying home to his wife after spending some hours with his mistress. There were a million reasons why someone might be walking quickly through this particular neighborhood of Aix at three in the morning—some harmless, some less so, but so many of which had not a thing to do with killing or stealing.

Weren't there?

She slowed down and eased around the corner, commanding her sneakers to be silent. He was not far ahead, less than half a block. Molly had to stop herself from calling out.

She stayed on his tail for several more blocks. At one point, he paused to dig in a pocket of his jeans, near enough to a streetlight, but Molly couldn't get a halfway decent look at his face. The he turned another corner and when Molly reached it and looked down the block, he was gone.

THE NEXT MORNING, Molly appeared in the salon with even more desperation for coffee than usual.

"Rough night?" asked Adèle, who was privately scandalized by the wildness of Molly's hair.

"Nightmares," said Molly. "Oh, yes, yes, yes," she said with rapture, taking her first large swig of hot, strong coffee. "Sometimes I think taking the first gulp is the absolute best moment of the day, and it's all downhill from there."

"How unusually pessimistic of you," said Michel. "Listen, I think it's past time we made a sumptuous dinner and ate up on the roof. We can't let all the upset in the neighborhood throw us off this way. The weather is supposed to be perfection all the rest of the week. Tell me some of your very favorite dishes and let's make a plan. What do you say?"

"Sounds great!" said Molly. "Hey Michel, I was wondering … have you introduced me to someone quite tall? Broad-shouldered and slim?"

"A man? What's his face look like?"

"Yes, a man," said Molly. "I don't know, a normal face."

Michel laughed. "That's the entire description, a normal-looking tall man?"

"Oh, forget it, it's probably nothing. It's funny—being in a new city when I'm used to living in a small village and knowing everyone, I keep thinking I see people I know. I can't tell you how many times I've thought I saw Ben on the street."

"You miss him," said Adèle.

"Well, of course. It's just my brain playing tricks. Probably the same thing with this tall fellow."

Michel leaned his head to one side and looked at her.

"All right then!" Adèle said, rather too loud. "I'm off, I've got a meeting and then I'll be back before lunch. Molly, did you want to spend the afternoon at that museum I was telling you about?"

Molly agreed, though truthfully, she wanted no such thing. After a bit of small talk, Molly excused herself from Michel and went to her bedroom, thinking she would make a good-faith effort to take her mind off crime and spend an hour reading a novel.

An hour passed while Molly's eyes ran up and down the pages of her book while she absorbed not a word. Eventually, her stomach growling, she decided to raid the Faures's refrigerator and wander around the neighborhood for a bit. Maybe Delano would be outside, or Berenice. Or she might get lucky and meet some other neighbor who revealed some chance observation that would prove helpful.

She was groggy and splashed some water on her face before heading downstairs, avoiding the creaky eleventh step out of habit. Surprised, she heard low voices coming from the salon, and she stopped on the stair and tuned in.

The voices were low and she could not make out what they were saying.

Molly crept downstairs until she could see inside the room. Michel's back was to her. She saw bare arms reaching around his back, hands with long fingers and manicured pink nails, pulling him close. Michel was kissing someone, but Molly could not see who it was.

Though of course she suspected, and she was not wrong.

Several ways to handle this, she thought, quickly deciding to clatter down the remaining stairs as loudly as possible, and cheerily enter the salon, enjoying (sort of) the way Michel and Apolline jumped apart and tried to pretend they hadn't been kissing like mad.

"Bonjour, Apolline," said Molly with a wide grin. "So nice to see you again. And re-bonjour, Michel," she said. "Well, I'd love to stay and chat but I'm afraid I'm going to be late to meet Adèle. She wants to try to get some culture into me so I won't be quite such a Philistine!"

She kissed cheeks with Michel before leaving, observing how flushed he was, and nervous.

That woman, Molly thought, once out on the street, shaking her head. It would be lovely for Michel to find someone special, and Apolline Cuvalier is decidedly not it.

❧ 28 ❧

"I swear I cannot stand another day of rain!" Frances complained, standing at the window of her and Nico's small apartment in what could generously be called downtown Castillac.

"The trees do not agree," said Nico, coming up behind her and putting his hands at her waist. He leaned his face against her straight black hair, sighing.

"Since when are you a champion of trees? I don't think I've ever heard you say the word 'tree' even once in all the time I've known you."

Nico laughed. "I have the day off. What should we do?"

"Bike ride?"

Nico laughed again, spinning her around and holding her in his arms. "Someday, that bike ride is going to happen. Even if little Leonardo has to be the one to teach you how to ride a bike." He patted her gently swelling belly.

"Leonardo? Oh no, sir, that's Émilie you're talking about. Or perhaps Cassandra, I haven't decided."

"Maybe it's both," said Nico, and ran to the other side of the sofa as Frances attempted to box his ears.

"Just to be clear," she said, sitting down and opening her laptop, "You know I couldn't be happier about this little bean. But twins is more than a bridge too far. So please, chérie, don't even say such a thing out loud. I don't want any of the powers in the universe hearing that as a wish."

Nico sat down next to her and swung his feet onto the coffee table.

"You haven't told Molly yet, have you," he said softly.

"You know I haven't. I'm a coward, that's the truth ... I just ... I mean, of course she'll be happy for us, I don't doubt that for a second. But feelings are complicated, right? Maybe not always exactly what we'd wish? Hey, I know the perfect way to spend this rainy day: let's look at baby furniture! We can order everything from right here on the sofa!"

Nico's eyebrows zoomed up. "Baby furniture?"

"Well, sure! I had friends back in the States who had practically a whole house full of new stuff. There's the high chair, of course, but also a play table, a bouncer, a swing, a sandbox, a playhouse—"

"Frances," said Nico, his tone agonized.

She turned her beautiful pale face toward his, showing remarkable self-control to keep from laughing. It was one of the absolute most adorable things about Nico, she thought—he was *so* easy to tease.

❧ 29 ❧

When Molly got up, the house was empty. Her friends had left no note, and Molly had a pang of feeling a bit like a neglected guest. Where were they always off to? A bit downcast, she wandered into the kitchen and made a plate of charcuterie and cornichons and took it up to the roof to sit among the greenery and breathe the fresh spring air. The salami was excellent, with a marked tang, and the goat cheese superb ... but Molly had a difficult time paying attention to what she was eating, as her mind raced around from thing to thing; it felt as though the unraveled threads were multiplying exponentially and she would never see a way to weave them into a coherent whole.

Unless what Berenice had hinted at was right, and there was only one murderer instead of three.

She heaved a sigh. When at a dead end, do some research. She went back to her room and settled in with her laptop.

Serial killers, whys and wherefores, history of, characteristics of, famous examples.

She did not really believe a serial killer was at work in the neighborhood. Because number one, they are exceedingly rare,

NELL GODDIN

much more so than the movies would lead us to believe. Number two, because a part of her wished it to be so, and she felt ashamed of this wish.

The research on serial killers was certainly interesting reading, if a bit grisly for Molly's taste. The more commonplace motives for killing someone were, in a way, understandable to her—jealousy, revenge, various kinds of desperation, even hatred—sure, these emotions weren't pretty, but who hasn't felt them all, at one point or another?

But according to Monsieur Google, serial killers were an entirely different sort. They killed for sport. For fun. Sometimes the murders had a sexual element, sometimes not. But there was no thread of humanity for Molly to grab onto, and reading some of their stories, she felt nothing but disgust and incomprehension.

BEFORE LUNCH, Molly went for a walk to clear her head. Whipping out her cell, she called Ben, though it was not their usual time of day for a chat.

"Chérie," he said softly, hearing her voice.

Molly melted a little. "I so much wish you were here right now," she said softly.

"So do I."

"Can I leap right in?"

"Of course."

"Okay, so I've been doing what little I can to follow up on the obvious suspects in each case. It feels a bit like doing an investigation with both hands tied behind my back and wearing a gag. But I'll tell you, Ben ... the fact is, even though the motives are good, I just ... have a sense I've been on the wrong track."

"Does Plouffe have an alibi?"

"Well ... no.

She paused. "Put that aside for a second. I know it sounds

dramatic, but I'm ... I'm wondering if maybe what we have here is a serial killer. One murderer, not three."

Ben said nothing. Molly breathed into her phone, cringing inwardly at the feeling that he thought she had lost her mind.

"I mean, look, I know—it sounds a bit over the top. But don't you think it's more than a little odd that there have been three murders in such a small area in a short amount of time? *Three*."

Ben got up and walked outside to try to clear his head. "A serial killer," he said softly. "I thought you were dead-set on Antoine Plouffe for the Trudeau murder."

"Well, I was ... and I wasn't. It did seem as though a case against him was building, and of course when that happens, it only further cements the idea of his guilt ... but ... if I'm honest? I think I was forcing it."

"You felt some ambivalence."

"Yes. I tried to put the ambivalence aside, telling myself I was only getting won over by his good manners. We both know murderers are not necessarily charmless beasts. I've done a bit of research and I don't know, one problem is that serial killers tend to have a certain pattern to their killings and I'm not seeing one here, at least, not the classic sort."

"So three different murderers make no sense, and neither does a serial killer?"

"That's about the size of it. Unless ..."

"Unless what? I do see why you're overwhelmed. It's a lot."

"Well, there *is* one thread, one thing that links all the victims together. It's not the same as what I read about—not ritualistic, or a characteristic of looks or gender. Something else."

"Yes?"

"Berenice pointed this out. For a variety of reasons, the victims were all, well, how to put this—not exactly the best of humanity. Cruelty and a propensity for violence is what links them together—to a spouse, a student, a young girl. The victims did these acts and none of them paid for it, no justice served, no protection or retribution for those harmed. So, I wonder—and I fully realize it sounds like the plot of a made-for-TV movie—whether the killer imagines himself or herself to be something of a vigilante. Getting to justice by any means necessary. Not a classic serial killer who has a sort of psychological pressure he is trying to release through murder, but someone with, you could almost say, an agenda of justice. However warped."

Ben didn't say anything.

"You think it's silly."

"No. I don't."

"The other confounding element is that all killers develop habits. These murders—suffocation, cut throat, and now unverified but possible strangulation—does that sound even remotely plausible, one person switching from one way to another like that?"

"Never say never," said Ben. "But you're right, the chances are doubtless low."

Another silence while they digested this.

Ben said, "I do think it's worth mentioning that there are reasons this appears to be a good idea that have nothing to do with the facts of the case. Please don't take this as a lack of confidence in your analysis or saying this idea is definitely wrong. But —it would make the whole situation a thousand times easier to manage, yes? You look for one perp instead of three. You focus on emotional instability, past trauma, a history of violence, grandiosity—potential qualities of serial killers or vigilantes.

"I can feel the relief myself in thinking I have only one killer to find, and I'm not even the one doing the investigating. I'm not saying that's all there is to it, not at all, just something to be aware of. And Molly—again, take this in the spirit it is meant, and not as criticism—I know you have no access to the gendarmerie or Yves Dupont. So forget about that. You can't just wander the streets, you've got to talk to more people, do some detecting.

You're being too passive. I can see why, the job is overwhelming. But you can do this, Molly Sutton, if anyone can."

Molly was quiet for a moment. "Thank you," she said in a low voice, which Ben could barely hear over the street noise. "I'm just realizing ... it's not even the fact of the numbers of murders or the complication of all the usual elements that go into solving cases. It's ..."

"Yes?"

"I've lost confidence in myself," Molly whispered.

"*You?*"

"I mean, three people have been killed within a few blocks of where I am. Yet what progress have I made, what evidence have I gotten my hands on? It's a joke. *I'm* a joke."

"Just stop it," said Ben. "You know perfectly well that in every case, almost every single one, there's a moment of despair. You just have to keep going and get through it. Beating yourself up accomplishes nothing. Investigations are almost always plodding work where you feel you are accomplishing nothing until that moment when disparate events start to connect. You know this, Molly."

"I do. I'm just telling you the thoughts that run through my head lately. Embarrassing though they are." Molly bit into her fifth cornichon and chewed a moment. "Listen," she said. "Let's talk about something else for a bit."

"I wish I had some interesting news from here—" Ben paused and then rushed on, "everything with the gîtes is going fine and I've really nothing at all to report. No worries on the home front."

"Even young goddesses opening the door without a stitch on?" said Molly, offhandedly.

Ben gasped. "Who told you?"

"I'm not on a desert isle with no way to communicate with the outside world," Molly laughed. "You have to know that if you tell Constance anything, that news will be all around the globe in a matter of minutes."

Ben laughed. "I do realize that, of course. It's just that she came over just moments after Briony ... well ... and I was chuckling to myself, and so I told her."

"And how *are* things with Miss Lark? Has she ramped up her efforts and begun banging on the door at all hours?"

"I've only seen her once since. She is staying on an extra week, which we can both be grateful for in this slow patch as far as paying investigations are concerned."

"Monster-sized rats, naked beauties—I feel like I've been missing out on everything," said Molly. "So tell me, have you seen the girls, Chloë and Giselle? I've sent them a postcard, but you know I worry."

"Just last week I saw them skipping down the sidewalk with bags from Pâtisserie Bujold. They seemed to be enjoying the day as much as any girls could wish."

"So glad to hear that. And what other news do you have of our friends? How's Frances? We've barely been in touch. Which is fine, I don't want to be blathering on about what's going on here when I don't even have a coherent story to tell, and I can barely think of anything else, so it's just as well. Though I miss her dreadfully."

"Of course you do," Ben murmured. "We'll all be so happy to see you when you finally get home."

THAT NIGHT, worn out from trying to appear interested in the Van Goghs at the Granet Museum, Molly picked at her rooftop dinner of chicken paillards sautéed in wine along with a glistening pile of garlicky string beans and crusty bread, then went to bed early, for once letting Adèle and Michel worry if they had done something wrong rather than the other way around.

Molly considered going back and asking directly what was going on, but she had this feeling that if the murders stopped, and the murderer was brought to justice—all would be right in the Faure household.

She went through her usual bare-minimum bedtime routine and dutifully got into bed, half-pretending to herself that she wasn't going to go out again.

Because she *was* going out, of course she was. Who could say, perhaps her presence the night before had scared the criminals off. She might be patrolling more than investigating, but that wasn't totally useless, right? Not her usual role, but whatever. She hadn't seen any gendarmes out last night, and why not? Shouldn't *they* be doing some patrolling, given the astonishing rate of crime in the small perimeter of the neighborhood?

The only question was whether she should try to get a few hours' sleep first, or just wait for her friends to go to bed and slip out then.

Molly got out of bed and went to the window, looking out at the quiet street. Maybe Ben was right, and she was forcing this idea of a serial killer to avoid slogging through the work of three investigations at once. Maybe she wanted to defer to Berenice because her own confidence was so low. Methodically, she ran through the murders once again.

Brule's murder may have had nothing to do with Liliane Chopin at all. Brule may have infuriated someone else for some reason completely unrelated to sexual assault. Maybe he smacked the wrong delivery boy.

And possibly the person who killed Madame Trudeau was a cousin who hated her for inheriting some family money and leaving the cousin out in the cold. Perhaps Louise Boulay had a secret gambling problem and owed money to the wrong people.

It is always a mistake to assume that the most obvious reason is the actual reason. Always a mistake to conclude that the neatest, most elegant explanation is the right one.

Then again—pushing in the opposite direction—could it be that the three murders *were* connected, and the most obvious suspects were all innocent? Maybe the Plouffes were incapable of murder (no matter how vigorously they might have privately celebrated Madame Trudeau's death). Maybe Delano was telling the truth—simply an innocent cry of anxiety—when he worried the authorities would pin his wife's murder on him. Maybe the Chopin family had moved on from what had happened with Brule, and Liliane had healed from whatever had taken place that night and begun a career in film with all thought of the incident buried in her past.

And if these most obvious suspects were innocent …

She put on her jeans, dark shirt, and sneakers again and crept into the hallway, listening. The sort of noise a breathing old house makes. No sound from down the hall in Michel's direction.

Molly went down a flight, listened, then down another. Into the kitchen and then to the street, carefully closing the front door. The paring knife in one front pocket of her jeans, the house key in the other.

It didn't feel all that great to be sneaking around behind her hosts' backs, but she knew that they would absolutely not be in favor of her going out, and might take steps to prevent it, though it was hard to imagine they would go so far as to lock her in her room. For a moment she amused herself by imagining escaping out of the window by a sheet tied to her bedpost.

All right, she said to herself, standing up straight and looking in each direction. Focus, Molly, focus. Attune your senses. Which way? There was a moon, but the night was cloudy and it disappeared just as she set out toward the Cours Mirabeau. She was grateful for the good streetlights and walked as quickly and quietly as she could, ears pricked. She was vaguely curious about what the Cours Mirabeau looked like at night, since she thought of it as a place of sunshine and busy cafés, artists at work, roaming groups of tourists. Not dark and still. Never empty, not even in the rain.

But Molly did not get to Cours Mirabeau that night. A half-block away, she heard a noise—it might have been a cat, she wasn't sure—a sort of cry, but muffled, strangled—

She peered between two buildings, quite close together, where the sounds seemed to come from. She heard footsteps, unhurried, not heading towards her. Molly ducked down the passageway. The buildings were both private houses, the windows on the ground floor, in fact all the floors, dark. She couldn't see where she was going and had her head turned slightly to listen, her hands moving along the sides of the walls to guide her.

The houses were not modest but neither did they extend terribly far back, and eventually, without having heard anything else, Molly's hands ran out of wall and she found herself standing in an open space with hardly any light to see by. She stood still, telling herself the cry had probably been a cat after all. The clouds over the moon got heavier and she found herself in a pitch-dark space she had no idea how to leave. She hoped she wouldn't stumble over a flowerpot and wake the neighbors, who were already on edge enough without Molly crashing into petunias in their backyards.

She only took a few steps into the darkness before stopping to listen again. Footsteps diminishing. She believed it was the same person, though of course could not be sure. If she could only see where she was going, she would have run toward the sound.

Just as she started to move ahead, her hands out in front of her, she heard a sort of whimper. Not quite—more of a grunt, really, and this time, it sounded distinctly more human than feline. Close by.

"Hello?" Molly said, reverting to English in her fear.

Silence.

Gingerly, Molly edged forward a few steps in the dark. "Hel-lo?" she shout-whispered. She turned her eyes up to the sky, willing the clouds to part.

Another, fainter grunt. Almost a sigh.

Molly got down on her hands and knees and crawled in the

direction of the sound. The ground was laid to stone, probably a terrace belonging to one of the houses, and uncomfortable on her knees. She felt her way under a wooden pedestal table and a chair, then around a large urn, and finally, the clouds still uncooperative and darkness nearly complete, her searching hands landed on a person, lying on the ground, on the stone, as still and immobile as a garden decoration.

❧ III ❧

30

B en startled awake.

He picked up his watch from the bedside table and saw that it was 2:30 in the morning. He fell back on the pillow, his heart beating fast. Had he been dreaming? Was Molly all right?

He tried rolling over and closing his eyes, but sleep was nowhere on the horizon, so with a sigh, he swung his feet to the floor. Bobo lifted her head and watched him.

Molly needs to come home, he thought. A feeling of something like dread bubbled up and he swatted it away.

Pouring himself a shot of cognac, he tried again to shake off the bad feeling. I'm probably just missing her.

That's all this is.

He poured a second shot, not believing his own lie, and got back into bed.

$\approx$ 3 1 $\approx$

M olly sat on the stone terrace next to the man, who lay on his back, still and silent. She had called *SAMU* immediately, then felt his wrist for a pulse. He was alive. She could not see well enough to know what he looked like, or whether he was someone familiar to her. She tried to remember the front of his house, since even being in Aix so short a time, she had surely walked past the man's door twenty times or more. But, of course, she had no idea whether he lived in the nearest house or somewhere else.

She felt impatient and worried. The man did not stir or make any sound.

The moon was only visible for brief moments as the clouds slipped past, and she was unable to make any sort of assessment of his situation, not that she was actually trained to do so; at any rate, she could not see well enough to make any guess about why the man was lying unconscious on this terrace in the middle of the night. Had he come out to call in the cat, and slipped and fallen? Had a stroke, a heart attack—occurrences that happened all the time, all over the world, every minute of every day?

She kept thinking of those footsteps, remembering how the

sound of them got softer, and wondering whether that person had been on this terrace, with this man, just moments before she got there herself.

It seemed as though emergency services were taking their sweet time, but when she checked her watch, five minutes had felt like half an hour.

Molly did not feel frightened, even though she was sitting alone in the dark with a person who may have been brutally attacked, with nothing but a paring knife to defend herself. If anyone nefarious is lurking about, he won't be able to see either, she thought. She closed her eyes to sharpen her hearing, but apart from the rustling of a tree branch in the slight breeze, the neighborhood was as quiet as ever.

If he *had* been brutally attacked—if this was yet another murder attempt, though so far the man was alive—did that mean that this man was also hated by the whole neighborhood, like the others? What had he done, or failed to do?

Where in the world was that ambulance?

Scooching closer to the man, Molly reached to feel for his pulse again. As she leaned on the stone near him, she felt something wet. She snatched her hand back, then wiped it on the stone, shuddering.

Molly could not see, so she did not know for certain. But she would bet almost anything that her hand was now covered in blood.

"OH, MOLLY," said Adèle. "I suppose this isn't the moment to chastise you? Because I want to very much."

"What *were* you thinking?" said Michel, pouring himself another cup of coffee. "You could have at least asked me to go along."

Molly smiled faintly. "You don't have to fuss, I'm completely fine. Just tired. I'm only sorry there was nothing to be done for

Monsieur Latour."

"I cannot stand the idea of you sitting there in the dark all that time next to a ... a body," said Michel with a shudder.

"He was alive at least some of the time," Molly said. "Not that it's any great consolation, but he went quietly."

"I hope he didn't suffer," said Adèle. "I didn't know Monsieur Latour personally, but he was well known in the neighborhood as the man who looked after the cats."

"He just had his family silver stolen a few days ago. A bad week altogether," said Michel.

"I've seen him putting out saucers of cream in the alleyway next to his house. Crooning to the cats who flocked there."

"That's very sweet," said Molly. "It does take some dedication to go out of your way for cats, when they are usually so ... unappreciative."

"You just haven't met the right cats," said Adèle. "When we were small, remember Pic-pic, Michel?"

"Of course I remember him. He bit my finger straight through to the bone and I was rushed off to the doctor's for a shot."

"Anyway, the cats are beside the point. Marius Latour is the point," said Adèle. "The medical people were quite certain it was murder? Perhaps he simply slipped and fell and hit his head?"

"Oh, they didn't express any opinions or talk to me at all, beyond asking when I had found him. I was just in the way. But they had lights, so I was able to see Latour clearly when they put him on a stretcher. I suppose it's somehow possible to get a head injury like that by falling on your terrace? But to be honest, sorry to say, I do not think it is very likely."

Adèle held up a palm. Her hands were shaking and she clasped them together firmly and pushed them into her lap. "And so, Latour makes four. I ... I'm feeling a strong urge to leave town. Listen: how about we throw some clothes in a bag, go to the train station, and just get on, go wherever the first train takes us. It will be a grand adventure, not knowing where we're going in advance!

What do you say? We could be on our way out of town, away from this ever-unfolding horror, within the hour. We could be eating sausages in Lyon for dinner, or pasta in Lake Como. There's literally no reason we can't escape this."

Molly sipped her coffee and looked affectionately at Adèle.

"Dearest," said Michel. He started to say more but instead took the empty coffeepot back to the kitchen for a refill.

"Lyon is quite beautiful, I've been thinking of it recently. You know I went to school there for a time," said Adèle.

Molly just looked at her.

"The rivers Rhône and Saône join right at the city, and the view from the bridges is spectacular. I would like to be standing there right this minute. And the local food is extraordinary. Have you ever had *la quenelle Lyonnaise?*"

Molly wanted to hug her but knew that was not the right thing for Adèle. "I do understand ... with your history, of course all of this is making you feel a bit tender, a bit vulnerable," said Molly. "All those memories must be flooding back of your family ... circumstance."

"The situation is simple enough, Adèle. You know Molly is never going to leave until these murderers are caught," said Michel as he returned to the salon. "So I'm going to choose to look at these murders as having the wonderful effect of keeping her here with us longer than otherwise. Not to mention the added bonus of having justice served once she catches the killers."

Adèle looked stony.

"Thanks, Michel, but you're getting a little ahead of yourself. I'm not going to be the one solving these crimes. I'm just a bystander to the whole thing," said Molly.

"Uh huh, sure," said Michel. To Adèle, he said, "I do promise you, though, when this is all over? We'll go someplace wonderful. Italy is a fabulous idea. Lake Como is lovely, certainly, and I was seeing the most amazing photographs of a festival in Spello where they make paintings on the street out of flower petals ..."

Adèle smiled at Michel but her expression was strained. They all drank their coffee, lost in thought for some moments before Molly spoke. "Do you mind if I ask just a few questions? I don't mean to sound like a gendarme interrogating you. But please, if you would, even just for something to do—tell me anything else you know about Monsieur Latour. His house is so close—did you see him on the street often?"

Michel shook his head and went back into the kitchen.

Adèle wiped away fresh tears with a linen napkin. "I'm trying to think, but Molly, I'm just ... overwhelmed."

Michel returned from the kitchen with a plate of baguette cut into slices and a fat wedge of gouda.

"It's yesterday's bread so a bit stale, but I'm about to faint from starvation," said Michel. "With everything going on, we need sustenance."

Adèle cut a chunk of cheese and ate it without bread.

"How about you, Michel? Do you know anything about Latour? Who his friends were, what kind of work he did, anything at all?" asked Molly. She was hoping to hear that Latour, like the others, was roundly disliked and been guilty of ugly deeds, but did not want to lead her friend down that road by force or by hint.

Michel shrugged. "I've got nothing, sorry to say," he said. "I spoke to him from time to time, just simple greetings, that was all. I can't help thinking that it's ... it's as though once the killings began, it gave people ideas. Suddenly murder, unthinkable before, has turned into a viable option."

"The social contract has frayed?" said Molly.

"Something like that. But that would be looking at the most dramatic explanation. Probably," said Michel, "what we're seeing is nothing more than a strange coincidence. Though I will grant you, 'strange' may not quite cover it."

Molly sat up straight, tapping a finger on her chin, thinking. If the Faures did not know what kind of man Marius Latour was, she would have to ask the only other people she knew in Aix: Émile and Berenice.

And given the pace of the killings, the sooner the better.

ADÈLE and Michel exchanged glances as Molly excused herself and left the house, saying she wanted to take a quick walk and think.

"I'll just say this: the timing of Molly's visit might turn out to be auspicious for the neighborhood, but not that great for Molly herself," said Michel. "I don't like her going out in the middle of the night, not at all."

"She takes too many risks," murmured Adèle.

"I know."

Michel stood up quickly, nearly spilling his coffee. "Tell you what. During the day, Molly is safe enough, don't you think? As she pointed out, the murdering and burglarizing takes place at night. So from now on, I will simply tail her when she goes out. She will believe she is alone, but I will be there keeping an eye on her."

"But you're not trained in such things, Michel. How will you manage it without her seeing you?"

"I'll figure it out. I have confidence in Molly, as should you. And I will discreetly make sure that if she does find herself in a bad situation, she won't be alone."

"I don't think this is a good idea. Will you be armed?" whispered Adèle, her face pale.

"I'll give that some thought," Michel answered gravely.

32

Famished and groggy from lack of sleep, Molly headed straight for Pâtisserie P. She would sacrifice a limb to be on her way to Pâtisserie Bujold to see her old friend Edmond Nugent and his delectable array of pastries, but Pâtisserie P would have to do.

The shop was crowded and she had to wait for several people to be helped. In line just ahead of her was a well-dressed young woman holding the hand of a small boy who was complaining that his shoes hurt. Molly wondered, as she had many times, how exactly did French women look so effortlessly chic? The woman wasn't wearing anything especially fancy or expensive but managed to look so pulled together, so gracefully stylish. The little boy complained again, scuffing his shoe. His mother gave no indication that she heard him. The boy twisted his hand away from her, and scowling, looked up at Molly. She made a silly face and the boy smiled shyly and hid behind his mother's legs.

At last Molly was back on the sidewalk holding a waxed paper bag with two fresh and delicious-smelling croissants, one almond and one plain. The plain croissant went down in a few rushed bites and she started in on the almond, barely registering its love-liness because she was so depleted from lack of sleep.

She wished she'd met the coroner the night before. The emergency team had paid no attention to her questions but rushed off with Monsieur Latour, whom Molly was fairly sure had already expired. They had not used the siren.

Turning back down rue Niccolo, she saw a man walking toward her with some urgency. Their eyes met. Molly slowed down, watching him. Was he heading for her, or just coming in her direction?

"Madame!" he called out, waving at her, and meeting her eyes with a penetrating look.

"Yes?" said Molly. "May I help you?"

"I am Patrice Jubert," he said, as though announcing he was president of France.

"Bonjour, Monsieur Jubert," said Molly, amused. "Is something on fire?"

Patrice looked impatient. "Fire is perhaps the one tragic thing our neighborhood is not concerned with, in this particular moment. You are a guest of the Faures, I believe?"

"I am. Molly Sutton, pleased to meet you," she said, holding out her hand, which he shook.

"I just knocked on the Faures's door but there was no answer," he said, with an accusing tone. "Well, I have some important news. If I may request that you let them know, at your earliest convenience?"

"Certainly," said Molly.

"Something very strange is going on. I can't explain it. I do not even try to explain it," he said.

Molly waited. Then realized he wanted encouragement. "Yes, what is it?"

"Murders and burglaries, that's our current reality. It's unthinkable but that is what we are facing. Violence breaking out. Windows broken, locks picked, neighbors struck down—

and who knows when these perpetrators will be caught? But this—what I'm about to tell you—is an entirely different ... I mean, let's admit, stealing, thievery—that's old as the hills, everyone is familiar with such crimes, though of course we do not wish for them to be running rampant here in our own backyards. But this new development ... this is something else entirely."

Molly had to admit, he had aroused her curiosity.

Patrice lifted his chin and stared into the clouds as though some important revelation waited for him there.

"Yes?" said Molly. "What development?"

"Several people on our street have reported receiving envelopes in their postal boxes or pushed through their postal slots. Anonymous brown envelopes, without an address or a return address, no writing or typing on them whatsoever."

He paused again and Molly prodded again. "Yes? And what was in them? Letters? Bills? What?"

"The envelopes contained money. Euros. Reports are that the amounts are not the same in every envelope but in all cases it is not insignificant. One person reported packets totaling fifteen hundred euros."

"Not pocket change."

"No, Madame Sutton, it most certainly is not. You must admit: this is not the usual thing."

"Yes, readily. In fact I can go so far as to say I've never heard of anyone randomly being given cash anonymously in their mailboxes. Or any other way, for that matter."

Patrice nodded. "Everything we take for granted has been thrown up into the air!"

"I don't know that you have to raise quite such an alarm," said Molly. "I'm sure there's some explanation, and, given that money is involved, I would imagine we won't have to wait forever to hear what it is. And so ... is this ... you want to me to tell the Faures about some people in the neighborhood receiving envelopes with

NELL GODDIN

money inside? Do you ... is there any more information? Are these people owed money by anyone? Do you have any more details?"

"There are no more details. It is so far three persons, or households, who have received such envelopes. Whether more have received them and not told anyone, I cannot say. They all evince shock and claim to have no idea where the money came from or why it appeared. Perhaps you do not find this surprising or notable, but I certainly do. Especially given the recent events, it is not only strange, but worrisome."

Molly started to make a wisecrack but stopped herself.

"Of course it is certainly better to have a wad of cash stuffed into one's postal box than to be stolen from, or God forbid, killed," said Patrice. "I am not saying all these things are of a piece, or have any connection, to each other. Yet it adds to the sense that the very ground upon which we walk is disturbed, and not to be trusted. We must be on our guard, ever vigilant! Please, let Michel and Adèle know. I appreciate your help in this matter."

And lifting his nose a bit in the air, he strode off, in the manner of self-appointed mayors everywhere, thought Molly with a smile. She watched him move down the street, wondering where she had seen him before. He must have been at the apéro, she thought, turning back toward the Faures's when Patrice disappeared around a corner.

MOLLY STOOD on the sidewalk a moment, wondering about wads of euros suddenly appearing in people's mailboxes. Then she turned back toward the Faures's, but something bright, a flash of a yellow blouse, caught her attention and she looked just in time to see Apolline Cuvalier and a girl go into a building that faced on Cours Mirabeau. Apolline's hand had rested on the small of the girl's back as they went through the heavy old door. Molly only saw them from behind, but the girl appeared to be around sixteen

210

or so, wearing a short skirt and white camisole, her hair tied back in a high ponytail.

The door closed behind them as Molly reached the building, which appeared to be a private residence. She could see curtains made of expensive fabric at the first-floor windows, and an enormous gilt mirror over a mantel. The door had no sign or plaque, only a brass knocker in the form of some kind of fantastic beast sticking out a long and unsettling tongue.

Molly crossed the street to get a different perspective. It was four stories, limestone, eighteenth century. The shutters a dark, beautiful blue. An elaborate iron gate with the initials VDC woven into it. The house was stately. Aristocratic. Whoever lived there had plenty of money, that was for sure, and also social position, probably both through generations. She grumbled to herself. She didn't trust Apolline as far as she could throw her, and the sight of her ushering that girl through the door in a proprietary way had stirred up even more distrust ... but what could Molly do? Well, for starters, she told herself, I can find out who lives there.

After turning down rue Niccolo, she realized she was practically at Émile's door. Why not drop in to see if he needs anything? Before she could talk herself out of it, she rapped on his door.

After another rap and nothing but silence, Molly was about to turn away when the door cracked and then quickly opened all the way, and Émile stood there grinning at her. "Chérie!" he exclaimed, reaching for her hand and pulling her inside.

"I hope I'm not intruding? I was just walking back to the Faures's and saw your door, and thought, well ..."

"I've been quite busy this morning," he said, brightly, after they kissed cheeks. "First, I'm feeling altogether invigorated just now; I've made it a habit to try to spend at least a few minutes working on some new skills, and I will not allow this illness to get in the way. And after that, I had my first visitor of the day, an old friend, Rodolfo Gallatine: a detective on the Aix-en-Provence force. We've known each other for years. He came by to fill me in on all the neighborhood goings-on. Of which, I am saddened and shocked to say, there are so many terrible things! Come, sit. Let me make you a coffee."

Émile's new treatment had really worked a miracle, Molly thought, watching him move down the hallway with far more liveliness than the last time she'd seen him.

So he's friends with a detective, she thought, a little flame of excitement beginning to burn in her chest. Was it possible Émile could arrange a meeting with this Rodolfo? Or even a phone call? Her hands began to sweat and she was so taken up with imagining how this new contact might go that for once she didn't snoop around the room while he was busy making coffee.

The lovely smell reached her and then she heard Émile on his way back. The house was narrow and long, just one room wide with a staircase and hallway along the side. The walls were plastered and freshly painted a bright white, so that despite the relatively few windows the interior didn't feel gloomy.

"Here we are," Émile said, coming back with a small enamel tray with two tiny cups of espresso.

"You are feeling better than the last time I saw you," said Molly.

"Today, yes. It's up and down," he said with a shrug.

"And I'm curious, what new skills are you learning?"

Smiling, Émile shook his head, "Oh, nothing too extravagant. This morning I've been patiently learning how to dice an onion correctly. You'd think a person living alone would have mastered that decades earlier! My dear wife has been gone since 1995, and she did all the cooking."

Molly made a sympathetic face but did not interrupt.

"I'm just lucky that so many people have been kind to me. They bring me food—which I still have little interest in, but it's a heartfelt gesture, and makes me feel I'm not completely forgotten —and even better, they bring me news. What can *you* tell me about the wide world, Molly Sutton? Or even the world just outside my door. My curiosity, I'm afraid, still exceeds my stamina."

"Well," said Molly wondering where to begin. "What has your detective friend told you?"

"He was just on his way home after a late shift when he got the call. Did you hear? Another murder last night. Dreadful, dreadful thing."

Molly paused. She looked at Émile, at his almost-wizened face, his bright eyes. "I was there," she said quietly. "Before your friend. I think I even heard it happen, or at least, I may have heard Monsieur Latour cry out when he was hit."

"Wasn't this in the middle of the night? Whatever in the world were you doing out at such an hour?"

Molly shrugged. "It's ... well ... the truth is, back home in Castillac, I'm something of a detective myself. A private investigator, not part of the gendarmerie of course. Just sort of fell into it. My reason for coming to Aix was simply for a vacation and to visit my friends ... but now ..."

"Your urge ... you want to set things right."

"Exactly. I'm due to go home, I have responsibilities I need to get back to ... but this situation, I can't just walk away from it. Partly I don't want to leave my friends behind if they're in danger, but ... to be honest, there's a kind of ... I don't know, I don't want to sound like I have delusions of being Superman or something," Molly laughed. "But the idea of leaving town when there's a murderer rampaging like this, right on my friends' doorstep? It's just ... I can't do it. It's unthinkable. I want them—and Aix—to be safe."

Émile nodded. "You don't trust the gendarmerie? I'll keep that a secret from Rodolfo."

"It's not that. I have quite a high opinion of gendarmes, I've met some very good ones, dedicated and talented at the job. It's more ... more like the situation feels to me like a ... I don't know, like a broken lamp that demands fixing. I can't just leave it sitting dark that way. If your friend solves the case, hallelujah! It doesn't have to be me. But it needs to be solved somehow." Even as the words came out of her mouth, Molly acknowledged to herself that she was telling a lie. She wished it were true that she didn't care who solved the cases, but strictly speaking, it was not. Nothing in her life was as satisfying as finding that one clue that nails a case shut, and that was just a fact.

"So tell me," she said, "is Rodolfo good? Do you think he's up to the job?"

"Oh, I expect he's done well enough. I wouldn't exactly call him Inspector Maigret, if you know what I mean. Any aid you can give will be much appreciated. You have had some success in this profession you fell into?"

Molly nodded. "I have. But this—this is different. I've been wondering—if I may be frank?—I haven't talked to anyone about this. It might sound ridiculous to you. But I've been wondering— without much to base it on—is it possible that the murders are connected? One murderer, not ... oh heavens, we're up to four."

Émile grinned. "You know, I have wondered the same. Not ridiculous at all, perhaps all of us in the neighborhood have had the same thought. Logically, it seems to me, it is a possibility that must be considered."

"That's what I think! Sure, it would be a rarity, but rarities do exist. No doubt the gendarmerie is doing loads of DNA testing, they should be able to see whether this theory has any merit or not. Oh for my own lab!" said Molly. "We will just have to muddle along using only our brains instead. So tell me, Émile: did you know Marius Latour? What kind of fellow was he?"

"A lover of cats," said Émile, with a smile. "He retired from his job at the post office, oh, three or four years ago. Unmarried. Had no family to speak of, I think he may have mentioned a cousin who moved to Germany? At any rate, Marius devoted his post-retirement life to the stray cats of the neighborhood. He took such good care of them that their numbers were ever-expanding, which brought him some disapproval amongst the neighbors. Cats—as you know, they inspire such devotion, and also hatred."

"I've known some beastly ones," said Molly, thinking with conflicted fondness of the orange cat, and wondering if Ben was leaving any food out for her. "Would you say Latour didn't have many friends?"

Émile considered the question. "He wasn't terribly sociable, that's true. But as you know, people are not all the same in that regard. Some love parties and being around other people almost every second. Others treasure their solitude. I would say Marius was on the introverted side, but not to an extreme. We chatted amiably when we saw each other, which was not rare since we lived so near each other and he was so often outside tending to his cats.

"I myself have far fewer friends than I would like. It isn't because I lack sociability, but ... and I don't believe I am making excuses ... more the result of some bad luck. My parents died when I was a young adult and I was an only child. They were both only children as well, so there was no extended family. I have had many friends here but some of the closest have moved away, others have died ..."

"I'm very sorry," said Molly.

Émile beamed at her. "I do not tell you these things to make you feel sorry! Loving people is always a risk. It's true, losing them to death or simply from their moving away, it hurts, it's painful. But that is only because I loved them. If you try to avoid the pain by avoiding love, what kind of life do you end up with?"

Molly smiled at him. "Did you always think about things this way, or is it a result of your illness?"

"Illness changes one, to be sure," Émile said. "Would you like more coffee?"

"I'd better not. What I should do is take a nap, but I seem to be resisting the idea."

"You don't want to miss anything," said Émile.

"Yes," said Molly. Clearly whatever debilitating effects the cancer and the treatment were having on him, his mind was sharp as ever. "Well, I don't want to tire you out." She got up and stretched her arms. "I do have two small questions, if you have the wherewithal?"

Émile opened his arms and smiled.

"That very grand house on the Cours Mirabeau, about half a block from rue Niccolo, this side, with the deep blue door—any idea who owns it?"

"Oh certainly. That would be Victor Chopin's house. His family built that house in the early 1800s. Lovely isn't it? Somehow none of the travails France has endured since then has done anything to diminish the great pot of Chopin money."

"Nice for them," murmured Molly, filing that away. "And one last thing—not to browbeat you! As far as you know, Latour was ... no one's enemy? Had not hurt anyone or behaved badly in any way you can think of?"

"The Marius Latour I knew was the most mild-mannered of fellows," said Émile. "Gentle, even."

Molly nodded, deeply disappointed.

"By all means, ask around. But as far as I know, he was a very decent man. Of course, anyone can have secrets, don't you think? Who can really say what any of us are made of, given unusual circumstances?"

Molly nodded. "True enough," she said, distractedly. "Ah well, it's always a mistake to try to force facts to fit a theory. If you think of anything else, about anything, please let me know? Can I give you my cell number?"

"Oh, are you saying I can be a sort of deputy? I can't cover the streets in the middle of the night! But I can at least keep my ears and eyes open and report anything back to you." Slowly Émile rose and fetched a scrap of paper and pen for Molly to write down her number.

"That would be more useful than you can imagine," Molly said seriously. "Keep this in mind: someone knows something, has seen something, has overheard something. We only need to find that person and listen when they speak."

Émile nodded, his expression both serious and grateful.

"Thank you, Molly, for giving me a real job."

They kissed cheeks on his doorstep and Molly was almost positive she saw a glimmer of tears in the corner of his eyes. For the most part, people just want to be useful, she thought. What would have been extremely useful was to find out that Marius Latour had been a scourge on humanity ... but alas, it appeared he was not.

33

That night, though exhausted, Molly slipped on the same dark clothes and headed out, key and paring knife in her pockets. The moon was still big and the sky clear, and with the help of the streetlights it was as bright as she could wish as she quickly moved to the end of the block and turned in a different direction than she had on previous nights.

Rather clumsily, and at first noisily, Michel followed. He was not used to trying to be silent when he moved, not used to creeping along in the shadows, trying not to be noticed or draw any attention to himself. He did not hear the door open behind him or see Adèle slip out as well. At a few points he forgot what he was doing and nearly called out to Molly to wait up.

Because of the brightness of the moon, Molly covered the neighborhood in short order, zigzagging along the streets and through the alleys, ears alert, eyes wide.

But on that Wednesday, she saw nothing at all out of place. She met no one on the street, saw no one, heard no one. The shops and houses were dark and quiet. Not a single sign of any murderer, or thief, or deliverer of euro-stuffed envelopes.

She did not even hear her friend awkwardly following behind her, cursing under his breath whenever she ducked into a dark alley.

As for Adèle? She had disappeared altogether.

❧ 34 ❧

Molly yawned all morning no matter how many cups of coffee she drank. Michel slept in. Of the three friends, only Adèle seemed to be on her best game.

"He's going to pick me up at one," she said to Molly as they straightened the kitchen after breakfast. "I'll just tell you right now—I'm nervous."

"And excited?"

"Yes, of course, that too. Maybe it's mostly that. I'm trying not to get my hopes up too much."

"Not easy."

"I mean, I do know that having a boyfriend doesn't magically make your life better. And also that I'm too old to be acting like a teenager with a crush."

Molly cocked her head while wiping the counter. "I suppose like most things, having a partner can make your life better and worse at the same time. More love is always good. But not necessarily always easy." She thought about her ex-husband for a moment, and how her marriage had had moments of happiness and of pain; she made a quick wish for Adèle, that she find someone decent and dependable, someone she could be herself with, someone who would be, no matter what, on Team Adèle.

The doorbell rang. Adèle looked at Molly with a shocked face. "Oh no, is that him? This early?"

"I'll get the door, maybe it's someone else. Run upstairs and get ready just in case," Molly laughed.

Adèle scampered upstairs as quickly as she could and Molly came to the door wiping her hands on a dishtowel.

But it was only a delivery, a small box from Pâtisserie P, sent by Émile.

FEELING PECKISH, Molly wanted to eat a meal by herself so she could collect her thoughts. She went to the closest restaurant on Cours Mirabeau and dropped gratefully into a wicker chair at a table with a dazzling white tablecloth.

"*Un kir, s'il vous plaît*," she said to the server, who nodded, and within minutes placed the drink in front of her.

Molly took a long sip, the beloved crème de cassis never failing to lift her spirits. And they needed lifting, that was for sure. Here she was, in the absolute epicenter of a veritable crime wave, and what had she accomplished? Nothing but a lot of hot-air theories and being too late to stop the murder of a gentle cat-man.

She turned her thoughts to Madame Trudeau, Matéo Brule, and Louise Boulay. Then to Antoine Plouffe, Liliane Chopin, and Delano Boulay.

Her eyes ran down the items on the menu but she did not see them.

Perhaps she should simply present herself at the gendarmerie and ask this Rodolfo Gallatine what she could do to help. He had a glamorous-sounding name, that was for sure; maybe he would be open-minded and glad to have her on board?

Ridiculous. How about asking Michel to throw a small dinner

party, and invite him? She wondered if Émile might be well enough to come, if it was only a few people.

Imagining the party, Molly leaned back in her chair and looked out at the stream of people walking by. A pair of dogs weaved in and out, chasing each other.

Then out of the crowd, Berenice appeared. It took Molly a moment to recognize her, since the older woman was not in her usual place on rue Niccolo and had no broom.

Molly waved. "Berenice!"

Berenice walked up to the barricade of the terrace. She had a strange expression on her face and Molly's stomach dropped.

"How are you? Is something the matter?"

Berenice tilted her head as though considering.

"Berenice, come join me for lunch!" Molly gestured to an empty chair at her table.

Berenice laughed. "I don't eat in places like that," she said, rolling her eyes.

"Oh come on, it's my treat!"

Berenice nodded and came around to the opening in the barricade, sweeping past the host with her nose in the air.

"I'm very happy you happened to come by. I would much rather have company at lunch, and Michel and Adèle are off doing this and that and I was on my own. And famished!"

"Thank you for the kind invitation," said Berenice, rather stiffly, as she scooted her chair up to the table and put the napkin in her lap, her hands resting in the French way on the edge of the table.

"So ... what's up? I know you a little bit by now," said Molly. "And I could see on your face—"

"It's not what you think."

Molly laughed to herself, since for once she hadn't jumped to any conclusions at all. "All right. What is it then? Have you had some bad news?"

"Quite the opposite, if you must know."

NELL GODDIN

"Won the lottery, then? Is there a lottery in France? I'm not a player so I don't keep up."

"Did you hear about the envelopes? The neighbors have been talking about it nonstop so you'd have to be a pretty dismal investigator not to know about them."

"The envelopes of money? Anonymous?"

"Exactly that. Well," she said, finally allowing the fullness of it to sink in and smiling broadly, "I got one."

"Berenice! That's ... it's very exciting! Do you mind if I—"

"Oh, I know you'll be asking for an accounting," said Berenice, smiling, dragging the moment out for full effect. "Let's just say that if I put the stack of euros on my kitchen table, the stack is not as high as a Napoleon but considerably higher than a calisson."

Molly and Berenice had much in common.

"Congratulations, then, that sounds ... well, it's incredible, isn't it? Has anyone got any ideas where the money is coming from? Or who is behind it?"

"I'm not going to spend it. Maybe not ever. What if we get ordered to return it? What if it's drug money or something like that? I shouldn't have told you."

Molly appreciated Berenice's face as beautifully expressive, but was unhappy to see it close down as firmly as though someone had slammed shut the shutters on a house.

"Not a word to anyone," Berenice murmured, and picked up the menu. "I'll have the steak tartare."

Molly repressed a grin. Berenice wasn't the easiest person she'd ever met, but there was something undeniably lovable about her. They chatted for a while about inconsequential things, including the weather, made their orders to the server—Molly asking for steak tartare as well—and watched people go by. Molly asked about Berenice's family and what she thought about Président Sarkozy and French politics.

She succeeded in not mentioning a single murder or person

connected with a murder, or even the mysterious envelope of money; she was mentally patting herself on the back for showing such restraint when Berenice said, apropos of nothing, "Just so you know, that woman who comes round to the Faures's—I warned you about her—she was mixed up with Matéo, before."

Molly's ears pricked up. "You mean Apolline Cuvalier?"

Berenice nodded.

"With Matéo Brule? How so?"

Berenice shrugged. "I don't know the ins and outs, obviously. I wasn't in the room with them. All I'm saying is, she used to come into our building. I keep an eye out for comings and goings. She used to come late at night. All dolled up, like she does. A tart, that's what she is, and I'm not afraid to say it."

Molly chewed a fingernail then took a slug of her second kir. "You're certain it was Apolline Cuvalier?"

Berenice waved a hand in the air and refilled her glass from the *pichet* of red wine she had ordered. "What I'm telling you is, she's nobody you want hanging around with your friend Michel. She's a bad piece of business, that one."

"Are you ... do you think there's some connection between Apolline and Matéo's murder?"

"Didn't say that. Don't know that. He was mixed up with the wrong people, and somebody strangled him. That's the beginning and end of what I know."

Taking a deep breath, Molly leaned back in her chair and gazed out at the Cours Mirabeau, then to the building on the other side where she had seen Apolline go in with the teenage girl.

"I doubt that," Molly said to Berenice. "I've got a feeling you know far more than you realize."

The old woman's eyes glinted for a moment and the corners of her mouth turned up almost imperceptibly.

Or maybe she does realize, Molly thought, and only wants to hold on to the information as long as she can?

𝕩 35 𝕩

After lunch (ending with a magnificent strawberry parfait piled with a hedonistic quantity of fresh whipped cream), Molly walked back with Berenice. They said their goodbyes beside her building, Molly looking up to Matéo's apartment on the third floor and wondering what, if anything, Apolline had to do with what had happened there. Now that the latest murder did not fit the pattern, it was time she fully let go of the serial killer/vigilante idea and buckle down to some actual investigation.

Molly used her key to open the Faures's door.

She heard crying.

"Adèle?" said Molly, coming into the salon and seeing Michel standing next to Adèle with his hand on her shoulder, as his sister sat in a chair with her head in her hands, sobbing. She did not look up. "Michel, what's happened?"

Please, not another murder?

Michel looked kindly at Adèle. "Dearest," he said to her, "I'm not going to try to think up something to make you feel better, because it's awful and there's no covering that up. Just ... talk to Molly, will you? She's a fan of Émile's as much as you are."

"Émile?" Molly felt her stomach drop for the second time that day.

"He was doing so well," said Adèle. "I mean, I'm not a doctor, obviously. But he looked so much better, didn't you think?"

"Yes," said Molly. "Definitely. Has ... something changed? I just saw him yesterday!"

"After Oscar stood me up, I went for a walk to try to compose myself." She paused and took a deep breath. "Eventually I stopped in to see Émile, and the doctor had just left," said Adèle, and choked on some more tears. "He's been given a month to live. That's it. A *month*."

"Oh no," said Molly. She pulled a chair over next to Adèle and sat down, putting her arm around her friend, and the two of them cried together while Michel went to make coffee.

"You know as well as anyone that it's not easy to move to a new city where you don't know anyone," said Adèle. "It's ... it's not something anyone does lightly, is it? Perhaps all of us who undertake such a move do it at least in part because we are trying to leave something behind? Something ugly?"

Molly nodded and wiped tears with her sleeve.

"There were moments when Michel and I thought we might have made the wrong decision. Aix is so lovely, and we wondered whether we had allowed aesthetics to guide us more than we ought to have. Because beautiful as it is, it's not like Castillac. It's a real city, with so many people, and it's easy to be lost in the crowd, fall through the cracks ... pick your cliché. We had not really grasped how much harder it is, at our age, to make the kinds of connections with people that make life worth living. We're not university students any longer, after all."

Molly managed a half-smile and slipped her arm around Adèle's waist. "And Émile is one of those connections," she said.

"He was the first person to reach out to us here. The only person, for many months. Even though he was already ill. He was not focused obsessively on his health, the way many sick people are—and please understand, I do not fault them for this, not at all. But Émile—he was different from most people. Somehow, he found a way to think of others even at a time of great strife for himself personally."

"I'm so sorry, and honestly struggling to make sense of it, he looked so good yesterday. In great spirits and the most energetic I'd ever seen him," said Molly. "And—what you say has been true for me, too, in my few weeks here in Aix. Émile is the one native of Aix I have made a friendship with. It feels like a real friendship, too, not simply following the social conventions."

"That is his great talent," said Adèle, and burst into fresh tears.

MOLLY MADE AN EXCUSE—WELL, a lie, not to put too fine a point on it—about needing to check back at a store for a shirt she had ordered, and slipped back outside. She had considered asking Michel and Adèle where she might find Patrice Joubert, but something had stopped her. They don't need to know everything I do, she thought, with a rather teenaged toss of her head.

So where to find him? Patrice hadn't struck Molly as a propitious source of information, but perhaps she had been hasty. He had seemed too wrapped up in his own importance to be anything like the keen observer she needed. On the other hand, he clearly enjoyed being in the middle of other people's business, and that might prove fruitful, if only she could find him.

Just after passing the Boulay house, she heard a door slam and turned to see Delano locking up and hurriedly setting off in the other direction. Molly turned and followed.

"Monsieur Boulay!" she said, when she had gotten close enough that she didn't have to shout.

Delano froze, staring down the street.

Molly touched his arm as she caught up to him, feeling his fear. "Monsieur Boulay, it's just me, Molly Sutton, guest of the

Faures's." She gestured at the Faure house, one door ahead of them. "We met the other day?"

Delano lifted his head slowly and looked near her face but without eye contact. Like a frightened animal, Molly thought. Apparently his abuser being dead was not enough to help him to feel safe.

"I'm on your side," she murmured in a soft voice.

Delano blinked hard several times. "They're saying she was strangled," he said in a low voice. "As though I would ever in a million years do such a thing."

"Who's saying that? The gendarmerie?"

"Coroner."

"Do you ... do you think you're going to be arrested? Sorry for being so direct, but if I'm to help you, I need to know what's going on."

Delano looked into Molly's eyes with the expression a ship-wrecked person might have seeing a boat headed his way. "Help?" he said, in the same quiet voice.

Molly took a long slow deep breath in, willing herself not to rush him. "How did you hear this news?"

"Well, it's curious—an anonymous call, first thing this morning. Man's voice, did not recognize it."

"But no visit from any gendarme?"

"Not yet. I'm afraid that afterwards I sat in the living room for hours, perched on the edge of a chair, waiting, unable to move."

"I understand." Something about this man broke Molly's heart, and she took one of his hands in both of hers. "It's quite frightening, thinking you're about to be arrested. For a crime you didn't commit," she added quickly.

His hand was trembling and Molly squeezed it. "Is there somewhere we could go to talk?" she asked softly. "For some privacy?"

Delano was staring at his shoe tops. He blinked slowly several times.

Patience, Molly said to herself, feeling none.

"Why don't you come to mine?" Delano said, with a poignant attempt to sound jolly, as though inviting her in to sample a fresh tart that was cooling on his kitchen table.

They turned back, Molly still holding his hand, which was clammy and cool.

"It's an odd time," he said. "Lived here my whole life. Was my parents' house, you see, I was actually born in the back bedroom, my mother having a fear of hospitals."

"Your parents, are they—"

"Long dead. Long, long dead." With his free hand, Delano wiped a tear from his cheek.

"I'm sorry," Molly murmured. She was curious about their stories, and about how Delano had gotten mixed up with someone who would beat him, but it was not the moment for all that. They reached his house and he let them in. The main room was not large. A fireplace, a worn settee, a small table by the door where Molly noticed a brown envelope, ripped open at the end, with no address. A couple of wooden chairs against the wall, a framed poster of a landscape with towering trees.

Delano sighed. "I don't believe I have invited anyone inside in years," he said. "Louise … she was not exactly … she was … not welcoming to guests. And she would not hear of spending money to give anyone food or drink. Oh, the fights we had about that, just after our marriage!"

Molly listened to his words and to what was underneath them.

"She did not like spending money?"

"Heavens no, she did not!"

"And you?"

He grinned and for a moment Molly could see a boyish side peek out. "For a nice meal? Some decent furniture? Yes, I most certainly would. What good is money just sitting in the bank?"

Molly nodded agreement. "First, let me say—you can't trust anything an anonymous caller says. So let's see if we can get verification from the coroner before getting too stirred up. Second, speaking of money—did you hear about some of your neighbors getting envelopes of euros in their mailboxes?"

"What?"

"According to Patrice Joubert, and verified by one of your neighbors, some people have been receiving envelopes stuffed with euros. Significant amounts of money. Do you know anything about that?"

"No, I do not. Are you accusing me of something?"

"No, no," said Molly. "I don't have any link between these envelopes and the murders. Just curious."

Curious about why, especially given the precarious place he found himself in with regard to law enforcement, Delano Boulay would lie about something that did not implicate him.

❧ 36 ❧

Chez Papa was packed to the gills for no apparent reason, and ranging down the bar were a lineup of Molly's favorites: Ben, of course, sitting next to Lawrence, who was halfway into his second Negroni; Florian Nagrand, the coroner, having a beer after a slow day—indeed, a slow month—at the morgue; Paul-Henri Monsour, the junior gendarme, digging into a plate of hot and salty frites; and Lapin, on his third glass of red, nursing his woes as he and his wife Anne-Marie had hit a bit of a rough patch.

All in all, the mood was typical, with various persons dealing with various contentments and various difficulties, ups and downs, sunshine and clouds.

Lawrence lowered his voice and leaned next to Ben's ear. "You might as well tell me. I do have spies, you know, so I'll find out sooner or later."

"What do you think I am hiding?" Ben said, with an unconvincing laugh.

"Obviously I do not know, or I wouldn't be importuning you to tell me. But I know it's something, I have eyes in my head. Does it have to do with La Baraque?"

"Oh no, nothing like that. I don't understand why everyone in the village thinks I'm capable of running Molly's business straight into the ground in a matter of days. I may not be the world's most naturally talented host, but I'm not a complete incompetent. For the record, there have been no more rat sightings. Not on my watch." He took a pull on his beer and gave Lawrence a look.

"Out with it then," murmured Lawrence. "I'd like to get this out of the way so we can move on to the matter of Briony Lark."

Ben rolled his eyes and snorted. "It's not a secret, as far as I know. They just haven't broadcast the news." Then he leaned next to Lawrence's ear and said, in the lowest voice he could and still be heard, "Frances is pregnant."

Lawrence's eyes got wide. "You're kidding."

"It's not as though getting pregnant is a monumental achievement. It does happen with some regularity," said Ben.

"Is this confirmed? Did one of them tell you, or you're just guessing?"

"I was chief of gendarmes, you know. I'm not without certain skills."

Lawrence sipped his Negroni, nearly signaling to Nico for a refresher before realizing he had plenty left in his glass. "I suppose the thing to say is that I'm happy for her. For them." He paused and made a theatrical sigh. "And I *am*. But we both know … this thing is a lot more complicated than that."

"Yes. Believe me. I probably should've told Molly straightaway—"

"—possible that she'll be nothing but pleased—"

Ben raised an eyebrow. "Sure she will."

Lawrence made another deep sigh. "You should tell her."

"Right. Or maybe I should let things play out the way they play out, and not interfere. It'll be fine. I'm sure she'll be thrilled, once … she gets used to the idea."

"It does feel a bit like the universe is slapping her in the face.

'Oh? You want a baby more than anything? Nah, we'll give one to your best friend who doesn't even like them.'"

Lawrence grimaced. He finished his Negroni and signaled Nico for another. He generally tried to stick to a limit of two, but these were trying times, and when he got up to leave, his legs were not quite as steady as when he came in.

Goodbyes took some time since Lawrence was friendly with everyone in the bistro. He waved to Ben as he left, deciding that there was no reason to tell him that he, Lawrence, was going to make sure Molly knew Frances's news as soon as possible. He would simply take a train to Aix and tell her himself, allow her to have whatever fit of envy she needed to have and get it out of her system before coming home and seeing Frances and Nico. It was surely not necessary that he do so; Molly was a grownup after all, and he had no doubt she would accept the news with joy once she had a moment to get used to it. But why not soften it for his dear friend, while using the excuse for a nice little trip south.

And as a side benefit, Lawrence did love a calisson, so he could get a few packages of those and kill two little birds with one stone.

A dèle had retired to her room. Molly stood in the hallway and listened for more crying, but as far as she could tell, the house was quiet. She went downstairs looking for Michel and found him in the salon, standing at the window.

"Are you waiting for someone?" Molly asked.

"You," said Michel, and when he turned, and Molly saw the expression on his face, she understood that he was not joking and that she needed to proceed with care. She smiled what she hoped was a friendly but not encouraging smile, and did not come any closer.

"Are you starving like I am?" said Michel. "Adèle's done for the night. How about we go out for a drink and something to eat?"

"Is there a particular place for good frites? I'm not in the mood for anything fancy. Just ... potatoes and salt, please, and plenty of it. With a kir. Perhaps a kir royale, it's been that kind of day."

"You're easy to please," said Michel, and gestured for her to leave the salon ahead of him. "There's a bistro right on Cours Mirabeau, if you don't mind a bit of a crowd."

"Not at all," said Molly.

Rue Niccolo was as calm as ever, with no one on the street save a teenager in a hoodie who disappeared around a corner.

They arrived at the bistro and took seats at the bar. The place was indeed crowded, with everyone from a Coke-drinking group of young women in jeans to older men in rumpled clothes nursing glasses of Pernod. A couple with a baby sat against the wall sharing a plate of frites, and from a distance, with relief, Molly judged the frites to be high quality.

"It won't surprise you to hear," said Molly, "that in the States you can get frites practically anywhere, but most of the time, they are blah."

Michel laughed. "You're not much of a patriot," he said, eyes merry.

"Why in the world is it be patriotic to believe a soggy, mealy frite is acceptable?"

"I would never suggest such a thing." Michel put his hand over his mouth. "Please, let's order and say no more about this. You're disturbing my appetite."

Molly laughed and spun on her barstool, which stopped pointing to her left; she could see behind Michel, where none other than Apolline Cuvalier was sitting down at a table for two with an older, distinguished-looking man. Molly swiveled back toward the bar, trying to keep Apolline in her peripheral vision. Was she on a date with that man? Molly stole another glance. It *looked* like a date, though Molly would be hard pressed to say precisely why.

What exactly was going on between Apolline and Michel?

Michel was studying the menu as though it was the main subject on his final exams and appeared to have no idea Apolline was so near.

The bartender sailed by with a bright orange drink topped with white foam, and Molly signaled to him. "A kir royale, when you have a moment. And a—Michel?"

"Whiskey, neat," said Michel.

Hm, thought Molly, not his usual.

She wished desperately that she were sitting close enough to eavesdrop on Apolline and the man. Furtively peeking in their direction, she could see the pair of them at the table, looking at menus. There was something cozy between them, something familiar, Molly thought. She leaned forward to see better. Her view was not perfect, but it looked like their legs might be touching underneath the small table.

Though the idea of Apolline and Michel being romantically involved had sickened Molly, now the idea that Apolline was cheating on Michel had her furious.

"It's a funny thing," she said, thinking aloud (not always the best idea). "Aix is rather like New York City, in a way. At least in a way that friends who lived there have described it—you've got this enormous city packed with people, you're lost in a sea of humanity—but actually, the city is a conglomeration of neighborhoods, and it turns out it's not at all unusual to run into people you know on the street."

"Well of course, because when you live in a neighborhood, you're going to the same fishmonger and the same newsagent. Are you starting to see people you know here in Aix?"

Molly swallowed hard. She'd made her own trap and then jumped into it. How to keep Michel from seeing Apolline?

Or—maybe it would be fruitful if he did see her? What was she trying to control, anyway?

This entire visit to Aix had been nothing but confusion, from beginning to end!

"Well," said Molly, "I don't want to cause any ... oh, never mind, I should just shut up. Just look behind you, but don't be obvious about it."

Michel sat up straight and turned on his stool. Molly wished she could see his face. He spun back around; his eyes were wide, but she could not read what he was feeling. "You mean Apolline?" He laughed, and Molly could tell the laugh was not genuine. "Are you—" he took Molly's hands and looked into her eyes. "Do you think there's something between me and Apolline?" He laughed, squeezing her hands. "You are ... you are the funniest, dearest woman!"

He leaned over and kissed her. Not on the lips but on the cheek, but as Molly would describe it later—only to herself—he kissed her cheek with *intent*.

"Are you ... are you saying there isn't anything ... that way ... between you?" Molly asked. "Not that it's any of my business."

"Depends on what you mean. Romantically, love? Not a bit." He laughed again, heartily, and this time Molly thought it was not phony. "Not even a little bit," he said, shaking his head with a wide grin.

"But I saw you kissing," Molly said, almost too quietly for Michel to hear.

He waved his hand dismissively. "Ah, I like kissing. Sometimes I feel ... I don't know the word exactly ... exuberant, I guess you could say. And the feeling rushes through me with such force and I want to grab the nearest beautiful and willing woman and kiss her. It doesn't necessarily mean anything." He looked at her carefully. "Do you think this makes me a terrible person?"

Molly laughed. "No, not terrible. Perhaps a bit reckless?"

"Perhaps if I were with the woman I most wanted, I would not be tempted to be reckless."

The bartender placed their drinks in front of them and gratefully they picked them up and sipped. Michel asked for two plates of frites and the bartender went off to fetch them.

"Michel. Perhaps this is overdue—I need to say—you do understand I am married—newly married, at that? And very happily so?"

He made a tragic face.

"And you do understand that I love you dearly and our friendship means so much to me. But ..."

"... I must content myself to yearning from the sidelines?"

"Sometimes you are very silly. Okay, you could put it that way. I understand that the whole point of flirting is to be indirect and make titillating hints, so just to be clear that I am not flirting, I will say it again, straight and directly: I am newly and very happily married. And that's how it's going to stay."

Michel nodded. He opened his mouth to rebut but then thought the better of it, then moved toward Molly and kissed her on the forehead. They sipped their drinks. It felt as though perhaps a line had been drawn under the past and they would able to start fresh, with some degree of ease restored.

Molly leaned back on her stool for another look at Apolline. "Who's the guy she's with, do you know?" she asked in a low voice.

Michel turned toward Apolline, not subtly.

"Michel!" Apolline cried, and Molly cringed.

Michel went to their table. Molly could not hear what was said but saw him kiss Apolline on both cheeks (not with intent) and shake hands with the man. She hoped he had the presence of mind to remember the man's name, but she had learned the lesson enough times that your average civilian does not pay enough attention to the important things. Their attention is easily diverted to the myriad things that are entirely secondary or tertiary or make no difference to anything at all.

"Victor Chopin," said Michel into Molly's ear before sitting on his barstool.

You don't say.

Molly took Michel's hand and pressed it. "Nice work," she said.

WHEN SHE AND Michel got home from the bistro, Molly faked a yawn and said she was going straight to bed. Michel, who for all his faults was anything but stupid, did not believe her for a second. Off they went to their bedrooms and waited some time to complete the charade, though Molly was anxious to get out to the streets; after the calm of the night before, she had a feeling tonight might be more eventful.

It had been a few days since the last murder. Was the wave of killings over? Did Rodolfo Gallatine or Yves Dupont or anyone at the Aix gendarmerie have the cases in hand? Was progress being made that civilians were not privy to?

Molly hoped so. At least—her better nature hoped so.

Such a shame about Marius Latour being a decent fellow. She supposed it was possible that the other murders were the work of a serial killer and Latour had been killed by someone else, but what was she supposed to do with that possibility? It made her feel ... and she did not like admitting this—defeated.

Doing her best to shrug that off, she donned her usual night-time costume, put the key and paring knife in her pockets, and crept downstairs, quietly closing the front door behind her.

Michel followed, only a smidgen less noisily than the night before, a little tipsy but intent on keeping Molly from harm.

It was just after midnight. Bright moonlight glimmered on the cobblestones at the opening to the alley where Molly stood, considering. Quickly she ducked down it, causing Michel to break into a trot to catch up. She had learned to walk without her sneakers squeaking, and once in the alley, she speeded up even more, reaching the center of the block where all the backyards converged. Hurrying, she cut down a small pathway perpendicular to the alley and crouched down behind a garbage can in the back of a stone house.

Molly had heard or felt the presence of someone following. Could be anyone at all, she thought. Thief, friend, gendarme. Drunk person. Killer. Absolutely no one at all.

The sound of footsteps got louder. Hesitant steps, once whoever it was had fully entered the alley and no longer had any streetlights to see by. The moon was on Molly's side and stayed hidden behind a bank of clouds.

Molly pressed herself against the stone wall, trying to make sure the garbage can completely hid her from view in case the moon popped out again. She held her breath but did not feel unduly frightened, telling herself she was in the middle of a city and all she had to do was shout for help if she needed it. Though a small voice, quiet and deep down, wondered whether people would rush out to help, in a city. Perhaps they were more likely to think someone else would step in, it wasn't their business.

The steps got closer and then stopped. Molly guessed the person was standing right at the small intersection where she had left the main alley. She strained to hear the steps continue, but they did not. She waited. She counted to twenty, slowly, but still heard nothing.

Was he waiting for her? Waiting for her to come out of hiding so he could pounce?

Molly rolled her eyes at herself. No one is going to be doing any *pouncing,* she thought. Chances are, whoever this is has some other reason for being out that has nothing to do with me. She stood up just as the clouds slipped away and suddenly everything was illuminated practically as though it were the middle of the afternoon. The alley was empty, and so were all the backyards as far as she could tell.

Taking a long, slow breath, Molly stepped from behind the garbage can, listening for all she was worth. Something streaked by to her left and she caught a cat's tail disappearing down the dark space between two houses. Her heart thumped.

More clouds appeared and slid over the moon, and in the darkness, she felt her way along, following the cat's path, one hand on each wall, praying she didn't stumble and worrying about which direction the person had gone and how he had managed it so quietly.

She reached the sidewalk and tried to figure out what street she was on, having lost her sense of direction. Checking both ways before stepping out under the streetlight, seeing no one, Molly breathed easier. It was quiet.

What am I even doing out here, she thought crossly. Well, I know the answer to that question perfectly well. I'm out here because I can't think of a single other thing to do. I'm out here because I feel helpless and useless and I can at least pretend I might accomplish something.

With a deep sigh, Molly turned back towards rue Niccolo. She went half a block, looking in every direction, listening.

She stopped. She turned her head, straining to hear.

A scraping sound. A sound of … metal on wood? And then … low murmuring.

Then silence.

She took a few steps toward the sounds, holding her breath, then stopped again. Moonlight dimmed, then brightened again, but Molly paid no attention, focused completely on what she was hearing and where the sounds were coming from. A few buildings down the block, there was another passageway, and quickly she moved down it, again using her hands on either wall to guide her.

The murmuring voices got perceptibly louder. The scraping stopped.

Molly kept going.

Just as she was about to come to the end of the building and the open space in the middle of the block, she kicked a watering can and the clatter was loud enough to raise the dead. Someone in the house shouted and lights went on.

Across the open space, which was crowded with indistinct shapes—some bushes, perhaps a fence, a charcoal grill—Molly thought she saw a figure disappear between two buildings. Quickly she followed.

And this time, at last, a bit of luck finally came her way, since the other end of the passageway was blocked by an ornate iron gate. Locked.

The figure, dressed in dark clothes so that Molly kept losing him in the shadows, reached the gate. Molly saw him grip it in gloved hands and shake it; the gate was old and strong, it rattled a bit but did not give.

I should probably turn around now, Molly thought to herself, as she hurried towards the dark figure in the hoodie, hand closing around the handle of the paring knife in her pocket.

SHE CAME CLOSER. The dark figure, back to her, was still gripping the gate, but not attempting to climb over it.

And then she was close enough, and the moon cooperative enough, that Molly could see exactly who was there, slumped with unmistakable teenaged extravagance, against the gate.

"Aleron!" she cried, a little too loud for one in the morning.

The boy shrugged. His eyes flicked at her and then away.

"What in the world are you doing out at this time of night? Do your parents—" Molly managed to stop herself from finishing that sentence and wasting any goodwill she might have earned with the boy the day she met him at the apéro.

Aleron lifted his chin. "My parents are bourgeois idiots," he said.

Molly couldn't help smiling.

"Perhaps they are," she said. "Does that have anything to do with why you're out roaming the streets when there are thieves and murderers about?"

"You're out here."

"I'm a private investigator. I'm supposed to be out here."

Aleron snorted, which, admittedly, hurt Molly's feelings.

"How do you know *I'm* not a murderer or a thief?" he said.

"Are you?"

The boy laughed. "Do you think murderers and thieves would answer that question honestly?"

"Well, you'd be surprised. Plenty of criminals have a real enthusiasm for letting other people know exactly what they've done, even when what they've done is something awful, not to mention illegal. It happens all the time, actually. In fact, in my professional opinion, I would say that the capacity of most people —criminals or not—to keep a secret, even when that secret is of real benefit to them, is quite limited."

"That's not me," Aleron growled.

"All right," said Molly.

They stood for a long moment in silence. She felt his loneliness and his frustration keenly and wished to help.

And perhaps he could be of help to her too?

"Aleron," she said slowly. "Is this a usual thing for you, coming out at night?"

He shrugged.

"I wonder … if you've seen anything. Heard anything. I've only been out for a few nights. I missed all the important stuff."

Aleron did not respond, but he made no move to leave.

"I mean, think of it, four murders in such a short span of time, in such a small geographical area. That's got to be … it's strange, you have to agree with that at least."

Aleron shrugged again. "It's got nothing to do with me," he said, with the dismissive self-centeredness so classic for his age.

"I wasn't implicating you. I was only wondering, since you're obviously a clever fellow, whether you've noticed anything … perhaps even something that at first seemed normal, but later, the thought of it comes back and sort of niggles at you. Know what I mean?"

Aleron cocked his head, which Molly took as a good sign.

"The murders don't interest me," he said.

"What?"

"I didn't know any of the people anyway," he mumbled. "And look, there are other people right in this neighborhood who are suffering. People who don't have enough money to get by, not really. What about them?"

Molly was taken aback. This was unexpected.

"I ... I'm sorry to hear that," she said. "My investigation is limited to the killings, though. I guess what you're talking about would require more of a political solution, which is outside my limits, I'm afraid."

Aleron hmphed in a way that made him sound like a grumpy old man, and Molly turned away so he could not see her smile.

"Will you walk me home?" she asked him. "A lady of a certain age probably shouldn't be out alone, what do you think?"

Aleron nodded but said nothing. Molly turned to walk down the passageway and he followed.

She stopped herself from taking his arm. "I keep ending up in these interior courtyards," she said. "And lose my sense of direction entirely. Every night I regret not bringing a flashlight, but I think I keep forgetting because I know it would not be discreet enough. Someone would probably call the gendarmerie thinking I was a burglar."

Aleron was not one for small talk, and he kept quiet as Molly chattered to him while they made their way back to the alley and headed toward the Faures's.

"Aleron!" someone whispered, close by.

The boy froze.

Molly grabbed his arm and tried to see who was there.

"What the hell?" the voice said. Molly saw a dark shape appear from behind some rosebushes.

"Run!" said Aleron, and the dark shape zigged one way and zagged another, heading not for the passageway with the iron gate but a different one on the other side of the house.

Molly held Aleron's arm with an iron grip. "Okay," she said, "it's time for a real conversation, my friend. And I want the truth."

꒳ IV ꒳

❧ 38 ❧

Molly slept until the sun had been up for hours, and then lay in bed thinking about what Aleron had told her. Occasionally she closed her eyes and let the mild street sounds float up through her open windows.

Then a crash. The sound of ... porcelain smashed? Inside the house?

Molly bolted upright. She must have misheard.

Another crash, then a piercing wail.

Molly leapt out of bed, threw on the dark clothes from the night before, and went into the hallway. Her expert eavesdropping skills were not required, as Michel and Adèle were going at it hammer and tongs, louder than Molly had ever heard them, in Aix or Castillac.

"And to think I welcomed her in this house!" said—or shouted—Adèle.

"It's not what you think," said Michel, more quietly.

"Oh really? It's spelled out right here on this piece of paper, isn't it?" said Adèle.

Molly crept down, where she could peek at them and hear every word.

"You do see, Michel? The grand total of our investment account, which is supposed to sustain us for the rest of our lives? You see that the number is less than *half* what it was only last month?"

"I ... it's ... Adèle ..."

"No, wait, my math is off. It's not even a third, dear brother. Let me say this as plainly as I can since the meaning appears to be escaping you: in the most frivolous and underhanded way imaginable, you have lost two-thirds of our money. *Two-thirds!*"

Michel walked over to the window and looked out, as though hoping someone would arrive to save him.

"Right, there you are, you've absolutely nothing to say for yourself. Same as it ever was, Michel. Always singing the same sad song. Poor you, being taken advantage of by some viperous female. What siren's song did she sing that would induce you to hand over so much of *our* money? You've been *defrauded*, Michel. Duped. Why didn't you just ask me—you know, your sister with the financial experience and knowledge?"

"You would've said—"

"Exactly! And then we would still be solvent."

Another crash, this time a soup tureen that, it is true, had a broken handle and an indifferent pattern.

"Did you ever think that *you* might bear some responsibility for these messes you get into? That it's *your* fault you get involved with these horrible women who take advantage of you?"

"Aunt Josephine was not some random person," Michel said. His voice was quiet, but Molly heard the fear in it, and the shame.

"I don't care! You still allowed it and participated in it. Just because she was our aunt didn't mean you were forced into going along with her every whim! The whole entire world can see the pattern of your life—everyone can see it but you! Apolline Cuvalier is Aunt Josephine all over again! How in the world can you not see that?"

Molly was tempted to try to referee but quickly talked herself out of it. Let them yell at each other and get that part over with.

Though to be fair, it was only Adèle who was yelling. "*Two-thirds!*" she cried, several times more. Another crash, and Molly could picture the porcelain hitting the wall. Shocked that Adèle was letting it rip in such a way, Molly was not judgmental of her; on the contrary, if one's brother has lost two-thirds of your money, throwing plates seemed, on the whole, like a harmless enough way to express one's wrath. At least it beat strangling or suffocating, right?

Michel did not meet his sister's shouts with shouts of his own. To Molly, his tone sounded like the quiet of defeat, and she rather wished he were shouting too, and the siblings were on more equal ground.

What in the world had he done? And Apolline—what was her game? Was she a scam artist, pure and simple, or was there more to it than that?

As THE FIGHT between the siblings raged on, Molly decided that the politic course of action for a houseguest would be to make herself scarce. She changed into a summer skirt and sandals and slipped out of the house without notice.

On the sidewalk, she heard Adèle shout "*two-thirds!*" once again.

The subject of money brought Aleron back to her thoughts, and she pulled out her cell and called Ben, wishing to hear his thoughts on the developing situations and how she should respond.

"Oh my, it's good to hear your voice," she said. "I thought you might be busy. How's Changeover Day shaping up? I feel just terrible that days keep slipping by and you're stuck with doing all the gîte work. Things here are ... *tricky*. I never expected to actually miss cleaning with Constance, but I do."

"I've got everything in hand," he said. "What's going on? Please tell me there have been no more murders."

"That opera Adèle wants me to see is next week. *Lucia di Lammermoor*, if that means anything to you. Anyway—well, several things, but let me start with this kid. Aleron Martel. He's, well, an absolutely *perfect* teenager so of course, I instantly adored him. Always got a sour look on his face, you know?" Molly laughed. "Anyway, I was out last night—"

"Molly!"

"I know, I know. I thought I would just make a quick turn around the neighborhood, go a bit earlier, just to make sure nothing was going on. The Latour murder was ... well, I guess it was just a few days ago, but it seems like longer. So, this neighborhood is typical: houses and shops arranged in blocks facing the street, with alleys and narrow passageways that lead to the interior of the blocks. These interiors are all different, block to block, there's no pattern—some have elaborate backyard gardens, some are paved, some sort of junky and not developed very well. In some, every backyard is walled or fenced, while others are open."

She paused. "Ben, are you there?"

"Yes. Waiting for you to get to the point."

Molly was taken aback. "Are you annoyed with me? Do you have something else to do right now that I'm keeping you from?"

"Sorry. That came out rude and I didn't mean it that way. I'm just curious about what you're going to tell me and you're really taking your time telling me what it is!"

Molly laughed, relieved, and sped up the story of the night before. "Anyway, I performed a bit of interrogation on Aleron, which turned out quite well, if I do say so myself."

"And?"

"Turns out *he's* the thief! The burglar who's been harassing the neighborhood for weeks. It's Aleron and his friend who've been breaking in and stealing for the last few weeks. A pair of *kids*."

"Huh. Not sure I'd use the word 'harass' to describe breaking and entering. Well, at any rate, it is good that you found him out."

"Wait, it's not like it sounds, it's more complicated. They're ... Aleron and his friend ... I guess you could call them teenage Robin Hoods? They're not stealing for beer money or some other selfish reason like you'd expect. They came up with this plan, it's, well, they call it political action, what they've been doing. Stealing, selling what they steal, and then giving the money to people in need. I'd heard from Patrice Joubert about these unmarked envelopes of cash showing up in people's mailboxes, and incredibly—because who ever heard of anything like this before?—it turns out Aleron and his friend are the ones responsible. 'Steal from the rich, give to the poor'—it's not just talk, they're actually literally doing it."

Ben didn't say anything for a moment.

"Hello?"

"Sorry, I'm trying to comprehend this. I mean ... I've arrested any number of teens over the years, as I think you know—"

"—Malcolm Barstow—"

"—only one of many. It's a difficult point in life, as we all understand once we live past it. Hormones, being on the brink of adulthood with everything that comes with that. Yet—I've never once heard of a case like this. *Political action* is what they're telling themselves?" Ben laughed.

"I think he's quite serious," said Molly. "He went on for quite some time telling me the political philosophy they believe is the basis for their actions. He's quite well read, I'll say that much. His friend's parents are in the antique business so he has a good eye for what will bring in quick money. And the bottom line—which I think you'll agree is impressive, no matter what your opinion of their plan—is that he and his friend believe that if you hold values, you should be willing to act on them. That if you claim to believe in something but spend your time playing video games or sitting in bars and doing nothing to actually support those beliefs ... well, Aleron has the utmost contempt for people like that."

"Teenagers wallow in contempt."

Molly shrugged. "Sure. But, well, it's true that he did help some people. One person who got an envelope was Berenice, and from what I can tell, she does struggle to make ends meet. The French social support programs are commendable, don't get me wrong, but they're not absolutely perfect, as I'm sure you'd agree."

"You're not advocating burglary," said Ben.

"Of course not. Though I do wonder what good a sapphire necklace is if it just sits in a safe all the time."

"Molly!"

"Sometimes I forget I'm married to a copper," she teased.

"Have you called the gendarmerie?"

Molly was quiet.

"Molly!"

"Well, I ... guess I have to? Aleron is a good kid. He may have come up with a bad plan, but his heart is in the right place."

"I'm afraid that good heart is going to land him in *La Santé*. From what you've said, we're talking multiple break-ins and many thousands of euros worth of property stolen. He's in a lot of hot water, I'm afraid."

Molly made a face. Ben was not saying anything she didn't already know, but she didn't like it. How could she turn the boy in? Yet, of course the Boisettes and the others should be able to get their belongings back, if that were even possible.

Would Berenice have to turn the money over to the authorities? Most likely.

"Well, let me change the subject for a moment," said Ben. He began a somewhat rambling story about meeting up with Madame Sabourin, Molly's neighbor. Molly tried to focus on what Ben was telling her, she really did. But on the street, people were walking by and she couldn't stop scanning the crowds looking for Apolline, or Delano Boulay, or the Plouffes. She couldn't stop trying to come up with a way to sit down with one of the detectives at the gendarmerie.

Trying to see why Apolline Cuvalier might have killed Matéo Brule or forced or hired someone else to do it.

Not to mention worrying about how to report Aleron and still protect him somehow.

"Look, I understand," said Ben, after asking a question and getting no answer. "Get back to what you're doing. We'll talk about this when you get home. And I hope you won't feel it as undue pressure if I say that I hope that will be very soon."

The thought occurred to Molly that if she went to the gendarmerie to turn in Aleron, possibly she could leverage the tip so that the gendarmerie would allow for collaboration on the murders. For the moment, she had some information they would very much like to get their hands on. What might it be worth to them?

Of course she did not want to use Aleron that way. Would need, somehow, to find a deal for him.

Not wanting to go back to the Faures's until she was sure the fighting had calmed down, Molly kept walking. She stopped at a vendor and tasted a bit of truffle salt. She moved quickly past the next vendor, which displayed beautiful handmade children's clothes.

Somehow Molly found herself outside Pâtisserie P and her stomach growled. The line was out the door and she stood at the end and happily turned her thoughts to pastry.

"I should have known I'd find you at the nearest pâtisserie," said a very familiar voice.

Molly whirled around. "Lawrence!" She threw herself into his arms and they hugged each other tight and then kissed cheeks.

"What in the world are you doing in Aix? I'm *so* happy to see you, I can't even tell you. I feel like I've been exiled from Castillac."

"An exile of your own making, I am at pains to point out," said Lawrence as they inched towards the threshold of the small shop. "So, tell me what's good here? I assume you've done a thorough inventory. I do love a calisson."

Molly stared at him. "Are you out of your mind? Those dry little bits of cardboard?"

Lawrence laughed. "How I've missed you. Please, don't hold back, I want to hear what you really think."

Molly got a salami and cheese croissant and was enraptured to find an exquisite version of her very favorite apricot pastry with a layer of custard cream, the apricots gently caramelized. Lawrence showed a rare ascetic side and ordered only a tuna sandwich on a small crusty roll.

A group of about ten people were walking up and down the Cours, changing "Do your job! Do your job!" holding signs that said: "Keep our neighborhood safe!" and "Flics suck!"

"I see the citizens are displeased," said Lawrence. "I don't blame them."

"I'm sure they fear for their lives," said Molly. "Understand-able." They walked down to the fountain, sat on the edge along with an artist drawing with pastels, and began to eat.

"So tell me everything! I've been having, well … things are complicated here. So much drama."

"Multiple murders, I hear?" said Lawrence.

Molly nodded. "Yes. And I haven't—but we don't need to go into all that." She took an enormous bite of her croissant and closed her eyes for a moment, appreciating the garlicky salami. "Plus Adèle and Michel are going through some things, too. So the visit has been a little complicated. I miss home like crazy. What's everyone up to? Do you think Ben's doing okay?"

Lawrence took a deep breath. He had only managed two bites of his sandwich, but he folded the wax paper around it and wiped his mouth with a paper napkin. "Molly, I could beat around the bush and think of some way to make this easier, but sometimes it's best to just rip off the band-aid. So here it is: Frances is pregnant."

Molly stopped chewing but otherwise did not change her expression. "She what?"

"Is pregnant."

"I heard you the first time."

Lawrence opened his mouth and then shut it again. He unwrapped the tuna sandwich, brought it to his mouth, and then lowered it without taking a bite.

Molly turned her head away, tears brimming up. She was so, so happy for Frances. And so, so envious.

"Frances always said she didn't want children," Molly said softly.

Lawrence nodded.

"Of course, I'm utterly happy for her."

Lawrence slid his sandwich into his pocket, ruining the lining, and put his arm around her. He said nothing, because really, there was nothing to be said.

WHAT MOLLY NEEDED JUST THEN WAS SIMPLY to be alone. Dear as Lawrence was to her, and as free as they were to share their feelings, even especially their less dignified, more embarrassing feelings—all Molly wanted was to close her bedroom door at the Faures's and flop down on the bed for a good cry. Not over Frances and her baby, but over the baby Molly did not have and was too old to have.

Lawrence took her hand. "I'm sorry to show up out of the blue like this, Molly dear, and I'm not expecting you to entertain me on the spur of the moment. If it's all right with you, I'd like to spend the day by myself, walking the streets of this gorgeous city. I need to track down some calissons—"

"Again, what in the world is the matter with you?"

Lawrence jerked his head. "Oh Molly. Was it a mistake to come? I just thought—"

"I'm talking about those dreadful calissons. Do I even know you at all?"

He grinned. "I am sure, my darling, that we will still be discovering each other many years hence. Now how about dinner? May I be so pushy as to invite myself to the Faures's tonight? I would like to be grand and invite everyone out for dinner, but I'm afraid my credit card might cry if I lose my head like that."

"Of course. I'll text you the address, it's right down rue Niccolo just over there. We usually eat around eight. But like I said, things have been ... unsettled of late. So if dinner won't work, I'll let you know."

They kissed cheeks and separated. Molly fairly flew back to the house, trying to hold her confused and violently zig-zagging emotions back while still in public.

All quiet at the Faures's, a lull in plate-throwing at least. A terrible image flashed through Molly's mind: Michel slumped in the salon, bleeding from the head, and Adèle upstairs packing, trying to flee the scene of the crime.

How could she imagine such a thing? What tricks our minds play on us when we're upset, she thought.

She shook her head, even slapped her cheeks lightly. Tried to laugh but failed. All this internal upheaval occurred in the brief time it took for her to climb the stairs and get to her bedroom, where she gently and with great relief closed the door and flopped on the bed.

Frances was pregnant.

Molly let the thought just sit in her mind, by itself, without any other thoughts crowding in. It wasn't easy. Her oldest, best friend, who had told her countless times that she had zero interest in being a mother, that babies were frightening and smelly creatures and she would happily leave the procreation of humanity to those more suited for and enthusiastic about the job.

Like Molly.

Molly heaved a gigantic sigh. Nobody ever claimed the world was fair, she thought, though it gave her little solace. Ever since she was a child, she had assumed she would have a family. Not out of any complacent desire simply to follow the conventional path, but because having children felt natural and right for her, something to look forward to when the time came. Only somehow—it never had.

Suddenly she was gulping with tears. Not because of Frances but for her own sense of loss, that felt endless, infinite, like she would never, ever get over it.

Eventually the crying stopped. Molly went to the bathroom and splashed cold water on her face, giving her mottled and puffy face a weak smile in the mirror. And then, quickly, before she could make any excuses, she sat down at her laptop and emailed Frances her warmest and heartfelt congratulations. She wished to add some sort of joke, because she and Frances joked with each other always. But in that particular moment, a joke was too much to manage and she couldn't think of anything. Besides, Frances knew this would be a difficult moment, which is exactly why she hadn't told Molly herself.

Hit send.

On to the next task, which was finding out how to contact Aleron.

Stepping into the hallway, she called out for Adèle and Michel and got no response. Berenice then, thought Molly, pausing for a moment at the top of the stairs, taking a deep breath, then another, and focusing all of her considerable powers away from her still-tumultuous emotions and instead on the problem of the murders.

❧ 40 ❧

The plate sailed through the air but to Michel it was almost floating, time having strangely, in the moment, slowed down, and he swerved his head to one side and dodged it without any difficulty. It smashed into the wall behind him, like the others.

"Adèle," he said, trying to keep his voice soft. "Adèle, chérie ..."

Adèle turned away, tears glittering in her eyes. "Don't come near me," she said, her voice low.

"You do understand—that I simply—I made a mistake? That I did not intend for any of this to happen?" he said.

No answer from Adèle.

"People do make mistakes," he continued. "I would venture to say—everyone does. That's not to excuse myself, or say it doesn't matter. Of course it matters. It's just the reality. And sometimes ... the mistakes are large. And I know, I know ... we are living together, have tied our lives together, and so inevitably, my mistakes become yours. I am so sorry for that. Truly."

Adèle did not move. Michel could not see her face.

"And also," he said, even more softly. "Your mistakes become mine. And so ... to change the subject a bit, I'm wondering, my sweet Adèle, if it is not time to think about ... taking steps?"

"*Steps?*" Adèle spat, her back still turned. "Your euphemisms aren't helpful, sweet brother. Just because you avoid calling a thing by its name doesn't take the meaning away. It's *your* behavior that's the problem, not mine! And I will tell you right now, loud and clear: I'm *not* going to the nuthouse."

"No, no, not that. A hospital. A *good* one, the very best there is. Where you could ... where they will ..."

Adèle shook her head slowly. She was smiling, which Michel very much hated to see because the smile had no joy, no warmth, and worse, reminded him of their mother. He watched her grip another plate with her fingers and braced himself.

"At least," he said, trying to make his voice as soothing as he could, "at least will you acknowledge that you could use some help, if proper help can be found?"

No answer, no movement from Adèle. Suddenly she stood up and announced it was time to get ready for a date with Oscar. Then she lifted another plate over her head, breathing heavily.

"It does seem as though if we're to have any plates left at all, something must be done," said Michel.

Another attempt at a joke that fell quite flat.

WHEN MOLLY CAME into the salon, Michel was at the window with his hands in his pockets.

"Bonsoir!" she said, perhaps a bit too heartily.

Michel did not turn towards her or speak.

What in the world, thought Molly. "Has something else happened?" she asked.

Michel shrugged. Then in a quick burst, he strode to the elegant drinks table in the corner of the room and poured himself a whiskey. A rather generous whiskey.

"Michel."

He took a long pull on his drink and covered his face with one hand. "I'm losing her," he said, barely loud enough for Molly to hear.

"Who? Sorry if I'm being dull-witted, I feel like I'm coming in halfway through."

"Adèle! She wouldn't stop. Just look!" Michel gestured to the broken porcelain on the floor and then to the marks on the wall where the plates had hit.

"Oh no," said Molly, at a loss. "Where is she now?"

"Getting ready for a date with Oscar. He's taking her to Janvier."

"That's the very expensive place over on rue Sanborn?"

Michel nodded. He drank off the rest of his whiskey and poured himself another. "You see, we have been down this road before. It's ... who can explain these things? ... it seems that despite Adèle's desiring a boyfriend, seriously and of course understandably, naturally—it seems that having any kind of romantic relationship ... even if only in her own mind ... sets her off."

"What do you mean, 'in her own mind'? And 'sets her off'?"

He sighed deeply and went back to his position by the window.

"She does seem very tense lately. I thought it was because of the murders."

Michel's shoulders moved in a barely perceptible shrug.

"Is there ... I notice you looking out to the street, like it's a part-time job," said Molly, trying to lighten the mood. "Are you watching for something in particular?"

"I discovered her last night, at 3 a.m., polishing silver and arranging flowers in the kitchen."

Molly frowned. "3 a.m.? Why?"

Michel shrugged again, theatrically. "Why anything? She's not sleeping. Plus she's got this thing, this new thing, about secrecy."

"Secrecy about arranging flowers? I don't get it."

"Exactly. There *is* no getting it. Because it's ... you know I hate saying this ... it's crazy. Unhinged."

They heard the clattering of Adèle coming downstairs in a hurry. She sailed past the salon without so much as a glance. Molly gave Michel a look, and as the door banged shut, she said, "I'm ... I'm going to catch up to her—" Michel did not answer. Molly understood that he was quite drunk. He put a hand to the wall to steady himself.

Something has got to be done, she thought to herself as she let herself out. My friends are completely falling apart right in front of me. She saw Adèle just at the end of the block and walked quickly to catch up to ask if she was all right—she wasn't all right, that was obvious enough, but at least Molly could express concern, give Adèle a chance to open up. Molly hurried, but the block was a long one and Adèle had a head start. She was walking with her face turned to the ground, legs moving quickly, arms rigid.

When Molly turned the corner, she was relieved to see Adèle not far ahead, though Janvier was in the middle of the block and she wanted to reach her before Adèle went in to meet Oscar. She was about to call out when Adèle walked right past Janvier without slowing down or so much as glancing in the door.

What? I have to add this to the growing pile of bafflements? thought Molly. She's not meeting Oscar after all? Had she told that to Michel for some reason when it was not true? Or had Michel misunderstood?

What in the world was going on? And where was Adèle going?

❧ 41 ❧

Molly was on her way back to the house when a slim figure in a hoodie approached.

"Bonsoir, Aleron. You act as though even the faint sunshine of dusk is poisonous," said Molly, ever amused, pointing at the hood.

Aleron scowled.

"I have ... let's call it a proposal. Do you want to come in? Only Michel is there, and he will give us privacy."

Aleron shook his head. "Follow me," he said, leading her away from Cours Mirabeau.

Molly walked behind him, trying to keep up. Aleron was lanky and long-legged, and Molly was not. His legs looked almost painfully thin in his black jeans, and though as far as she knew the boy was well fed and had decent parents, she felt a burst of compassion for the young man that made her chest ache.

After some twists and turns down a narrow street Molly had not discovered before, they came to a little pocket park tucked in between a small cottage and a much grander house. A cherry tree was in full bloom, and they settled themselves on a wooden bench underneath it.

"Lovely," said Molly.

Aleron scowled.

"You go first," said Molly. "What's on your mind?"

Aleron smoothed his palms on his thighs. Molly could feel how nervous he was.

"Look," he said. He glanced up at the roof of the small cottage, where Molly saw some tiny plants growing among the shingles. "I just ... I don't know how to go about convincing you, but so ... I want to ask, if you please, Madame Sutton ..."

Molly cocked her head.

"... if you would *please* not report us. Me and Luc. To the *flics*. I mean, look, I know that politically, you're not ... like, this whole thing was a project we came up with and had nothing to do with any of this other stuff, with the murders or anything like that ... we're actually accomplishing something good, you know? At least we're trying. We're working to make things more *fair*."

"I'm not sure the Boisettes would agree with you about that." She held up a palm to stop him from interrupting. "I do give you credit for wanting to do a positive thing. I'm not criticizing your intentions. And I don't want to have a discussion about the merits of what you've done because that won't get either of us anywhere. My opinion doesn't matter anyway. The fact is, you and your friend are in a heap of trouble. Serious, life-changing trouble. Do you understand that the value of stolen property is a determining factor in judging the severity of a crime? I mean—you didn't just pinch a few apples from a fruit stand. You stole very valuable jewelry. And silver."

"Well, a few apples wouldn't have solved anything at all, would they?"

Molly shrugged. "I'm not talking about your goals. I'm talking about the trouble you're in, right now. That you have to face up to and make some decisions about."

"If you think we're turning ourselves in—never. We'll leave town."

Molly watched some cherry blossom petals drift to the

ground. "Do you really think you're going to get away with it?" she said softly. "How did you imagine this was going to end?"

Aleron looked at the ground. He scuffed his sneaker and looked away.

"You may have no respect for gendarmes, but they aren't all idiots," she said. "They know who accepts stolen goods, they can track things in ways you can't imagine. I'm sure you and your friend wore gloves and took precautions—I hope you did!—but it's virtually impossible to break and enter and spend time in a building and not leave any evidence of your presence behind. You must know how easy it is to find DNA these days. Don't you watch any cop shows on TV?"

"Television is the opiate of the masses."

Molly grinned. "Indeed. But perhaps spending some frivolous hours being sedated with some good TV might have stopped you from carrying out this plan, which was, I'm sorry to say, doomed from the start."

Aleron jerked his face towards hers. "What, do you know something? Have you already reported us?"

"I have not. But I will have to, eventually. I'm sorry about that, but my feelings about it, as I said, aren't relevant. I respect your values and intentions, Aleron, I honestly do. But the methods ... the important point is: I fear you are likely looking at a long prison sentence that will have no benefit to anyone."

Aleron looked so young, in that moment, that Molly could see what he had been like at age five. She wanted to hug him but did not.

"It's just that you're the only person who knows," Aleron pleaded. "What if we promise to stop? Will you not tell on us if we swear we won't do it anymore?"

Molly shook her head. "I'm afraid I can't do that. And listen—this is not why I'm not going to keep quiet, but I'm curious—did you try to break into the Faures's?"

Aleron looked uncomfortable. "But we didn't."

"You scraped up the paint. I heard you."

Aleron looked down at his shoes and mumbled, "I told Luc you lived there. Go somewhere else."

Molly felt tears spring to her eyes, moved by the boy's loyalty to someone he barely knew. She tapped her fingertips on her thighs, considering. "Tell me how you got into the Boisette's safe? From the way people are talking, it sounds like the flics are focused on professional burglars. Burglars with serious skills."

Aleron grinned. "Luc's a total nerd. Flunked out of school but can teach himself anything. You've heard of the internet?"

Molly smirked. "Well, good for him. I hope you can both stay out of the slammer—maybe I have an idea that might benefit us both. Something I'd like to ask you to do that might help your situation."

Aleron looked wary, but he was listening.

"There's no question that the authorities are desperate for these murders to come to an end," Molly continued. "The whole city is clamoring for justice, people are understandably afraid, and there has to be a great deal of political pressure to solve the murders and put an end to this violent chapter in Aix's history. If you could be instrumental in that process, in helping determine who is responsible, perhaps things will go a little better for you. Taking responsibility, trying to help the cause of justice—it's the sort of thing judges very much like to see."

"And how am I going to do that? I'm all ears," said Aleron, his breaking voice dripping with sarcasm.

It was a credit to Michel, and lucky for me, thought Molly, that when life gets tense, he ramps up his efforts in the kitchen.

"So very French of you," she said to him while helping him wash butter lettuce for the salad.

"We take consolation wherever we can get it," he said, his face glum. Adèle was back. She had offered no explanation about the date with Oscar and her fury had barely relented. She was not throwing plates, not muttering *two-thirds!* every few minutes, but her expression was stony. Even while she sat quietly, you could feel the rage bubbling along, with no sign of abating.

"At least we still have enough plates for dinner," Michel whispered to Molly, which was almost, but not quite, enough to make them laugh.

Lawrence rang the bell and Adèle let him in with such *froideur* that Molly overcompensated to try to make him feel welcome. He and Adèle had known each other in Castillac only as acquaintances, and Adèle was still sensitive about the Castillacois knowing more about her family history than was comfortable. The primary reason for moving away, for Adèle if not Michel, was precisely to avoid having to face people she did not know well but who knew all about Aunt Josephine's murder, her mother who killed her, the entire sordid family saga. It was still talked about in Castillac, years later.

Adèle heaved an enormous, put-upon sigh, crossed her arms, and looked out the window. She squinted. Molly noticed the fingers of one hand trembling. Michel stayed in the kitchen finishing up dinner while the two women and Lawrence sat in the salon awkwardly exchanging pleasantries until the discomfort reached a sort of agonizing peak.

Lawrence stood up. He fluttered his fingertips, something he did when he was nervous.

"Are you late for an appointment?" Molly asked, trying to be funny, but the remark fell flat.

"Perhaps," said Lawrence. "I'm very sorry, Adèle. I've come at a bad time and the last thing I intended was to make a nuisance of myself. I think I'll just pop back to my hotel and take a long, luxurious bath. It was good to see you again, and I hope we'll meet again sometime in the future."

He made a courteous half-bow and walked quickly toward the

door. Molly looked wide-eyed at Adèle, waiting for her to stop him, to apologize, to say something ... but she did not.

"Lawrence!" Molly called, going after him.

Michel appeared with a tray of *gougères*. "What have you done with our guests?" he asked his sister, yet another joke that fell quite flat.

❧ 42 ❧

The next morning, relieved to leave the Faure house, Molly made Émile the first stop, eager to press him on the subject of Apolline.

"I'm so utterly happy to see you," said Émile, as he and Molly settled into their chairs with cups of espresso. "When I'm feeling poorly, I don't mind being cooped up quite so much, but on a day like this, when for some reason I've got a little burst of energy— it's an agony to be stuck in this little house every second, cut off from everyone. So—please—tell me everything, dearest heart! What is happening on rue Niccolo, in Aix, in la belle France, and the world!" He threw his arms wide and grinned at her.

Molly laughed. For all his dire prognosis, the man seemed more full of life than most people. "I'm afraid that'll take some time. Where to start?" She sipped her espresso and smiled back at him. "My grasp of world affairs, at the moment, is a bit weak. Haven't had time to keep up with the news much lately."

"How are Michel and Adèle faring? Are they still finding Aix to be congenial, after all the recent unrest? I haven't seen Adèle as often as usual. I hope I haven't done something to put her off."

"Oh, I'm sure not. She was quite upset by the news of your prognosis," Molly said. "As am I."

"Ah, of course. What people cannot understand, who have never received such news, is how deeply sorrowful the dying are, not just about ourselves, but about being forced to upset people with bad news. The feeling ... it's as though we're disappointing everyone we love, which is the last thing we want to do. It's all absolutely silly since obviously no one escapes death. It is strange, but—and please understand, I say this making no claim to be a saint, or anywhere approaching one—telling others the bad news is far worse than accepting the news oneself."

Molly nodded, thinking about his words. "Humans are funny creatures, aren't we? We know death comes for all of us, but none of us actually believes it. Not deep down. It happens to strangers, not people we love. Not *us*."

"Just so. Even now, I struggle with it. At the last appointment, my doctor was ... well, let us simply say that he did not offer me any shred of hope, and leave it at that. Again, not making myself out to be special—I do not fear death, I have had time to orient myself to it, and made my way over that daunting fence, thankfully. But still, even after the words of the doctor—which as I said, offered no comfort or hint of possibility, no chance for escape no matter how slight—even still, I find myself thinking that for *me*, somehow, some way, there will be an exception ..."

Molly and Émile smiled at each other, and she felt the warmth and the sorrow in it. She reached for his hand and gave it a squeeze.

"If you're game, there is something pressing I'd like to talk over with you. That might help with the case. With at least one of the murders."

"Please," said Émile, his eyes sparkling.

"Well, it concerns the Faures, sort of indirectly. It's about Apolline Cuvalier. Do you happen to know her?"

Émile looked at the corner of the ceiling while considering. "Ah. Apolline. An interesting person."

"How so? I'm curious about your perspective."

"Well, you could simply call her ambitious, and leave it at that. If you wanted to go in more deeply, you could say that she enjoys using people for what she can get out of them, and then tossing them aside. She is a manipulator, a rather grand one, and from the little I have seen, I would imagine that often, she succeeds in achieving her goals."

"So, not a fan," said Molly with a quick laugh. "You sum up my thoughts exactly. The question is, how far does she go? How about her connection to Matéo Brule? You know they were involved in some way, though I don't know whether it was sexually, romantically, or just business."

"With a person like Apolline, these things often do not have clear boundaries. It could be any or all of them. Do you have any particular reason to think she murdered Brule?"

"Well, no actual evidence, beyond her association with him. But that doesn't mean she didn't. Or didn't arrange it."

"Murder for hire?"

Molly had a vision of Ben shaking his head. "No, no, that's getting way ahead of ourselves. All I'm saying is that I don't trust her, and I'd like to know more about her connection to Brule. I can't say she's a suspect, but ... she keeps popping up where she does not belong. And she has ..." Molly paused, not wanting to spread her friends' dirty laundry all over town. "She has behaved badly with the Faures. Lured Michel into some bad investments."

"Plenty of untrustworthy souls everywhere, I'm afraid. Even ourselves from time to time, don't you think?"

Molly shrugged off a feeling of impatience. She enjoyed Émile's philosophical rambles but at the moment was after less ethereal conversation.

"I'm curious, Molly. Not to take you off track—but would you say that intuition plays a large role in your investigations, generally? If that is not too personal a question?"

"Not too personal at all," said Molly. "My husband Ben and I have discussed this endlessly. Because intuition is very, very valuable to an investigator. It can be a way that the less accessible part of your brain works some things out, makes connections that your rational brain cannot. But—it can also be dangerous, where without realizing it, you allow yourself to be influenced by feelings that aren't actually relevant or are biased.

"Anyway, the short answer is yes and no. And as my intuition applies to Apolline Cuvalier, I believe she is guilty. Maybe only guilty of financial fraud, which might have nothing to do with Brule. Or maybe it does."

"Have you had any luck talking to people in the neighborhood? I'm sure it's not easy trying to get anyone to talk to a stranger, and an American on top of it!"

"True enough. I've been able to do quite well in Castillac, but Aix is so much bigger, and my accent is jarring to people, and yes, it's been difficult. I wish I could swing by your friend Gallatine's office and have a long chat with him."

They sat in quiet for a few moments. Molly's mind would not settle.

"I hesitate to say anything," Émile said quietly. "You know my affection for Adèle, certainly. Although we only just met when they moved here, my relationship with her has been a real treasure in my life. She comes and spends time sitting and talking, without impatience, without any sense that she's just checking a box on a list and can't wait to get on to the next thing, the way it is with some. Yet ... at the same time ..."

Molly cocked her head.

"Well, let's see, how to put it gracefully. The last thing I want to do is speak ill of her, so please understand that is not my intention." He took a short breath. "On a number of occasions, Adèle has struck me as ... not quite stable, do you understand me?

Mentally, emotionally not quite ... as she should be. I don't want you to think I am judging her! But I do fear ..." he looked down at the floor. "She appears rather fragile, is all I mean to say."

Molly nodded. "She's been quite upset lately. Though surely she has plenty of good reason to be upset." She remembered the night before, when Adèle had been so rude to Lawrence, but decided to keep it to herself.

Émile shrugged. "Well," he said, eyes bright, "I have some news myself to give you, that I selfishly hope you haven't already heard so I can get all the credit for passing it along."

"Yes?" Molly polished off her espresso and put the cup down on a mahogany side table.

"Rodolfo Gallatine was kind enough to stop by yesterday evening." He paused, smiling, to see if Molly was curious.

"And?" she said, alert.

"And Rodolfo says an arrest is imminent. The way he describes it, police work plods along behind the scenes and everyone thinks nothing is happening, but the work is getting done, it's painstaking and slow and sometimes it goes on with no good result ... but not this time. He is confident they have the guy."

"So the killer is a man?"

Émile spread his palms on his thighs. "He did use that pronoun, I believe, yes. Though I must also issue a small disclaimer that my treatments have not been terribly kind to my brain, and I might be mistaken."

Molly furrowed her brow. "Did Gallatine say which murder the arrest is for?"

Émile made an exaggerated shrug. "He does not shower me with details, I'm afraid."

Molly frowned. Had Gallatine made progress with the Trudeau murder? Or Latour? Or Boulay? Brule? It was impossible, this situation! Too many bodies! Too many suspects!

Molly had to clamp her mouth shut to avoid slandering Rodolfo Gallatine, whom she had no reason to distrust. She understood that her irritation was about desperately wanting to be the investigator with the guilty party in her sights, not perched on the sidelines, a spectator, nothing more.

WITH DETECTIVE GALLATINE on the verge of making an arrest, Molly figured she might as well start packing for the train back to La Baraque and Ben. Even if Gallatine had only solved one murder, she thought, it's high time to accept defeat and get back to my real life.

The prospect of home did give her a warm feeling in her heart, but, Molly being Molly, it was not quite enough to dispel the despondency at not being able to contribute even the tiniest bit to an arrest. She felt like a failure.

Just one last thing: she would go to the gendarmerie and see what she could do for Aleron. Straight in through the front door, no more excuses. And if the conversation opened an avenue for her to participate in the remaining investigations, that would be icing on the cake.

There was a bit of hubbub around the entrance, with a few uniformed gendarmes heading out in a hurry, past another group of protesters shouting and waving signs in the air. "Do your job and keep Aix safe!!" "Murderers behind bars!!!" People were frightened and angry, and who could blame them?

She approached the counter, pausing for a moment to consider which detective she wanted to speak to. "Is Detective Dupont available?" she asked, figuring she would go with the lead on the case. The man behind the counter did not look up. He pushed a button and mumbled into a headpiece, then told her to wait on a bench by the door, Dupont would come when he could.

Molly tried working on a list of questions for Detective Dupont but gave up, more comfortable winging it once she could see Dupont's expressions and reactions to their conversation. She was hoping for a friendly sort of man, who would share her belief in Aleron and want to help him as well as solve the murders. Finally, a small woman with her hair in a tight bun came out from around the counter and pointed her to Dupont's office.

"Bonjour *Inspecteur* Dupont, thank you for seeing me." She went quickly through an introduction, telling him something of her experience working with the gendarmerie in Castillac, while watching him carefully. He was good-looking—what was it about gendarmes?!—though she sensed some hardness, some sternness in his character, as though he would not suffer fools, or mistakes, or a badly mixed drink, gladly. Or at all.

"… I have loved visiting your beautiful city and—" she saw he was irritated and sped to the point—"anyway, if I can be of any help at all, I want to do so. I'd like to ask a rather delicate question: if a person is guilty of a criminal act, nonviolent but serious, would I be correct in thinking that if that same person could give information leading to an arrest in a different criminal act— murder, let's say—then perhaps some leniency might be forthcoming?"

Dupont stared. Molly had the impression he was clenching his fists under the table. Yes, he was good-looking, but he did not have the softness around the edges that Ben had. Not softness exactly, it was more … empathy. A willingness to see the pathos behind terrible acts, even if the person committing them had to be arrested.

"What I'm asking is whether a perpetrator's regret at his actions and willingness to further justice might be helpful in the eyes of the law?"

Dupont blinked, letting his eyes stay shut for a long moment. "Madame Sutton, I do not know what may have given you the idea that I have time in my day for these vague and hypothetical ramblings. I can assure you I do not." He stood.

Molly scrambled to her feet, her face pink. "Well, I heard that Gallatine is on the point of an arrest for at least one of the murders, so congratulations for that."

Dupont cocked his head a fraction of an inch, narrowed his eyes, but said nothing. Molly left the station with as much dignity as she could pretend to have.

Well, that couldn't have gone worse, she thought, heading back to the Faures's.

And also ... Frances was pregnant.

"You look like you've lost your last friend on earth," said Berenice, approaching Molly on the sidewalk, broom in hand.

Molly tried to smile. "Oh ... I'm ... it's just ... well ... you have these ideas about yourself, and sometimes events occur or don't occur and you realize that these ideas aren't maybe as real or as true as you think they are."

Berenice cocked her head. "Philosophical," she said, and began to sweep even though she was not in front of her own building.

Molly heaved a sigh. "My best friend is going to have a baby."

Berenice shrugged.

"Which of course is wonderful news. But you know, she never wanted children. Yet that's what she's going to get."

Berenice shrugged again. "Madame Sutton, you're old enough to know—anything in life, it's got pros and cons. You marry, or not. Have children, or not. Move to another country, or not. Pros and cons, no matter which way it goes."

"Philosophical," said Molly with a small smile. The image of Dupont narrowing his eyes at her flooded into her mind, and she could only wish that Frances's baby was the only thing to feel unsettled about.

"You haven't said much about Louise Boulay," said Berenice. "You got something against Louise?"

"I caught Delano in a lie. He claimed to have no knowledge of the envelopes of money, when I saw one sitting on a table in his living room, just as you described it. Why lie about something like that, unless you have a penchant for hiding the truth? I have to admit that since then, I've felt less solid about his innocence. I mean, come on, he was being routinely abused. He has the strongest motive possible. Actual, real-live self-defense is about the best motive there is. And of course, he had means and opportunity as well."

"You told me he said he didn't do it, that he loved her."

"Mm. Yes, but that's a liar talking. The truth is, Berenice—I have no idea."

The women watched a pigeon hop along the sidewalk looking for crumbs.

Berenice kept sweeping. "And then there's Apolline Cuvalier," she said.

Molly waited. A tiny, indomitable spark of hope flickered in her chest.

"Well, I'll tell you, you got me thinking about her," said Berenice. "Apolline Cuvalier was in and out of my building, all times of the day or night. Sometimes bringing girls with her. Girls at that awkward age, no longer children but not yet grown up, if you see what I mean. And men. Usually older, dressed in good suits."

"She was bringing these girls to Matéo Brule's apartment?"

Berenice swept ferociously for a moment, then leaned on the broom. "I didn't like it. It didn't look right, to my mind, girls that age should be home in bed."

"Was one of those girls Liliane Chopin?" Molly asked quietly. "Was she going to Brule's before he attacked her—they knew each other?"

Berenice didn't answer at first. Then, turning her back and sweeping along the base of the building where dirt tended to pile up, she said, barely loud enough for Molly to hear, "If you put a glass on the ceiling, and press your ear to it, you can hear every word of what's being said above. I imagine an investigator like yourself knows a trick like that already."

It's not as though police detectives were infallible, Molly thought. Gallatine *could* be mistaken. Errors happen all the time,

NELL GODDIN

intentional and not. And I don't even know which murder he's got someone for.

She understood full well that she *wanted* Apolline to be guilty. But that didn't mean the woman wasn't innocent.

"Okay," said Molly, taking a deep breath. "How about I take you to lunch, and you tell me everything you know. You've been holding out on me, Berenice, and that has got to stop."

"Bistro Maxime and you've got yourself a deal."

ALAS, the conversations Berenice reported were a little spicy but nothing actionable or even close to it. Molly enjoyed a garlicky sausage and an enormous pile of perfectly cooked frites, a green salad with that signature lemon-mustard dressing that any French restaurant makes flawlessly, but all Berenice had to give her were wispy bits of nothing. Talk of margin calls and float along with some ham-handed innuendo.

They were tantalizing bits of nothing, Molly had to give her that. But at this stage, tantalizing was far short of what was required. Apolline and Brule had partied together, they had frequently stayed up all night, it sounded likely that drugs were involved. Apolline had brought underage girls to Brule's but Berenice could not confirm that one of them had been Liliane Chopin. Or that anything illegal had taken place, beyond the drugs. She had swindled Michel, that was clear enough, and Molly didn't think it was a leap to guess that the men in good suits might be part of the financial fraud, whether helping Apolline set it up, or as victims themselves.

And if the relationship with Brule broke bad? Let's say she and Brule had a spat about something, and he threatened to blab to the authorities about her financial scam. He wouldn't even need to know that much about it for her to want to shut him up.

"The thing is," Molly tried to explain to Berenice as they considered the dessert menu, "I've heard through the grapevine that an arrest is imminent, and the target is male, so not Apolline. Now of course, my information could be incorrect, or the arrest is for one of the other murders. Or the detective could be making a terrible mistake. Heaven knows he must be under a ton of pressure to solve the case as quickly as possible. There were protesters outside the gendarmerie earlier today.

"But in order for me to stop that train and divert attention to Apolline—that will take something dramatic, you understand? Something rock solid. Something beyond what I've got. It feels like I'm on the right track; I just can't quite connect the dots."

She remembered seeing Apolline with her hand on the back of that girl as they went into the Chopin mansion on Cours Mirabeau just the day before. A pushy gesture, even proprietary. It had struck Molly as all wrong even though on the face of it, simply putting a hand on a back was harmless enough, and with the right person, might be merely affectionate.

A strawberry parfait had just been set in front of Molly when her cell buzzed.

"Excuse me," she said to Berenice. "Hello?"

"It's Aleron."

"You have anything?"

"Meet me at the same bench. I'll be there in ten."

He hung up.

Molly looked at her watch and then longingly at her parfait.

"Berenice," she said, hopping up and pulling out her wallet. "I'm sorry to rush off but I've got no choice. Thanks for everything and I'll talk to you soon." She put a pile of euros on the table, gave a brisk wave, and set off for the bench under the cherry tree, her heart pounding.

❧ 43 ❧

"So yeah," said Aleron, nodding, his face barely visible under his hood. "I don't know, did you expect me to find evidence she's a murdering maniac? Because I didn't exactly find weapons dripping in blood. But still, Apolline's was a little fishy."

"Tell me." Molly scooted to the edge of the bench, holding her breath.

"Her apartment's in a good building. It's a surprise, how bad most people's security is. Luc and me, we got in easy through a window in back."

"The less you tell me about breaking the law, the better."

Aleron rolled his eyes. "You're the one who—"

She put a hand on his arm. "I'm not criticizing. Please, go on."

"OK, like I said, the apartment is rich, expensive. But it doesn't look like anyone lives there, really. I mean—it's not settled in, like."

"Describe it for me?"

"Cardboard boxes stacked along the living room wall. Some expensive clothes hung up on portable racks, also in the living room. There's nothing on the walls, no knickknacks, no photographs. Nothing in the refrigerator except a bottle of water and a few bottles of champagne. It's *bare*, see? Like nobody's actually moved in. Or maybe, whoever did is about to move out. Half packed up."

Molly nodded, thinking.

"That's about it, really. There was one little thing you'll probably be interested in," said Aleron.

"Yes? Are you going to make me beg?"

"In the bedroom, there was a small table with a drawer next to the bed. Walnut, I'd guess, ugly. Anyway, the drawer had the usual stuff—tweezers, some coins, a pair of glasses. And also some little plastic vials with colored tops."

Molly waited. "Is that supposed to mean something to me, little plastic vials? What are they for?"

Aleron laughed. "For a private investigator, you live a sheltered life."

"Yeah okay but what are they? So far there haven't been any poisonings, if that's what you're getting at."

"They're for coke. Or more likely—crack. I'm not into drugs, personally. But I know that's what those vials are for."

"How many?"

"Five or six?"

"Oh." Molly heaved a sigh. "That's not exactly enough for drug-running, is it?"

"Maybe not, but it's still illegal."

"Says the expert in the law," said Molly with a quick grin. Aleron rolled his eyes.

They sat quietly, lost in thought, the city sounds of Aix murmuring around them. The cherry tree dropped some petals. Molly had hoped for something better. Something she could show Dupont and Gallatine and make their heads turn.

Molly said, "So just to sum up, your take is that it's a hideaway, or maybe a party space—never meant as a place to live?"

"Sure, could be any of those," said Aleron. "An interim place to stay before moving on." His hands were jammed deep into his pockets, and he crossed his skinny legs. "I mean, how would I know? I looked around for murder weapons, but you wouldn't expect anyone but a complete idiot to leave anything like that lying around. And from what I hear, that would only be a knife, and everybody has those."

"I can see the advantages of having a criminal on my team," said Molly.

Aleron jerked his head up.

"Joking," said Molly. "Thanks for doing this. We didn't get anything juicy, which is disappointing for sure. We'll just have to keep at it."

He shrugged. "Whatever she's up to, she's not leaving it out for anyone to see."

"Too bad," said Molly. "Why can't we have a sloppy criminal?"

Aleron snickered and loped off, leaving Molly despondent on the bench, watching the cherry blossoms fall.

✣ 44 ✣

Molly tried Ben and the call went to voicemail. She was so sick of being all up in her own head, endlessly talking to herself about the murders, and going in circles—so if Ben wasn't available, she'd just have to talk things through with whomever she could find.

In under ten minutes she was back at the Faures's, and just as she guessed, Michel was in the salon with a drink, looking out the window with a glazed expression.

"Listen Michel, and I mean this with love: it's time to snap out of it. I know you're upset about losing the money and getting duped by Apolline. Anyone would feel the same. But you can't just stay stuck like this, my friend. How about you help me figure out what in the world is going on in your neighborhood? Surely that would help Adéle feel safer. Get your revenge, if nothing else. Are you game? I need your help!"

Michel looked at her and closed his eyes for a moment. "Oh, Molly," he said, but did not continue.

"Come on, talk to me! How did Apolline rope you in? Give it to me, step by step, even if it is painful to relive."

Michel put a hand over his eyes and emitted a small burp.

"It's important, Michel. Can I get you some water?"

"That would be nice."

Molly trotted into the kitchen and poured two big glasses of Evian. He was drunk, again, but maybe not so impaired that he couldn't help her understand Apolline's tactics. Maybe.

"Drink this," she said, back with the water. "Now give yourself a quick slap in the face, you don't look awake."

"You're very take-charge this morning," Michel said, eyes still not all the way open. "And for the record, I'm plenty awake. Unfortunately."

Molly rolled her eyes. "Look, Michel. You're a clever man. How did Apolline lure you into dropping your guard so she could steal your money? Was it simply that the tale she told of making quick money was so convincing? Or was there more to it than that?"

"What difference does it make? What's done is done. Adèle will never forgive me, and I don't blame her. Besides, there are worse things ... than not being rich. *Much* worse."

"Oh, for God's sake, Michel. Drink some more water. I know Apolline was hanging out with Matéo Brule. Did he have any part in the financial scam?"

Michel shook his head.

"I was thinking she was involved with drugs, maybe bringing teenagers to Brule's place to get them hooked. But then I realized —that makes no sense. She wouldn't be operating on the level of a street drug dealer, for one thing. And five or six vials isn't—"

"Vials of what?" Michel perked up a bit.

"And what about Victor Chopin? Is he involved with the financial scam? Was he ever around when you were talking investments with Apolline?"

"Molly," said Michel. Slowly he ran a hand over his face. "You're making everything so complicated when it is very simple. Freshen this for me, will ya?" He held out his glass, not the one with water.

"Pass," said Molly, irritated. "Okay tell me, how is it simple? And how do the underage girls figure in? Wait—Apolline was using them as bait, wasn't she? Roping in wealthy older men with these innocent teenagers, selling the men on her fraudulent schemes while they were distracted by the girls—that's it, have I got it now?"

Michel's head dropped back and he moaned. "Just make me a fresh drink then, that would be fine."

Molly stood up. "You're useless," she said, feeling angrier at Michel than she ever had in their long friendship. "You're being selfish and self-indulgent and there are murderers out there that the gendarmes don't seem to be able to catch. I could use your help but you're giving me less than nothing."

Michel brought his head back up and looked at her with one eye closed. "I can't really help, for reasons I do not want to go into. But I can tell you this much: Apolline has ruined my bank account, but she didn't kill anyone. I can guarantee that, though I am well aware that my word is not exactly gold-plated these days."

"Why do you say that?" asked Molly. "What makes you so sure?"

Michel lifted his shoulders in the most Gallic of shrugs. "Because it is true. Actually, if you want to know, Apolline is probably going to be the murderer's next victim. I love you, Molly dear, but you've got it all backwards."

Backwards?

Wait, *what?*

THE NEXT VICTIM.

In a rush, Molly understood why Michel avoided being explicit. It was distasteful. Not distasteful—heart-breaking.

Because who did they know who had a motive for killing Apolline?

Who did they know who was behaving erratically, who seemed

to have lost any capacity for self-control, whose rage and taste for retribution was apparently unstoppable?

Molly's head drooped as she allowed herself finally to hear what Michel had said, and believe it was possible. So, she thought, Michel is frozen, he can't be the one to turn her in, it falls to me to stop her. Molly took a deep breath and tried to find some inner strength. It took many deep breaths.

Ears ringing and with an ache in her chest, she thought: Rodolfo Gallatine is on the wrong track, same as I was. I've got to hurry to the gendarmerie and beg him for five minutes. And then —find Adéle.

Her mind kept racing. She had known Adèle was struggling, had known her mind sometimes went to dark places, but somehow Molly had never allowed herself to consider …

She started to run. The gendarmes may toss her right back out on the street, she understood this of course, but she had to try talk to Gallatine before he made an arrest. There was not a moment to be lost.

NOT TWENTY MINUTES LATER, Molly stood on the steps of the gendarmerie, more confused than ever.

Trying for a presentation of professionalism with a jot of charm, she had entered the gendarmerie and approached the young woman at the desk. The young woman was neatly coiffed, her cap jaunty, her uniform and manner above reproach. Molly wanted to find fault in her because she had told Molly something so unbelievable that Molly wanted to discredit her, but to Molly's disappointment and utter bewilderment, she found no reason not to take the young woman at her word.

What the gendarme said was: there was no detective by the name of Rodolfo Gallatine working at the Aix-en-Provence gendarmerie. Nor was there a Rodolfo Gallatine working in the gendarmerie of any neighboring cities. No Rodolfo Gallatine on the point of making an arrest.

Rodolfo Gallatine, as far as the gendarme knew, did not exist.

Well.

Émile had described Gallatine so vividly that Molly had half a crush on him. The image in her mind was so clear, so compelling —a rather dashing detective with a head of unruly dark hair, a strong nose, full lips, perhaps a willingness to cut bureaucratic corners when it suited him—had she made this man up out of nothing? Had she misunderstood Émile that dramatically?

She did not think so... but she was not immune to daydreaming, she knew this about herself.

Émile had been quite specific about Gallatine, the position he held at the gendarmerie, and the fact that he was poised to make an arrest for at least one of the murders.

Perhaps Émile had been hallucinating? Some side effect of his extremely arduous chemotherapy, or ... who knew what painkillers or mind-altering drugs he might be on? Or did he ... perhaps he couldn't resist telling her something he thought would make her happy, even if it was made up, even if the happiness would only last a moment? Did he hope she would head back to Castillac none the wiser?

Molly shook her head. The bafflements just piled up, one on top of another. She had to find Adèle and get her somewhere safe, where she could do no harm to anyone else. Or herself.

Oh Adèle, thought Molly. If only there had been a way to help you before you took this dark, dark road. I failed you.

❦ 45 ❧

Saturday night and Chez Papa was packed. Ben paused outside, not sure he was in the mood for it. He could see Frances perched on her stool at the end of the bar, Nico joking with Lapin and Marie-Claire Levy. He scanned the crowd for his old friend Remy but did not see him. The air inside was smoky and Ben could tell, without having opened the door, that it was one of those nights when something was going to happen. His detective's intuition felt it, even standing outside on the sidewalk.

A sudden break-up, an ugly secret revealed, a proposal ...

Perhaps whatever it is will be a good thing, he thought, turning the door handle and pushing his way inside.

"Ben!" shouted Lapin, gesturing for him to come to the bar. "We were just talking about you. Are your dainty little ears burning?"

Ben smiled. His ears were the opposite of dainty, something Lapin had teased him about for decades. "I'm sure it was a flood of compliments," he said. "Nico, the usual, if you would be so kind."

Nico nodded and reached for a beer glass. Ben leaned over and looked down the bar, trying to catch Frances's eye, but she was leaning on her elbows and did not look up.

"It's going to be good to have a little one around here," said Lapin, gesturing at Frances and beaming as though he were the father.

"Yes," said Ben, trying to look cheerful. He wondered how Lawrence was doing in Aix.

"I often wish I had married earlier, so I could have a swarm of little ones underfoot," said Lapin dreamily.

Ben laughed. "It isn't too late. Anne-Marie is younger than you. And in far better shape," he said, poking his friend in his voluminous belly.

"Now, now, there's no need to get personal," said Lapin. "It's only—you know—I like the *idea* of a swarm of little ones. But I am not quite so sure I would like the *actual* little ones in and of themselves."

Ben nodded. For himself, he was quite sure what he would like, but knew that fate does not generally pay all that much attention to what we like or not. He finished his beer quickly and motioned to Nico for another.

Frances suddenly sat up very straight and put one hand on her belly. "Nico!" she said, and her ever-attentive husband left Marie-Claire and came to her. "Something feels funny. I'm worried … I'm worried something is going wrong." Frances grabbed Nico's hand and squeezed the blood out of it.

"Feels funny how?" Nico asked.

His lack of panic had already calmed Frances down and she giggled. "I'm being ridiculous," she said softly. "Honestly, I never understood what worry is until now. Every little thing—things I wouldn't have given a second thought to before—seems like a possible apocalypse. And plus my body, it's just … so unfamiliar, so strange to me now."

Nico came around the bar and put his arms around her. He kissed the side of her neck and then nibbled on her earlobe.

Frances cackled. Ben leaned forward and their eyes met. And both wondered: how was Molly doing, and was she ever coming home?

❧ 46 ❧

How to find Adèle? Molly could think of no better idea than staking out the location of her next victim. Of course, Michel could be completely wrong about that, but no other options presented themselves. At this point, Molly suspected that Oscar—never actually seen by Michel or herself—was a figment of Adèle's disordered imagination and that it was unlikely Adèle was on a date with anyone.

It was night, and night was when the murderer struck, every time.

Molly turned back to Cours Mirabeau. She was sweaty when she got to Apolline's building. Second-floor lights were on, Apolline's floor. And then—thank heavens—Apolline herself walked to the window and looked out.

Molly quickly looked down at the ground. She counted to ten. Then slowly lifted her head and looked back at the window. Apolline was gone but the light was still on. Molly stared at the three windows facing the Cours, barely allowing herself to blink. From time to time she saw Apolline moving about the room but only from the chest up—there was no way to see what she was doing. As far as Molly could tell, Apolline was alone.

Perhaps if I rang the bell, and she let me in, I could warn her ...

Figuring there was nothing to lose, Molly strode over to the building and checked out the intercom. There were four brass buttons with no names, presumably one for each floor, one apart- ment per floor. The building had an understated grandeur about it and Molly appreciated the wrought iron over the glass door.

She pressed the second button, which made an understated grandeur sort of buzz. Molly did not expect Apolline to let her in, but she hoped she would at least ask who was at the door.

No response.

She thought of how Michel's day must have gone, with Adèle in such a rage, and how complicated it was to love someone capable of such violence. She thought of Émile and his fantasies of dashing detectives who came to visit. Molly shook her head. She wanted desperately to protect these people and this city she had instantly loved the minute she arrived here. Hopelessly, she pounded on the door.

There was no one in the foyer to respond to the pounding, and Molly walked away, but not so far that she couldn't see the light on and any movements in the front room of the second floor. At least, she thought, if I can't get in, maybe Adèle can't either, and Apolline is safe for now.

Five minutes ago Molly had been sure that Apolline was a killer. And now she was standing watch to protect her. The situa- tion was certainly ... unstable, and she could sense that her mind, body, and spirit were not yet integrated. Molly felt as though she were in a movie, or a dream, where you could take nothing for granted because everything was going to shift in some way you couldn't predict, and all you could do was try to adapt and not even try to comprehend, not in the moment anyway.

There was a little tickle at the base of her skull, not intuition exactly, just a slight inclination, an impulse that would not be ignored.

There was nothing to do but stay and watch. If she could catch Adèle before she could act again—and put a stop to the madness—Molly would wait all night, if that's what it took.

❧ 47 ❧

It took a long time for the Cours Mirabeau to empty. Molly had to struggle not to get caught up in the small dramas unfolding around her—parents discussing how to discipline their errant teenager; a couple arguing about whether and where to have a nightcap; an unsteady old man in scruffy clothes who had had too much to drink.

Hours passed. The night sky was clear and she could see a few stars despite the lights of the city. Every time her attention was pulled away from Apolline's windows, Molly dragged it back. She stared at those lit-up rectangles until she could see them in detail with her eyes closed, though there was not much to see: no curtains, no furniture, nothing on the pale-yellow walls. Every so often she saw the top half of Apolline crossing in front of a window and Molly felt some relief. But she was forced to admit that standing watch out on the Cours was imperfect protection for Apolline at best. Molly did not even have the paring knife with her, if it came to that. Maybe she should text Michel for Apolline's number and simply give her a call—why had she not that of that before?

Because Apolline would think she had lost her mind, that's

why. They were not exactly on friendly terms, and she could hear Apolline laughing in her face as she hung up on her.

Molly stretched, yawning, and took one last glance at Apolline's windows. No Apolline. But just as Molly was about to turn away, she stopped. There was a change in the tableaux she had been staring at for so many hours: a figure in a dark hoodie had appeared at the edge of the window on the right and slipped behind a door. Molly stared, straining to see, but the angle from the ground only allowed her to see from the chest up. The person stood still, clearly hiding behind the door, face tilted to the floor.

The hoodie ...

Not Aleron. It *couldn't* be Aleron. It was hard to judge from where she was, but she thought, she hoped, the figure was not tall enough to be Aleron.

Molly jumped up to stand on the bench and stared again. There was no way to see who it was even though the face was now turned to the window, because it was covered; the person was wearing a balaclava or something similar under the hoodie.

A balaclava. In Provence. In springtime.

Molly ran to the door of the building and again pressed Apolline's button, then the buttons for the other two apartments. No answer.

She felt frantic. The tickle at the base of her skull had turned into a cold finger of dread. She had to get upstairs before it was too late.

MOLLY BANGED HARD on the door, rattling the glass under the wrought iron. She pressed Apolline's buzzer again, hopelessly, unable to think of what else to do. Then, in a flash, she realized that Aleron and Luc had broken into the apartment the night before and that he—or Adèle, it had to be Adèle—must have gotten into the building from the back, and she could follow that same route.

She ran around to the side of the building. A long passageway separated it from the building next door, and Molly flew along it, looking but finding no door, and no windows broken or jimmied open.

Finally, by the back corner, a few steps led down to a door to a basement, but it was firmly locked and covered with cobwebs. Molly scrambled back up the stairs and considered. Behind the building was a garden, which was well-tended, good smelling ... and fenced. It was mostly a decorative fence, thankfully, wooden, and only about five feet high. Without pausing to consider, Molly launched herself at it, jamming her feet into the space between slats and with much groaning, pushed herself over the top.

Her shirt rode up as she pushed herself over, and the top of the fence sliced her unprotected belly.

"Ouch!" she said, out loud, lifting her shirt to see a bleeding gash about six inches long. Well, it's not deep, she thought, and it's an old shirt anyway. She put her palm over the shirt and compressed the wound, still focused on how to get to Apolline's apartment and somehow keep Aleron out of more trouble than he was already in.

The back door—a beautifully carved, art Deco specimen—was locked. But with relief Molly saw that the window towards the other corner of the building was open. She tried to press her hands on the sill and lift herself up, but the croissant-eating had been a bit out of control lately and she could not manage it.

She spied a bucket just under the window and stepped on that with one foot. With a deep breath she hoisted herself up onto the sill and slipped inside.

Through a sort of utility room to a corridor, and up the back stairs. She tried to move quietly, knowing she was barging into a situation she did not understand.

A very, very quiet voice inside her head asking, *is this wise?*

The building had four apartments, one per floor. She crept upstairs to the second floor, Apolline's, and faced another door.

Surely it would have been locked? How had Aleron gotten through? Holding her breath, Molly put her hand on the handle and pushed.

Click.

The door moved, and Molly was inside.

❧ 48 ❧

M olly stepped into a hallway leading to the kitchen. She crept as quietly as possible, trying to hear where the person in the hoodie and Apolline were.

The apartment was deadly quiet. No sound of a person, a dog, or a television. Not so much as a ticking clock.

A phone rang. She heard Apolline pick up. The tone of her voice sounded easy, not stressed, though Molly was not quite close enough to make out what she was saying.

Where was Aleron? Was it Aleron? Adèle? What was she walking into, anyway?

The door from the kitchen to the rest of the apartment was closed. Molly pressed her ear against it and could hear Apolline's voice more clearly. Something about catching a train, then complaining about not sleeping well.

Molly squinted her eyes, thinking. She heard footsteps that sounded like heels on parquet, making her heart race, but the steps did not get louder. Must be Apolline, pacing in the living room while she chatted on the phone.

Molly hoped it was not Michel she was talking to.

Where was the person in the hoodie?

Senses on high alert, Molly crept through the kitchen to the back hall, looking in the pantry and a broom closet, anywhere the hoodie might be hiding. She wondered what kind of trouble she would be in if Apolline caught her.

She reached the end of the hallway, to the opening of the living room. What she saw was Apolline sitting in a club chair with her legs crossed, cell phone pressed to her ear and looking out of the windows that faced on Cours Mirabeau. And creeping up behind her was the figure in the hoodie, holding an object overhead. A marble sculpture, thought Molly, for an instant not believing what her eyes were seeing.

And in that moment, in a flash, the tickle at the back of her head and the events of the last days fell into place, in coherence, and she knew exactly who was in that hoodie.

"Émile!" she shouted, loud enough to rattle the windows.

Apolline jumped and turned around. The sculpture came down hard but landed on the back of the club chair instead of Apolline's head.

Apolline screamed.

Émile stared at Molly.

"You're not Adèle," said Molly, her brain trying to catch up to her own thoughts. "Or Aleron."

"No, chérie, I most certainly am not."

Apolline had called the emergency number and was barking into her phone.

"Come on," said Molly, pulling Émile by the arm. "You need to get out of here fast."

M olly and Émile reached the back stairs quickly enough, but she could see that he was too frail to take the stairs anywhere near as quickly as they needed to. She stepped down a few steps and urged him to climb onto her back, and with more strength in her legs than she would have guessed she had, began trotting down to the ground floor, Émile holding on tight, like a wizened jockey in a hoodie.

Oh God, thought Molly. This must be a dream, or some kind of joke. I cannot be carrying Émile on my back having just seen him try to clock Apolline Cuvalier in the back of the head with a marble sculpture of a horse.

This cannot be real.

But her aching back said otherwise. She reached the window where she had followed Émile inside and squatted down so that he could stand on the floor again.

"I'm going through. Then I'll help you." Blood was trickling onto the waistband of her pants from the cut, but she didn't notice it. She scrambled through the still-open window and turned around, half-thinking he might have disappeared in those few seconds.

But Émile was docile. He looked depleted and grateful for her help. He stood looking at her for a moment. "I'm sorry," he said. "I don't have the strength to hoist myself up."

"Just lean over the sill as best you can, and I'll pull you through," said Molly, her ear cocked for the gendarme's siren.

With some effort, she managed to get him out, though he collapsed on the ground, his legs like jelly.

"How did you get in here?" Molly said, her tone urgent and not especially kind. "You couldn't have climbed over that fence, how did you get in?"

Émile, slumped against the building, pointed to the other side from where Molly had climbed in. A gate stood open.

Molly took a deep breath, trying to consider the options, but her thoughts were screeching in one direction, then another, utterly disorganized and fragmented.

She leaned down in front of Émile. "Climb on again," she said. He was so light, no heavier than a child. It was easier to piggy-back him than try to hurry him along.

The gendarmes would be there any second. Molly heard someone running down the stairs of the building and guessed it was Apolline, who had recovered from the shock and was coming after them.

"Come on!" she urged Émile. "There's not a second to lose!"

With a grateful and tired expression, Émile reached his arms around her neck and did his best to lift himself onto her back. "Thank you, chérie," he murmured into her ear.

But Molly shook her head and didn't answer. She needed time to think. To try to piece together, finally, the truth of what was going on. But at that moment, time was something she did not have.

Over the weeks in Aix, she had come to love Émile. And so in the moment of understanding, when at last she knew who had been killing neighbors on rue Niccolo—she knew it to be true but it did not compute. Her friend had been standing behind Apolline about to clock her over the head with a marble horse. Molly saw it, she knew she had seen it, and yet her brain had even still steadfastly refused to take it in.

With Émile holding on tight, his head tucked into her neck, Molly took off, first down the passageway to the blessedly empty Cours Mirabeau, and then quickly across it and into the warren of narrow streets on the other side, having no plan except to get the two of them as far from any gendarmes as possible.

IT DIDN'T TAKE LONG for Molly's legs to wear out. She couldn't take Émile back to the Faures's, or his own house, not with gendarmes coming after him. No place was safe. In the end, because her legs were wobbling and she couldn't think of anything better, Molly ducked down a passageway between two buildings in a part of town she did not know, hoping the interior of the block was not fenced or walled off but would afford them a moment of privacy and rest.

She did not intend to protect him from the law, not at all. But her mind was fractured and she needed a moment, just a moment, to allow everything to settle. And for Émile to explain himself, if he could.

The moon was sort of cooperating, and she could see at least the vague outline of things. She set Émile down and held a finger to her lips. He nodded. Taking his hand, she crept along, moving quite slowly, eyes as wide as possible to improve her vision.

Bam! One foot straight into a trash can.

They stood very still. Molly could feel Émile's hand trembling. She had a quick flash of Ben. "Help," she murmured to him, then shook her head at her own foolishness.

They crept to the end of the passageway. In the back of the building to the right was a small terrace, with several metal chairs and a loveseat with cushions. She pulled Émile over and sat next to him, still holding his hand.

"All right now," she said, her low voice cracking. "Tell me what in the holy hell that was all about! What have you been *doing?*"

Émile sat hunched over, seeming to have shrunk, almost as though he were no longer human but a scruffy stuffed animal about to tip over to the ground. He looked at his feet and for a long time did not speak.

🐝 50 🐝

"**É**mile," Molly said, trying and failing to speak more gently. "Let's start at the end instead of the beginning. What were you doing in Apolline's apartment, dressed like a jewel thief?"

She was experiencing a strange and unusual thing: her mind was not leaping around as it usually did, trying out different hypotheses to explain recent events. Instead, it felt as though her brain were frozen. That in the moment she saw Émile about to strike Apolline Cuvalier in the back of the head with a marble sculpture of a horse, everything she understood about anything had suddenly failed to make any sense at all, and no amount of shuffling details around was going to put it right.

"I understand that I failed," Émile said, at last. "But you surprise me. Do you not feel even a little bit pleased?"

"Pleased?"

Émile waved his palms in the air. "I do take responsibility, apparently it was a poor plan, I simply do not have the requisite strength any longer ... I should have been more patient, come up with something different. But my dear Molly, you must understand—you know my prognosis—I am running out of time. It's

315

not just what the doctors have said. It's ... I can feel death coming. It's palpable. Like a looming shadow, coming ever closer."

"And so ... you thought you would take Apolline with you, for company?" Molly winced at her sarcasm. She could not find the right tone.

"In a manner of speaking, yes," said Émile. "Do you really not understand? Here I am, on the very brink of death, a place I have been inhabiting for months. It does things to your mind, Molly, and not all of those things are terrible. There is the potential for glory in it—yes, truly! Of course, inevitably one thinks of all the things one never managed to do—heaven knows I wanted to spend a holiday in Australia and see the Great Barrier Reef—but still ... mixed in with the regret, is .... is a sort of freedom. An opportunity to do something *large*. For the benefit of humankind."

Molly stared at him. She heard his words, but the meaning was still not coming through.

"I don't have to worry about human punishments or constraints," he said. "I am somewhere between heaven and earth. Dying, yet strangely invulnerable."

Molly heard a new tone in his voice. A sort of confidence. With an edge of steel.

"What would an arrest matter to me now?" he said. "Or a trial, or jail? Bring it on," he added, chuckling.

"Did you just *chuckle?*"

"Indeed. My perspective is no longer earthly, you see. I observe events here on this planet, here in France, in Aix, from a long distance away. We are mere ants, Molly, and so little of what we do matters at all."

Molly put her head in her hands. Then she sat up straight, cocking an ear, worried about who was looking for them. Émile was capable of spouting his philosophical gibberish all night and she wasn't going to just sit there and allow them both to be arrested.

"I thought you would be pleased," he said, showing his irritation. "Mademoiselle Cuvalier treated Michel most abominably, after all. You were the one who told me this—do you not find any satisfaction in the idea of retribution, of justice? I thought that was your stock in trade?"

Slowly Molly turned to face Émile. In the moonlight, she could see that incredibly, he was smiling.

"Are you saying ... I need you to spell this out. You ... you were going to kill Apolline, as ... as payback? For fleecing Adèle and Michel?"

"Absolutely! Why not? The gears of justice are irreparably rusted stuck, I think you'll agree? Do you believe the force of law and order was going to bring the money back?"

Molly just stared, her eyes wide. "And the ... the others?" she whispered, finally.

IT WAS PERHAPS the most bizarre half hour of her life, sitting on a loveseat next to a man she had thought of as a kindred spirit, while he described in horrifying detail how he had murdered Madame Trudeau, Matéo Brule, Louise Boulay, and Marius Latour. All to, as he put it, "improve the neighborhood." Molly had been right after all, what seemed like ages ago—the murders were not random, but the work of a serial killer. A man she had, until moments ago, respected. And very much cared about.

Had she missed a million signs? Surely the invention of Rodolfo Gallatine should have immediately clued her in that something was very wrong. She tried to focus on what Émile was saying. At least, in his telling, he had not enjoyed snuffing out the lives of his neighbors. There was a tone of regret. And also ... of pride.

She had to keep repeating it to herself, to make it real: her friend Émile Moreau was a serial murderer, an insane and violent man.

And she was sitting next to him on a loveseat, alone together under the moonlight.

Émile spoke with a bright and smiling expression of the service he had performed for his beloved city, and how much better the lives of the neighborhood would be now that his victims were no longer there, victims whom he judged to have demonstrated such bad behavior that everyone else would be much better off without them.

Molly listened without asking any questions. It occurred to her that she might be in danger, sitting so close that their legs touched from time to time. But each time the thought came to her, she shook her head slowly. She was not in danger, because she did not fit the type Émile was interested in killing: she was not from the neighborhood, if nothing else. And he would not kill her to keep her quiet, because apparently, now that the killing spree was at an end, he did not mind being found out.

"Here's what I suggest we do," said Émile, once he had finished his story at last. "I think you should go home. Leave me right here. I am too weak to walk, in any case. I had rather imagined being taken by the gendarmes in some familiar place, perhaps by the fountain on Cours Mirabeau, though most probably it would have happened in my own little house, without any fanfare. But here is just as good. It's simply a detail that doesn't matter, don't you see, Molly?"

Molly just stared. Her body was trembling from top to bottom, inside and out.

"No matter," Émile said, cheerfully. "I am prepared for what's next. This comfortable love seat is as good as anywhere else to wait for the inevitable. But there is no reason for you to be any more mixed up in this than you already are. Apolline will be reporting that you barged into her place of course, and I'm gravely sorry for that, Molly. I can at least tell the flics you had no idea what was going on. You've obviously done nothing wrong, and I hope that fact will save you from too much bother."

"Bother?" Molly whispered. She shook her head again as though it would help shake her thoughts into some kind of sense.

"Just go home," said Émile, whisking his palms toward the passageway. "Goodbye, my friend. You have given my last days a great deal of pleasure, I hope you know that. Now go along." He turned away from her then, and seemed again to shrink into himself.

Molly stood up. She paused for only a moment and then walked away, leaving Émile sitting on the edge of the loveseat like a small bird.

She walked quickly, wanting to get her blood stirring, as though she had been dipped into an icy pond. Just as she reached the Cours Mirabeau, she stopped. With a rush, she felt everything Émile had told her finally settle into her mind, finally coalesce into truth. She pulled out her cell and called the emergency number, and with a bittersweet reluctance mixed with relief, told them where they could find the serial murderer of Aix-en-Provence, March 2008.

51

"I know it's sudden, but I have to get home. I've already packed and made a train reservation. I hope you won't think me impossibly rude," said Molly to her hosts. "And I'm going to miss *Lucia di Lammermoor* after all."

"Well, it does feel just a bit as though once the murder was solved, you were done with us," said Michel, pretending to mope.

Adèle's eyes were unfocused, and she stared at a spot on the carpet. She had said nothing more than "bonjour" so far as the three friends poured cups of morning coffee and congregated in the living room. Molly watched her carefully.

"You know that's not it," said Molly, shooting Michel a look. "I'm just missing La Baraque so dreadfully."

"And Ben," said Michel.

Molly nodded, with a smile. "Yes, absolutely. And it's true, I feel a lot better about going home, knowing everything's back to normal around here."

There was a pause. Things were not exactly normal, after all. The Faures had considerably less money than they had only a few days earlier, for one thing. But they had the good grace not to correct Molly on that point.

321

"Tell us what he said," Adèle said, still looking at the spot on the carpet.

"She means Émile," said Michel.

"Yes, of course. My train's not for another hour. There are still plenty of holes, as there always are … but I can tell you what I know. The broad stroke, as I said last night, is that after Émile got the cancer diagnosis, he began thinking about his legacy. Totally normal, right? Probably what everyone in that position does, but Émile took it very seriously. Was he leaving the world better than he found it? That was the question that haunted him. You know how he is, he does love a philosophic ramble. And later, when the doctors told him he only had a few months … his thoughts took quite a turn. He felt he had nothing to lose, that no punishment would matter, that he might as well sacrifice himself for what he kept calling "the greater good." And … this idea seemed to give him, I don't know how to put it, maybe … delusions of grandeur? He honestly appeared to be taking an immense pride in what he did. Believed he had accomplished something very positive that would be celebrated, that his neighbors would be grateful for."

"Did you tell him any different?"

Molly was taken aback. "Do you think I should have? I … did not. It didn't seem like a wise course of action, arguing with a serial killer. But," she added, cocking her head, "I didn't congratulate him on a job well done, either. He knew I disapproved but it seemed like he was so high on his imagined glory that it didn't bother him."

Michel shook his head. "And what about you? Surely the gendarmes are going to want a word with you after you barged into Apolline's apartment?"

"I've been wondering about that," admitted Molly. "But wouldn't they have shown up by now? I could hardly fall asleep last night, worrying about it. But after it got to around 3 a.m., I realized that perhaps Apolline didn't want gendarmes poking around her apartment. Obviously my suspicions about her being a killer were off the mark, but that doesn't mean she's not up to something she shouldn't be."

"Tell me about it," said Adèle.

A silence, as the three friends thought various thoughts, and decided to keep them to themselves. Molly was reviewing with private horror the fact that she and Michel had suspected Adèle was the killer. The rages, the made-up boyfriend, the history of trauma and violence in her family—Molly had resisted the idea but had felt herself slowly becoming less and less sure, and then, to her shame, convinced.

She avoided making eye contact with Michel, not wanting to see him feeling the same.

"I'm certainly glad he didn't manage to kill Apolline, for our sakes," said Michel. "It's just so inside-out, a man who, like you've both told me, loved philosophy so deeply. Did he miss the part about right and wrong? About not playing God?"

All Molly could do was shrug. "I wish I knew," she said. "I feel like a pretty crummy detective, I've got to say. I sat in that man's living room and talked with him for hours, and never suspected a thing. I allowed my personal feelings to influence what I was thinking to an alarming degree. I'm ... to be honest, I'm ashamed of myself."

"Molly! You saved Apolline and you did figure it out in the end. Not so shabby."

"The thing I keep going back to," said Adèle, "is that Émile was doing so poorly, physically. With chemo and all the rest, how was it possible for him to carry out these murders? He looks so frail, so weak!"

"I know," said Molly. "I've been wondering if I might have caught on a bit sooner if he had not seemed so feeble. His physical state seemed to be an automatic disqualification. Though honestly, when I think about it now—sometimes when I visited he seemed like two times the man he'd been on the earlier visit. He was reinvigorated, almost reborn. As though his sense of righteousness transformed him physically, if only briefly. You know those stories of mothers lifting trucks off their children, having sudden superhuman powers when an emergency arises? Maybe it's something like that. He believed so fervently in what he was doing, that he summoned up the strength to do it when the opportunity arose.

"Not sure I would call breaking into someone's house and strangling them an opportunity," said Adèle.

"Poor choice of words," said Molly. "Madame Trudeau, by all accounts, was feeble herself, so I imagine that was not much of a challenge. I asked him how he managed to slit Matéo Brule's throat. And—it was so creepy, how Émile explained with such an expression of self-satisfaction on his face. He made up some excuse so that Matéo let him into his place, and then pretended to have something in his eye. When Matéo leaned close to have a look, Émile whipped out a blade and cut him. Just like that."

"Just like that," said Michel, shuddering.

"Cold," said Adèle.

"Indeed," said Molly.

"And what was Matéo's crime, exactly?"

"According to Émile, the reports of sexual assault were legit."

"Then I'll admit I am glad he's no longer living down the block," said Adèle.

"Adèle!" said Michel.

"I'm joking. Sort of."

"Can we drop this subject?" said Michel. "I feel as though all we've done for ages is talk about death, and I am absolutely over it. I wish you were staying a bit longer, Molly, I'd whisk both of you off on a road trip to the beach!"

"Tempting," said Molly. "Extremely tempting. But all I want right now is a walk in my woods with Bobo flying out ahead of me. I have never in my life missed home so much. And I hope the two of you will come for a nice long visit. I've got plenty of room —you wouldn't believe all the improvements and additions I've

EYE FOR AN EYE

done—so no worries about that. Please do come. And we will cross fingers that Castillac will be murder-free for your entire visit."

"Ha!" said Michel, taking a surreptitious glance at Adèle, who had had enough of murder a long time ago. "I know I said let's drop it—but just … one more question. Émile says he was ridding the neighborhood of persons he deemed no better than garbage. So all right, we don't agree with his conclusion but we can agree that Madame Trudeau tortured her students, Louise Boulay her husband, and Matéo we just covered. But that still leaves Marius Latour. Did Émile unearth a horrible secret life nobody knew about? What in the world did the gentle cat man do to get on the list?"

Molly dropped her head. It was wrenching to talk about.

"Marius stepped out of his apartment with a dish of milk just as Émile was coming home from Brule's. He was covered in blood. Their eyes met. Émile claimed that even though Marius did not call the gendarmes immediately, Émile could not trust him. So …"

"… so he killed a perfectly innocent man," said Adèle.

"I'm afraid so," answered Molly. "He accepted that eventually he would be caught and arrested. But wanted to put that off as long as possible. To 'finish the job,' as he put it."

They drank their coffee, and then made more, but for the moment, nobody had anything more to say about Émile Moreau.

❧ 52 ❧

Molly had done a poor job of managing her travel plans, and thus spent hours in the Libourne train station waiting for a connection. So even though she had tearfully hugged Adèle and Michel that morning, the goodbyes feeling more laden with emotion given all that they had been through, it was after dark when the taxi finally bumped its way into Castillac.

"Oh hey, I've changed my mind," Molly said to the driver, not Christophe but someone new whom she did not know. "Instead of taking me to my place, you can just drop me off here."

After paying and getting her bags, she let an enormous grin break out at the sight of her beloved village. She wanted to savor every detail: the golden stones, the small back-gardens, the uneven sidewalks. The murmur coming from kitchens where villagers were still at dinner or washing up. The smell of spring in the air, cooler than in Aix, herbaceous and alive.

While she stood, listening and smelling and looking around, a cuckoo started up and she laughed out loud.

Molly made her way down the street, in the direction of La Baraque, wrestling her bags along and taking everything in. She hadn't called Ben or anyone to let them know she was coming.

Maybe she would swing by Chez Papa for just one kir before heading down rue de Chêne for home.

The one string of lights shone in the scrawny tree outside and the sight made Molly's eyes well up. She peeked through the window and saw Ben at the bar talking to Lapin. Nico pouring a glass of wine. Marie-Claire Levy leaning close to a man she did not recognize. Even Madame Sabourin, Molly's next-door neighbor, was perched on a stool at the bar, looking a bit uncomfortable with her back very straight.

And there was Frances.

Oh, Frances.

Molly pushed her way inside, dragging her bag, one of which now had a wonky wheel. She walked up behind Ben and whispered in his ear.

He turned around. The expression on his face—amazement that turned into a look of such warmth and joy—made tears roll down Molly's face as he wrapped his arms around her and squeezed her tight.

"Thank God you are home," he said softly into her ear.

"Yes," she answered, kissing him on the forehead and then on the lips. "Oh, how I've missed you."

"Hey hey," said Nico, sliding a kir in front of her. "Long time no see." Molly smiled and thanked him, squeezed Ben's hand, and walked to the end of the bar.

"Frances," she said, and then her throat closed up with all the feelings and there was nothing to do but put her arms around her friend and hug as hard as she could.

"It's crazy, right?" said Frances, once the hugging was done.

"Indeed," said Molly, wiping a tear from her eye and putting a hand on Frances's belly with an ear-to-ear grin. "But the absolute best thing in the whole entire world."

EPILOGUE

Aleron Martel and his friend Luc managed to wrangle a deal for only three months of jail time, by going undercover and providing information that brought down an entire multi-national network that sold high-end stolen goods. They attempted, during their three months serving time, to convert the other inmates to their political persuasions and enjoyed some success at this.

Michel convinced Adéle to go to a renowned institute that was a sort of combination wellness retreat and mental health clinic. She spent several months there and came out feeling entirely rejuvenated, grateful to Aunt Josephine for paying for it.

Émile Moreau was arrested fifteen minutes after Molly called the gendarmerie. He was booked and taken to the city jail of Aix-en-Provence. Although given his rights, he talked with animation detailing his crimes to the arresting officers, those at the station, and then at the jail.

In his first night there, Émile curled up on the bunk with the brown blanket he was given, looking like a small bundle of person, no bigger than a dog or a little child.

When Émile was brought a tray of breakfast, the officer called to him but got no answer. The vigilante murderer had died peacefully during the night.

In the end, it was a heart attack that took him, and not the cancer he had suffered from for so many months. In Aix and in Castillac, his demise was discussed and evaluated: was it a fair death, to be taken so soon after capture, before any trial? Or had his victims been deprived of justice a second time?

It was exactly the sort of conversation Émile would have savored, a fact which was not lost on many of the people who were engaged in it.

GLOSSARY

Chapter 1
rue ... street
gîtes ... weekly rentals
jardinière ... flower pot

Chapter 2
La Baraque ... literally, a shack
chérie ... dear
à toute a l'heure ... see you later

Chapter 4
merde ... poop (vulgar)

Chapter 5
gendarmerie ... police station

Chapter 6
SAMU *Service d'Aide Médicale Urgente* ... ambulance service

GLOSSARY

Chapter 8
calisson ... cookie, specialty of the region

Chapter 9
bouillabaisse ... seafood stew
fougasse ... a bread similar to focaccia, with herbs and olives or bacon

Chapter 13
Excusez-moi de vous déranger ...I 'm sorry for bothering you

Chapter 14
santé ... to your health

Chapter 15
ma chérie ... my dear
tabac ... newsstand/tobacconist
Maman ... Mom

Chapter 16
bonsoir ... good evening
apéro .... cocktail party

Chapter 17
hors d'oeuvres ... pre-dinner snacks

Chapter 25
pot de crème ... French version of pudding

Chapter 38
La Santé ... French prison

Chapter 40

froideur...frostiness

Chapter 42
    meuf...slang for woman (like "chick")

ACKNOWLEDGMENTS

This book was on what sometimes felt like a never-ending journey.

My deepest thanks to the quick-witted and sharp-eyed people who helped turn a hot mess into a real book: Nancy Kelley, Tommy Glass, Paul Ardoin, whitneyrbwrites, and Barbara Mosley.

ABOUT THE AUTHOR

Nell Goddin has worked as a radio reporter, SAT tutor, short-order omelet chef, and baker. She tried waitressing but was fired twice.

Nell grew up in Richmond, Virginia and has lived in New England, New York City, and France. She has degrees from Dartmouth College and Columbia University.

www.nellgoddin.com
nell@nellgoddin.com